LIFEBLOOD OF THE THIRD REICH

"This is the Daimler-Benz complex," the American officer said, running a pointer across the lighted screen. "The complex covers a thousand acres, employs some twenty thousand workers, and includes three main factories. Our intelligence tells us that at the present time they're turning out at least 15 to 20 tanks a day. As Colonel Sutterlin pointed out, unless we knock out Daimler-Benz, Field Marshal Von Runstedt might get enough tanks for his Army of the West to stop our drive from the Rhine."

The officer then raised his pointer to the emptiness of the sky. "Somewhere up there," he said, "there are over a hundred ME-109's and FW-190's to challenge any attempt to hit Daimler-Benz. And you can be certain—the best pilots in Germany are flying them!"

ALSO BY LAWRENCE CORTESI

The Last Outlaw
Gunfight at Powder River
Trouble in the Big Tusk
Rogue Sergeant

TARGET: DAIMLER-BENZ

LAWRENCE CORTESI

LEISURE BOOKS   NEW YORK CITY

A LEISURE BOOK

Published by

Dorchester Publishing Co., Inc.
6 East 39th Street
New York, NY 10016

Copyright © MCMLXXX by Lawrence Cortesi

All rights reserved. No part of this book may be reproduced or transmitted in any form or by any electronic or mechanical means, including photocopying, recording, or by any information storage and retrieval system, without the written permission of the Publisher, except where permitted by law.

Printed in the United States of America

Chapter One

By March of 1945, after the surprise capture of the Ludendorf Bridge at Remagen, the Allies had established a bridgehead across the Rhine River at the town of Remagen itself. The Russians, meanwhile, had been mauling the Germans on the eastern front for over two years and only one question remained: how soon would the two Allied armies meet at the River Elbe? Thus, the prospects for victory in Europe during World War II appeared only months away. By summer, the Allies would surely force Germany into unconditional surrender.

In Germany itself, groups of high-ranking officers had already met in clandestine conclaves to ponder the probability of total defeat. How could they acquiesce to the Allies, with minimum problems for the German people and for the German armed forces?

However, fate intervened, bringing hope to the Germans and doubt to the Allies. The two World War II adversaries would find themselves in one last desperate fight. The confrontation would center around the heretofore insignificant, almost forgotten former automobile factory—the Daimler-Benz complex at Marien-

Germany, and on the outcome would come quick victory or a prolonged stalemate in Europe.

General Richard Todd, the chief of staff for the American 8th Air Force based in England, considered the Germans a still formidable fee, despite the American-British sweep across France and into Germany, and despite the Russian drive across Eastern Europe. "We know the Germans have a devastating weapon in the V-2 rocket. We also know they've developed a superior jet plane that can easily outdistance and outmaneuver our best conventional planes. There are also rumors that the Germans are developing a new, horrifying bomb that has the TNT equivalence of a thousand-plane bomb load. If they can use this new armament to support their huge army, we could be in extreme difficulty. The Germans must be defeated before they can develop any of these weapons to change the course of war."

General Todd's statement rang with truth. The German army on the western front alone still numbered 25 infantry divisions and 15 Panzer divisions. The Luftwaffe possessed nearly 2,000 planes, of which more than 200 were the new, dreaded jet aircraft. And they still sent occasional V-2 rockets into England. But the German military suffered one severe shortage to make use of these still considerable military resources—a shortage of fuel. The Panzer armies stood immobile, the Luftwaffe remained grounded, and the V-2 rockets lay idle on their pads.

Field Marshal Gerd Von Rundstedt, commander of the German Armies of the West, issued a blunt public statement: "Without fuel, we can do nothing. As far as I am concerned, the war is over." After the Americans established two more bridgeheads across the Rhine, one at Wessel and one at Cologne, Von Rundstedt became even more pessimistic. Without fuel, he was unable to shuffle around his tank and infantry units to stem the widening American bridgeheads at the three points on the east bank of the Rhine River. "We have no gasoline to operate our armor," the German commander said. "There appears no way to halt our enemies."

Von Rundstedt had reason to feel dejected. Since mid-1944, the Allies had concentrated their air power on communications, airfields, and fuel resources. The American 8th Air Force, the British RAF, and the American 15th Air Force in Italy had knocked out almost every major crude oil refinery and synthetic oil refinery in Germany. They had destroyed most of the major railroad bridges, marshalling yards, and railroad pikes. The Germans could only transport troops by truck, but they had little fuel to move even these vehicles.

General Todd told reporters in early March: "In a few days or a few weeks, all enemy transportation will cease. Our ground troops will be able to waltz through Germany." Todd and other Allied military leaders knew, of course, that Germany continued to build aircraft and V-2 rockets in underground factories. But he was confident that the rockets and jets were too little and too late. "Without fuel, these planes and rockets are mere piles of junk."

But then came a Russian setback. On 11 March 1945 the Red Army suffered an unexpected loss in occupied Hungary that astonished the Allies and Germans alike. The defeat would give the Germans the one thing they needed to continue the fight—precious fuel for their planes, tanks, and vehicles.

The 6th SS Panzer Army had been temporarily transferred from the western front to the eastern front to break a siege by the Russians against 100,000 German troops trapped in Budapest. When the Panzer units emerged from the Bakony forests in Hungary, the unexpected German appearance from the remote western front surprised the Russians. The Reds hastily formed a patchwork unit to stop the 6th Panzer. However, the German armored units drove the still unorganized Russians southward. The Tiger tanks skirted Lake Balaton and opened a wedge south of Budapest.

The Russians had finally stopped the German attempt to relieve the German garrison at Budapest. But, in the process, the Russians had neglected the oil fields at Lake Balaton. Before the Russians could defend or destroy these fields, the German tank units had siezed the petroleum fields. They quickly established a defensive ring of tanks, artillery, and infantry around the fields. When the 6th Panzer commander, General Joseph Dietrich, reported his coup to Berlin, the German Minister of Production, Albert Speer, was elated.

The Germans still possessed the nearly intact oil refinery at Ruhland. During 1944, Allied bombers had struck the refinery several times. But when German crude oil supplies dried up, the Allied air commanders had switched their efforts to the synthetic refineries. The Germans, meanwhile, had repaired the Ruhland complex, perhaps out of habit, an instinctive routine in Germany after a heavy strategic bombing raid.

At any rate, within hours, the Germans sent all available motor fuel trucks and railroad tank cars to Lake Balaton. Within a day, oil-laden tankers were speeding back to Ruhland, where petroleum workers could refine the precious black gold.

The Allies were stunned by the sudden turn of events. General Richard Todd told his wing commanders: "With oil, they can operate their hundreds of grounded planes, especially the new jet aircraft. They can refuel their Panzer divisions. The war could last another year, maybe longer if they have time to develop their new, sophisticated weaponry."

Field Marshal Von Rundstedt, when he learned of the Lake Balaton conquest, sent an immediate communication to Production Minister Albert Speer. "The oil fields have won us a respite, one that can stem the possibility of total defeat. We must take full advantage with immediate fuel allocations on the western front, along with more tanks and aircraft. The longer we delay the Allies, the better will be our chances for a favorable peace."

General Dietrich Peltz, commander of Fleigerkorps

Reich Fighter-Bomber command in Berlin, called the seizure of the oil fields a rare opportunity. The Luftwaffe commander hardly expected the windfall at Lake Balaton to save Germany from defeat. However, the new supply of oil would enable the Luftwaffe to again fly its hundreds of grounded planes and thus offer stiffer opposition to the Allies.

In fact, General Peltz wasted no time in capitalizing on the sudden success in Hungary. Within two days after the Lake Balaton coup, the Luftwaffe resumed an aggressive role on the western front. The Germans, utilizing 100 JU-87 bombers, grounded for weeks for lack of fuel, soon conducted heavy raids on the Allied bridgeheads on the Rhine River. On 13 March, JU-87's conducted 400 sorties against the Wessel and Cologne bridgeheads. Meanwhile, FW-190's, employed as fighter-bombers, conducted nearly 200 sorties every few hours against the 9th and 1st American Armies staging areas on the east bank of the Rhine.

A new Allied bridgehead across the Rhine at Oppenheim brought a new, near-fatal Luftwaffe response. The German air ministry had organized its first jet bomber unit, KG 51, under the command of Oberstleutnant Hans Kowaleski. The unit included 40 Arado bombers in two staffels and 40 ME-163 jet fighter planes. The dreaded AR-234 jet bombers struck the Oppenheim bridgehead on 13·March with 150 sorties. The swift, twin engine jets proved too elusive for either American anti-aircraft fire or for American fighter plane interceptors. The American ground units watched in awe, for the jet bombers, although causing minimal damage, had hurt the GI's psychologically. The Allied plan to sweep eastward from the Rhine to link up with the Russians had suffered a biting sting.

General Peltz fully recognized the Allies' apprehensions. He knew the enemy was especially fearful of the German jet aircraft. Field Marshal Von Rundstedt told Peltz the aircraft had indeed shaken the Allies, and, if the Army of the West had enough tanks for the hundreds of trained and willing Panzer personnel, Von Rundstedt could make things even tougher for the Allies. Peltz agreed. A one-two Luftwaffe-Panzer punch might well stop the Allies.

"We now have fuel," General Peltz told Von Rundstedt, "and I shall ask the minister of production to resume full tank production at once. We will replenish your Panzer units with all possible speed." To keep his promise to Von Rundstedt, Peltz met with Production Minister Albert Speer who listened carefully to the commander of Fleigerkorps Reich, for Peltz had a good reputation as a military strategist.

General Peltz had been a member of the Luftwaffe since 1935, and at the outbreak of the war he had commanded a staffel of dive bombers in Poland and Russia with remarkable success. During the Battle of Britain, Peltz had commanded air units in France. He had also been active as a Luftwaffe commander in the Mediterranean during the Allied invasions of Africa and Sicily. In December of 1944 he was transferred to the Fleigerkorps IX Fighter Command to rebuild the German fighter force. Finally, in February of 1945, he took command of the Fleigerkorps Reich for the defense of Germany.

So Minister Speer had great faith in Peltz's loyalty and leadership qualities. Therefore, Speer considered carefully General Dietrich Peltz's suggestions for two vital needs.

First, Germany must initiate a crash program to train hundreds of jet fighter plane pilots for both a defense of Germany and for tactical operations against Allied ground troops. Second, Germany must respond to Field Marshal Von Rundstedt's request for more tanks.

"We have new jet aircraft coming off assembly lines each day," Peltz told Speer, "and now we have fuel. We must have pilots. And, as for tanks, we have an almost forgotten tank factory at Marienfelde."

"You mean Daimler-Benz?" Speer asked.

"Yes," Peltz answered. "New tanks would raise the

morale of the Panzer soldiers. They will show the same new aggressiveness as have our Luftwaffe pilots. We can stop the Americans and British at the Rhine. If we conduct massive jet aircraft attacks, we will surely discourage the Allies in the west. We can then shift Panzers with jet aircraft support to the east to stop the Soviets."

Albert Speer stroked his chin, meditating.

"It can be done," Peltz insisted.

"I agree," Speer said. "We will begin a crash program to train jet pilots and I will order a full resumption of tank production at Daimler-Benz. But," Speer pointed, "can you assure us that Allied bombers will not destroy the Ruhland refineries and the Daimler-Benz tank factories?"

"I will draw up a plan with my staff to make Ruhland and Daimler-Benz the most heavily defended areas in Germany," Peltz promised.

On 15 March, General Dietrich Peltz called a staff meeting of his Fliegerkorps Reich Luftwaffe commanders.

"The recapture of the Hungarian oil fields has offered us an opportunity to win a favorable peace. We have more than enough aircraft to aid our cause. Luftflotte VI on the eastern front numbers 1800 aircraft, stretching from Riga to the mountains of Yugoslavia. With pilots to man them, we can stem the advancing communists. And, we have already seen how Luftflotte II in the west, and especially KG 51's jet aircraft, have disrupted American and British activities on the Rhine. Production Minister Speer has promised a priority effort to train more jet pilots. We can then accelerate our aggressive Luftwaffe sorties in both east and west."

"We understand this," a staff member answered.

"But, is there time?" another staff member asked.

"Time is not on our side," General Peltz admitted. "But we can win time if Field Marshal Von Rundstedt delays the Allied advance from the Rhine. To do this, the Field Marshal needs tanks, hundreds of tanks, and it will be our duty to see that he gets this armor."

Then General Peltz gestured to an aide who lit up a huge photograph on the screen. "Daimler-Benz, gentlemen," Peltz pointed, "the huge tank production complex at Marienfelde, the greatest tank producing plant in Europe. The minister of production has agreed to resume tank production here at full capacity, around the clock. Not only will Field Marshal Von Rundstedt get all the tanks he needs, but so too will our Panzer units in the east get needed tanks. Such armor, along with jet aircraft support, could change the course of the war. It will be our responsibility to see that tanks roll out of the Daimler-Benz assembly lines unmolested by Allied bombers.

"Fortunately," Peltz continued, "the Russians have concentrated their efforts at the Vistula River so that our newly-won oil fields are in no immediate danger. The Allied air forces appear obsessed with destroying our air bases and communications, so they have slackened their strategic air strikes on our industry. As we train more jet pilots on a twenty-four-hour basis, so too must we defend Daimler-Benz and the Ruhland refinery around the clock."

"But surely, Herr Peltz," a staff member questioned, "the Americans must know of Daimler-Benz and Ruhland. They must know that oil and new tanks will strengthen us in every military area. They must surely know that any delay will enable us to increase our jet power and V-2 rocket techniques." The aide looked at the lighted photograph. "Will not the Allied air command also be looking at this photograph?"

"They will," General Peltz nodded. "That is why I have called this conference. We must devise a plan to make the Daimler-Benz plants at Marienfelde and the refinery at Ruhland the most heavily defended sites inside Germany. We must organize a defense of such magnitude that any Allied attempt to bomb Ruhland or Marienfelde will result only in disaster for the enemy.

None of the general's aides answered. Despite Peltz's reputation, they were not sure he could devise a means to stop a massive Allied bombing raid against anything in Germany.

The Allies learned soon enough that Germany had moved swiftly after the capture of the Lake Balaton oil fields. Allied espionage agents in Germany quickly informed London that the refinery at Ruhland and the Daimler-Benz plant at Marienfelde had begun a twenty-four-hour production schedule. General Richard Todd expressed a real fear and he met with General Omar Bradley, the American commander of the 12th Army Group on the Rhine. The sudden oil boon had boosted the morale of the Luftwaffe, General Bradley complained bitterly to the 8th Air Force chief of staff. If Allied planes did not contain these new German jets, the resurgent German Air Force could decimate every bridgehead on the Rhine.

"With increased tank production and an aggressive Luftwaffe like these jets at Oppenheim," Bradley said, "we could have a real problem driving into Germany."

The Allies had expended too much effort in gaining a foothold across the Rhine River, Bradley told Todd. Allied victories had lessened the German will to fight. In recent months, German soldiers, disillusioned by unceasing setbacks, had surrendered by the thousands rather than die in a senseless cause. Fanatic SS officers had taken charge of many Wehrmacht units whose discouraged officers preferred surrender to a useless slaughter of their troops.

General Bradley did not want to lose the initiative east of the Rhine. If the enemy delayed the Allies, such a delay might encourage German military leaders, the common German soldier, and non-combatant civilians to find new hope and to stiffen resistance. The Allied armies in the west must continue their offensive against Field Marshal Von Rundstedt. This meant no tank replacements for the wily German commander and no fuel for the German jet aircraft.

"The Germans need time," Bradley told Todd, "and it's the one thing we don't want to give them."

"I agree," General Todd answered.

The only question: who would conduct these vital air missions against Ruhland and Daimler-Benz? When would such a mission go? Bradley left the answer to General Todd, who on 15 March 1945 met with his staff at 8th Air Force headquarters in London. For a full morning, they discussed potential raids on Daimler-Benz and Ruhland. When the conference broke up, none of the staff members said anything—not to their subordinates and not to curious foreign correspondents. However, the reporters had already guessed that the meeting's agenda had included the Daimler-Benz tank factories and the Ruhland refinery.

Despite the aura of secrecy from the Allied air command in London, rumors of an impending air strike against these two German targets soon reached every man in the ETO. Todd had not met with Bradley to talk about the weather; and Todd had not subsequently met with his staff all morning to play poker. 8th Air Force airmen guessed that the Germans would do everything possible to protect their oil refinery and their tank production plant.

Allied airmen knew the hazards of air attacks deep inside Germany. Combat bomber groups as well as fighter groups of the 8th Air Force remembered vividly the hundreds of fellow airmen who had failed to return from such a mission. Similarly, the 15th Air Force in Italy also carried honor rolls of fellow airmen who had crossed the Alps for a raid in Eastern Europe and who had failed to return. True, Luftwaffe resistance had been spotty for the past few months. But now, with new fuel supplies, the German Air Force might again assert itself, as evidenced by their recent aggressiveness with jet planes at the Rhine bridgehead of Oppenheim.

In addition, Allied airmen had heard plenty about the new German jet: its speed, power, and accuracy; its great superiority over the most capable conventional Allied fighter plane. The Germans had been using jet fighter planes since October of 1944. And on 3 March 1945, during the Allied bombing raids over Magdeburg and Brunswick inside Germany, jet fighter planes, the ME-262 Snowbirds, had appeared for the first time as an organized unit. They had pounced on the bombers like invisible streaks from the sky, knocking several bombers out of the air before the crews and fighter escort pilots knew what had hit them. Certainly, any attempted air strike against Daimler-Benz or Ruhland might bring swarms of jet fighter interceptors after attacking bombers.

Still, the rumor of an upcoming strike against Daimler-Benz at Marienfelde or against the refinery at Ruhland aroused an eager spirit among Allied fighter pilots and bomber crews. Despite apprehensions, most of them wanted the chance to participate in these potential strikes.

At the small Remitelli airdrome in Cattólica, northern Italy, the black fighter pilots of the 332nd Fighter Group had also heard the rumors of air strikes over Daimler-Benz and Ruhland. They too understood the horror of the 3 March air strikes at Madgeburg and Brunswick, where jet pilots had shown utter contempt for the P-51 escorts while the German pilots scattered nearly ten times their number of bombers during the aerial assaults. These Negro fighter pilots also guessed that the Luftwaffe would save their best shots, the jet fighter planes, to defend Daimler-Benz and Ruhland. Allied intelligence in Germany had confirmed the steady production of jet fighter planes and jet bombers. A couple hundred of these might appear over Daimler-Benz or Ruhland to meet an attacking American bomber force. P-51 pilots, like these of the 332nd, would find their Mustangs too inferior to stop the German jets from pulverizing the attacking bombers.

At a coffee table in the 332nd messhall, Lt. Roscoe Brown of the group's 100th Squadron looked across the table at Captain Bill Mattison, the CO of the 100th Squadron.

"Do you think the rumor's true, Captain?"

"It's true," Mattison answered. "If the Nazis turn out enough tanks and jet planes, and enough fuel to operate them, they can stop our guys from overrunning Germany. That would mean more time to increase jet plane production. And," Mattison pointed, "those jets might not only cover the skies over Germany, but they might come right down here and knock us out of Cattólica."

"Who do you think they'll send in there?"

"I don't know," Captain Mattison said, "probably the 8th Air Force."

Lt. Roscoe Brown scowled and slammed his cup of coffee on the table. The 332nd had been as eager as the hundreds of other American fighter pilots in Europe to go on this vital raid, despite the apprehensions. Brown would have relished the chance to hit Ruhland or Daimler-Benz. Besides conducting tactical ground support missions, the 332nd had also escorted 15th Air Force bombers on raids into southern Germany and Eastern Europe. But, as usual, it seemed that the 8th Air Force would get the glory again.

Lt. Roscoe Brown looked at the enveloping night that now settled over the dormant P-51's on the 332nd's Remitelli airfield. It was getting late and Brown was sure that General Todd, at his headquarters in London, had no doubt made his decision. Todd would no doubt send an 8th Air Force wing on these vital missions.

The lieutenant's eye caught a disjointed ridge among the darkening silhouettes in the Apennine Mountains to the west. Suddenly, he felt as isolated as this lonely ridge, for not only was his 332nd Fighter Group segregated from the rest of the 15th Air Force, but the 332nd and all the other 15th Air Force units always took a back seat to the glory boys of the 8th Air Force.

Lt. Brown had guessed correctly—the 15th would take a back seat again. On the evening of 15 March 1945, General Richard Todd issued Field Order 613 to the commanders of the 3rd Air Division and the VIII Fighter Command of the 8th Air Force. The commanders of all groups in these units would report to 8th Air Force headquarters in England at 0700 hours on 16 March 1945 for briefing.

The order disappointed the airmen of the 15th Air Force, including the black pilots of the 332nd Fighter Group. The Negro fighter pilots at Cattólica, the Lonely Eagles, could not guess that within a week they would play a major role in the sudden confrontation brought on by the German capture of the oil fields at Lake Balaton.

Chapter Two

Daimler-Benz: throughout the twentieth century the name has been synonomous with expensive, custom-made automobiles like the Mercedes-Benz passenger car or the 3-Litre Grand Prix racing car. Between 1926 and the advent of World War II, some dozen years later, Daimler-Benz racing cars had won 53% of Europe's Grand Prix races. The success of Daimler-Benz engineering reached its apex in 1938 when Daimler-Benz Litres placed first, second, and third in the Swiss Grand Prix.

The greatest names in European racing during the 1920's and 1930's drove Mercedes-Benz automobiles. The honored drivers Caracciola and Nuvalari, the incomparable Lang, and the Englishman Sean could trace their successes to Mercedes cars. And, of course, the German racing ace, Kurt von Brauchitsch, who would be one of Germany's first jet fighter pilots, won his sixteenth Grand Prix race with a Mercedes-Benz 3-Litre car.

Two men—the firm's director, Dr. Wilhelm Haspel, and the firm's chief engineer, Dr. Fritz Nallinger—were responsible for the superior quality of Daimler-Benz products, including the Mercedes-Benz passenger car.

Throughout the 1930's, Haspel and Nallinger rejected the idea of packaged, assembly line automobiles, and insisted on custom quality. And, despite the high cost of a Mercedes vehicle, the company never lacked customers for either its private passenger car or for its 3-Litre racing car.

But the Kurt von Brauchitsch victory at the Swiss Grand Prix in 1938 became the last success for Daimler-Benz on a race track until the early 1950's because the aura of war had spread across Europe. Germany had tasted easy victories in Austria and Czechoslavokia and her war machine went into high gear. Daimler-Benz could not escape the inevitable changeover to military hardware. In early 1939, the Third Reich called on Daimler-Benz to commit itself to war production and the Mercedes factories were soon turning out ball bearings, aircraft engines, military trucks, and the incomparable Tiger tank.

By the end of 1939, the Daimler-Benz industries of Germany included five huge production plants. The factories at Mannheim and Stuttgart in western Germany produced military trucks and personnel carriers. The plants at Sindelfingen and Gaggenau were turning out aircraft engines. The largest plant, a thousand-acre site in the northeast suburb of Berlin at Marienfelde, was producing ball bearings and Tiger tanks. Totally, Daimler-Benz employed nearly 33,000 workers, with 21,000 of them at the Marienfelde complex which included three large factories and several auxiliary plants. During World War II, this complex turned out more than half of Germany's tanks, while her factories at Sindelfingen and Gagganau turned out the aircraft engines for most of the Luftwaffe.

Because of its priority production, Daimler-Benz employees were among the highest-paid workers in Germany. They were well-fed and well-housed in company housing projects. Even forced laborers from conquered countries received good pay and good housing, earning as much as most native Germans. They enjoyed a living standard far superior to the standards of their own native lands.

Finally, Daimler-Benz offered workers bonuses in the way of food, clothing, and other material wants for efficient, full-effect production. Thus, the factory hands at Daimler-Benz plants considered themselves the elite among German war workers. Their morale was high and their loss to military conscription was low.

No doubt, Dr. Haspel and Dr. Nallinger were responsible for the superior efficiency and high-grade production at the Daimler-Benz plants. They deftly met the challenge of war production, for both men had been swept up in the martial air of patriotism that had radiated throughout Germany during the 1930's. Dr. Nallinger's engineers at the Mannheim and Stuttgart plants designed two of the finest aircraft engines of World War II, the in-line engine for the famous Italian 202 fighter plane and the 603 engine for the twin engine ME-210 fighter-bomber. Not until 1944, with the appearance of the P-51 Mustang, did the Allies possess an aircraft engine to match the Daimler-Benz 202 or 603.

And yet, if Dr. Nallinger's Daimler-Benz aircraft engines were superior, his tanks were the best. Nallinger had designed Germany's most potent weapon—the Tiger tank. The Tiger became the most ominous vehicle in Europe, far superior to anything turned out by the Allies.

The German Tiger, heavy and mobile, was armed with the famed 88 cannon, the most accurate field gun in the European war. Dr. Nallinger's tanks had tumbled across Eastern Europe, knocking out 17,000 Russian tanks to a loss of only 500 of their own. In Africa, Rommel's Tigers had swept across the deserts against the less capable British tanks. At the Kasserine Pass, the German Tigers decimated the American tank units. In Western Europe, neither the French Renault nor the British Cromwell could stop the German Tiger, as German armored divisions barrelled to the Atlantic coast. Every German commander—Rommel, Von Rundstedt, Reisdel, Deitrich, and others—praised Dr. Haspel and Dr. Nallinger for the Daimler-Benz tank.

But, as the war dragged on, events worsened for Germany; by the end of 1944, Allied air fleets had completed a year of steady bombing against German war production. During 1944, waves of B-17's, B-24's, and English Lancasters had flattened the Daimler-Benz aircraft engine factories at Sindelfingen and Stuttgart, and a few months later an Allied air fleet devastated the personnel carrier plant at Mannheim.

Then, from late 1944 on, the Allied air fleets began concentrating on airfields, communications, and oil facilities. Thus, Germany had suffered only one minor raid on the huge Daimler-Benz Tiger tank complex at Marienfelde, with small damage. The Allies had rightly concluded that destruction of oil, airbases, highways, bridges, and railroads would neutralize both German tank and Luftwaffe units. Not until the surprise seizure of the Hungarian oil fields in March of 1945 did the Allies look again at the Daimler-Benz plants in Marienfelde. For more than six months, the plants had produced minimally, mostly because Germany had little fuel, so there had been little need for more tanks.

But now, on 14 March, the Fleigerkorps Reich commander, General Dietrich Peltz, held his meeting in the expansive Daimler-Benz boardroom at Marienfelde, the northeast suburb of Berlin. Present in the board room besides Peltz were General Adolf Galland, commander of the Jagdverband 44 jet fighter unit; Colonel Johannes Steinhoff, commander of the Geschwader 7 jet fighter unit at Lagar-Lechfield; Dr. Wilhelm Haspel, director-chairman of production at the Daimler-Benz industries; and Dr. Fritz Nallinger, the chief engineer for Daimler-Benz.

"I'm impressed with what I've seen," Peltz began, "tanks already rolling off the assembly line. But, enemy agents have also seen this activity and they have no doubt informed our enemies in London. The Allies will surely attempt an air strike on these factories. So," Peltz looked at General Galland, "I am here to learn if you have followed the steps I suggested to prevent any destructive air strikes on the Daimler-Benz factories here in Marienfelde."

"We have carried out your suggestions, Herr Peltz," General Galland answered. "We have taken strong measures. I have prepared my Jagdverband 44 to defend Daimler-Benz. Colonel Steinhoff has equally prepared his Geschwader 7 to defend the refineries at Ruhland."

General Peltz nodded but he looked at General Galland with a tinge of embarrassment. Galland, who had risen to the head of a fighter command during the course of the war in Europe, was now reduced to a mere Jagdverband leader, a post usually reserved for a colonel.

Galland, beginning his air career in 1935 as a staffel commander, had constantly been at odds with Hitler and Goering. He might never have risen above the rank of oberstleutnant had it not been for a brilliant career as a fighter pilot and fighter gruppen kommodore. In the 1930's he had led the famed Luftwaffe Condor Legion in Spain. At the outbreak of World War II, he had led the Geschwader II unit during the devastation of the Polish air force. In Italy, he had commanded the K-6-54 Fliegerkorps to wreak havoc throughout the Mediterranean. During his career, he had downed over a hundred enemy planes to rank among Germany's five top air aces.

By mid-1944, Galland had risen to the rank of general and command of Luftflotte II on the western front. But then, with the advent of the jet aircraft, he had complained bitterly when Hitler wanted to produce jet bombers instead of jet fighter planes. Galland and other Luftwaffe kommodores knew that Germany needed a fighter defense against the daily, massive raids over Germany. He had even duped Messerschmitt into believing that a quarter of the jet production schedule should be devoted to fighter plane production—against the wishes of Hitler.

By the fall of 1944, Galland had formed the first jet

fighter unit under the command of Major Walter Nowotny, Germany's great air ace with 258 enemy kills. Nowotny was subsequently killed by P-51 pilots in November of 1944.

In the same fall of 1944, General Galland had initiated *Der Grosse Schlag* (the Big Blow) on the western front. He had mustered hundreds of fighter planes to harass Allied bombers. On the 8th Air Force raid to Schweinfurt in 1944, Galland's pilots had knocked more than 10% of the 500 bombers out of the air and heavily damaged half the rest in an air battle ever known as Black Thursday by the American 8th Air Force. And it was General Galland who directed the German Air Force during the Battle of the Bulge to give the Germans the first initiative in this campaign.

But by January of 1945 *Der Grosse Schlag* had failed because of superior Allied air power, a lack of experienced German pilots, and a lack of fuel. The failure gave Hitler the opportunity to relieve Galland of his Luftflotte II command. However, because Galland enjoyed great popularity in Germany, Hitler made no attempt to reduce Galland's generalleutnant rank and he allowed the fighter ace to work with jet fighter pilots. Finally, in February of 1945, Galland agreed to lead a new jet fighter jagdverband and he was now ready to use this unit in defense of Daimler-Benz.

Adolf Galland returned General Peltz's embarrassed look with a resolute gaze of his own. "My responsibilities, Herr Peltz, regardless of rank or position, will always be carried out with loyalty and determination. I will do my duty here."

General Dietrich Peltz answered with a nod.

"We have 60 ME-262's, two gruppens, assigned to Jagdverband 44 for interceptor duty," Galland continued. "I also count on your assurance that a third gruppen of 30 jet fighter planes will shortly arrive to bring our jagdverband to full strength of 90 aircraft. The pilots of JV 44 are among the best-trained airmen in Germany, thanks to Colonel Steinhoff. I believe, Herr Peltz, that we can prevent any Allied attempt to destroy the Daimler-Benz factories here in Marienfelde."

"With a mere 60 aircraft?" Peltz grinned. "If I did not know you better, Adolf, I would say you were talking great foolishness."

"They are enough to disorganize even the largest Allied air fleet," General Galland answered. "You saw what our Snowbirds did to the Allies during their bombing sorties against Magdeburg and Brunswick two weeks ago. We can do the same here."

General Peltz nodded again and then looked at Colonel Johannes Steinhoff.

"Be assured, Herr General," Steinhoff said, "we will use the twelve aircraft of Geschwader 7 to full advantage, although we had hoped to bring JG 7 to full gruppen strength of 30 aircraft. While General Galland's JV 44 is our principal weapon against any Allied bombing attempt on Daimler-Benz, we will not hesitate to bring our own ME-163 jet fighter planes from Lagar-Lechfield to help out. And, should the Allies attempt to attack the Ruhland refineries, General Galland will come to our aid with JV 44."

General Peltz studied Colonel Johannes Steinhoff. The slender colonel had joined the JG 7 jet unit, the first for the Luftwaffe, in the fall of 1944. He had served under the celebrated Major Walter Nowotny while Steinhoff was clocking more jet fighter plane time than any other man in Germany. He had become so efficient and knowledgeable in jet aircraft that he had also devoted much of his time to training new jet pilots for both the ME-262 and the ME-163 jet fighter planes. Steinhoff had been among the first jet pilots to take on the endless waves of Allied air armadas that flew over Germany day after day, and he had downed more Allied aircraft during his short tenure as a jet pilot than he had shot down in all his years as a conventional 109 or 190 pilot. The pilots of JG 7 worshiped him, and Peltz felt grateful that a man like Steinhoff would join Galland in the defense of Daimler-Benz and Ruhland.

"I'm sure, Colonel, that you and General Galland will work well together," Peltz told Steinhoff. Peltz than looked at Galland. "I have readied several conventional geschwader ME-109 and FW-190 fighter units. We have transferred these fighter units throughout Fliegerkorps Reich. All told, we can muster up to 200 operational planes to meet any challenge of an Allied bombing raid on Ruhland or on Marienfelde."

"Colonel Steinhoff and I will be ready," General Galland said.

"Fine," General Peltz said. Then he gestured. "I have also put the Flaknachtrichs 1-9 and 1-13 anti-aircraft units on full alert. These anti-aircraft guns stretch for dozens of miles to the west—at Ijmuiden, Swollo, Wittenburg, Standal, and other towns in the Dummer Corridor. They are skillfully trained to fill the skies with flak against enemy bombers. Also, they have the latest flak guns, up to 60,000 feet. To the south of these Daimler-Benz and Ruhland plants are the flak guns of Flacknachtrich 137. They too have the latest flak guns with accuracy up to 60,000 feet."

Further, Peltz told Galland, he had personally recruited the best anti-aircraft gunners available among the dozens of flaknachtrich units in Germany. No youth corps or patriotic women were among the gunners in the batteries of Flaknachtrich 1-9, 1-13, or 137. The gunners had long experience. They knew the speed of American and British heavy bombers and they knew the altitudes at which these bombers flew. They had mastered the technique of the box fire, coming up with a new barrage after the first unit had loosened its own barrage.

If the American or British bombers came from the west, they would need to fly through 150 miles of steady, relentless anti-aircraft fire from the 1-9 and 1-13 flakenrichers. If they came from Italy to the south, the enemy bombers would meet a hundred miles of box pattern flak from Flaknachtrich 137's six batteries. Hopefully, the flak batteries would down or damage dozens of bombers before the bombers reached the target.

And these enemy bombers and their fighter escort planes would face two or three hundred German interceptors, including the jets of Galland's JV 44 and Steinhoff's JG 7. Hopefully, while conventional planes engaged the enemy escorts, the jet fighter plane units would deliver fatal body blows to the attacking enemy bombers.

"What of the north and east?" Galland asked Peltz.

General Peltz frowned. "Our flaknachtrich and air units are limited in these approaches to Daimler-Benz and Ruhland. But, since we do not anticipate any aerial attacks from these directions, we have minimized our protection to the north and east in favor of heavy protection to the west and south. Such air attacks, should they come, will come from England with a remote possibility from Italy. So we have concentrated heavy anti-aircraft defenses in the Dummer Corridor and one Flaknachtrich to the south."

"And what of our alert system?" Galland asked.

"If we have any shortcomings against an Allied saturation raid, it will not be in the early warning system," Peltz answered. "We have reshuffled our jagdführer warning systems and we have moved them intermittently westward all the way to Holland and southward to the Alps. The relay of jagdführer alert systems will not only report the approach of any enemy bombers, but they will also track their flight patterns. Our jagdführer operators will know the whereabouts and altitude of enemy planes at every moment. They can warn us in plenty of time if an Allied air fleet approaches Daimler-Benz or Ruhland. You can be sure, Adolf, our fighter pilots will be in the air soon enough to meet enemy bombers while our flaknachtrich gunners give these bombers no respite."

General Adolf Galland nodded at the general, apparently satisfied. Now, Peltz looked at Dr. Haspel and Dr. Nallinger, the two civilians at the conference.

"I can assume, Herr Haspel, that these plants are operating at full capacity?"

"Yes," Dr. Haspel answered. "We can turn out twenty

tanks a day. Within a month, Field Marshal Von Rundstedt will have replacements for most of his Panzer divisions. As soon as we got the request from Minister Speer, we held a meeting with plant supervisors to resume full tank production. Our supervisors, in turn, have encouraged our workers to respond faithfully to this new opportunity. For the past two days, we have been operating at full capacity. By the time this conference ends, Herr Peltz, Tiger tanks will be off the assembly line, ready to join Field Marshal Von Rundstedt's Army of the West."

"500 new tanks in the next month," General Peltz mused. "Surely, with so many tanks and with the aid of our refueled Luftwaffe, Field Marshal Von Rundstedt can deter the Allied offensive from the Rhine."

"Yes," Galland said.

"And you may be assured, Herr Peltz," Dr. Nallinger now spoke, "these latest tanks will be of the same high quality that won us our great victories across this continent."

"Then in two months we will have enough tanks to defend ourselves against encroachments from both east and west?" General Peltz asked.

"Yes, Herr Peltz," Dr. Nallinger answered.

"We can produce the tanks, General," Dr. Haspel now spoke, "but only if you can protect these factories from air raids. While I appreciate the enthusiasm of Colonel Steinhoff and General Galland, I am still apprehensive. In truth, the Luftwaffe has failed utterly over the past year."

Now, General Dietrich Peltz frowned. True, the Luftwaffe had grown more and more ineffective during the past year. They could not muster enough fighter planes to drive off the hordes of Allied bombers; and the ME-109's and FW-190's were not capable of stopping the new American P-51 fighter plane.

General Peltz glanced at the opposite wall of the board room at the photograph of Adolf Hitler and then scowled. It was his fault that Germany was not better prepared to defend the Fatherland against incessant, saturating Allied air attacks. The Führer's erratic behavior had been the ultimate cause of the Luftwaffe's failure.

Peltz remembered that Johannes Steinhoff and General Adolf Galland had pleaded in vain with Hitler and Goering when the Messerschmitt industries were ready to produce jet aircraft. Designers Alexander and Wilhelm Messerschmitt had been working on a jet aircraft for two years. In October of 1943, Wilhelm Messerschmitt had announced to the Luftwaffe high command that they were now ready to produce in mass production a jet fighter, a jet bomber, or both. Men like Peltz, Galland, and Steinhoff had insisted that Messerschmitt produce jet fighter planes to defend Germany against Allied strategic bombing. But the erratic Führer, still dreaming of world conquest, had insisted that Messerschmitt produce jet bombers to again blitz Great Britain as in the glory days of 1940.

"The flying bombs have brought England and her American Allies half to their knees," Hitler had raved unrealistically. "We will add jet bombers to the V-1's and V-II's, and the Allies will be forced to capitulate in the west. We can then smash the communists in the east."

While Luftwaffe leaders like Peltz and Steinhoff had shown dismay at Hitler's suggestions, General Galland had expressed outrage. Galland had called Hitler a fool and Goering an inept egotist who could not realistically see Germany's need for jet fighter planes. Galland had pointed out that every factory knocked out by Allied bombers had reduced Germany's capacity to fight. Swarms of new jet aircraft could change the tide of war and give Germany an opportunity to beat back the Allied air fleets with their superior jet fighter plane.

But Galland's pleas had fallen on deaf ears. Hitler had condemned Galland for his wild insults and Goering had merely agreed with the Führer while he continued to parade about with his fancy uniforms and self-awarded medals.

When Hitler threatened to strip Galland of his

Luftflotte II command for his insolence, General Peltz had intervened. The Luftwaffe leaders and even German ground commanders had seen the logic in Galland's thinking, so German commanders everywhere pressed for the production of jet fighters. Goering and Hitler had finally acquiesced and stopped the production of jet bombers. But the haggling had continued for two many months before Messerschmitt had finally gone ahead with the mass production of the ME-262 Snowbird fighter plane.

The delay may have been fatal. Not until the fall of 1944, nearly a year and a half after Messerschmitt was ready to mass-produce jets, did the first ME-262 fighter plane oppose Allied bombers.

Now, in the board room of Daimler-Benz industries at Marienfelde, General Dietrich Peltz switched his glance from the portrait of Adolf Hitler to General Adolf Galland. Peltz suddenly felt compassion for the man who had suffered humiliation and loss of command for his efforts; and Peltz knew that Galland's unrestrained complaints had at least given Germany a chance.

At the moment, Germany possessed 700 jet fighter planes, with more coming off the underground assembly plants every day. If Germany could win enough time to train pilots for these jets, the Luftwaffe would surely have a superior air force. They might even regain control of the skies over Germany. General Peltz now looked at the skeptical Dr. Haspel.

"I can only say, Doctor, it appears that Colonel Steinhoff and General Galland have spared no effort to defend your plants against enemy attacks. I am satisfied." Peltz paused. "And what of yourself, Dr. Haspel? How is the morale of the workers here? And what have you done to protect these workers in the event your plants do suffer an air raid?"

"The morale of our workers is high," Dr. Haspel answered. "As for protection against air raids, we have constructed concrete bunkers as well as tunnels under our slag piles to accommodate every soul at Daimler-Benz. They can be in these protective areas within minutes after a red alert."

"Fortunately," Dr. Nallinger said with a grin, "until our troops regained the oil fields in Hungary, our workers were not too busy. They had ample time to conduct air raid drills."

General Dietrich Peltz returned the grin before his face sobered and he scanned the men about him. "We have, unfortunately, suffered mass damage at most of the Daimler-Benz factories in Germany, but fate has spared the factories at Marienfelde from serious air raids. The Tiger tank and our jet fighter planes constitute our last hope for peace without unconditional surrender. Marienfelde must be defended, for we can be certain the Allies will send their bomber fleets here."

"We can only promise to do our utmost, Herr Peltz," General Galland said.

"We can ask for no more," Dietrich Peltz answered. Then, he sighed. "If there is nothing else to discuss, we can consider this conference over." But Peltz did not end his meeting with any Heil Hitler saltue; nor did anyone in the expansive board room of Daimler-Benz remind the commander of Fliegerkorps Reich of his oversight.

And as Colonel Johannes Steinhoff, General Dietrich Peltz, and General Adolf Galland left the Daimler-Benz board room after the morning session, a Tiger tank had indeed rolled off the assembly line.

On 16 March 1945, General Earl Partridge, commander of the American 8th Air Force's 3 Air Division in Elvedan Hall, England, sent a communication to the 13th and 45th Bomb Wings at the Bury St. Edmonds heavy bomber field in England.

"Prepare seven groups of B-17's, 336 aircraft, for a vital mission deep inside Germany. TO at 0500, 18 March 1945. You will receive no field orders. Instead, both group and wing commanders of these units will report to 8th Air Force headquarters at 0800 tomorrow, 17 March, for briefing with General Todd, Chief of Staff, 8th Air Force."

The 3rd Air Division commander sent a similar communication to the commanders of the 3rd Air Division's 47th and 93rd Combat Bomb Wings to prepare another 226 B-17's for an 18 March mission with TO at 0500 hours.

On the same morning of 16 March 1945, Brigadier General William Kepner of the VIII Fighter Command, from his headquarters at Bushey Hall, England, sent directives to the commanders of the 67th and 64th Fighter Wings.

"Prepare fourteen groups of P-51 long range fighter planes for escort mission. TO at 0530 hours, 18 March 1945. You will receive no field orders. Instead, both group and wing commanders of these air units will report to 8th Air Force headquarters at 0800 hours, tomorrow, 17 March, for briefing with General Richard Todd, Chief of Staff, 8th Air Force."

Both the bomber and fighter wing commanders had often received mission requests for an assault as a matter of routine. The field orders for such missions generally entailed a simple communication, leaving to the wing commanders the duty of organizing and consolidating the flight patterns. Further, the field orders usually designated the principal and secondary targets.

Thus, the bomber and fighter group leaders of these six wings had immediately guessed that General Richard Todd, the 8th Air Force chief of staff, had something special in mind or he would not be calling for a face-to-face briefing. And, with the rumors of the past two days, the wing commanders and the group commanders could easily surmise that their units had been selected for a vital raid against the Ruhland refinery or against Daimler-Benz at Marienfelde, Germany.

Chapter Three

From a distance, the huge quonset hut at Thorpe Abbott, England, might have been a circus tent. But the expansive, half cylinder of metal constituted the briefing tent of the 100th Bomb Group, known as the "Bloody 100th" because they had lost more planes over Europe than any other 8th Air Force air unit. The big interior of the quonset hut allowed about 500 airmen, the combat complement of a B-17 group, to gather inside and listen to the group commander as he briefed the men over a microphone.

By 0430 hours, the morning of 18 March 1945, Colonel Fred Sutterlin, CO of the 100th, arrived on the podium in the hut, holding a sheaf of papers in his hand. Occasionally, Sutterlin paused to listen to the distant growls of B-17 engines preflighting on the field, or he studied the dozens of waiting combat crews. The flyers had been jabbering among themselves since they arrived because the briefing for the airmen in the briefing tent had already guessed the day's target.

The 100th Group airmen knew that Colonel Fred Sutterlin had been to a 3rd Air Division meeting yesterday along with other group commanders of the

13th, 45th, 47th, and 93rd Bomb Wings. And they knew that fourteen P-51 group commanders had also attended the high-level briefing. General Earl Partridge, CO of the 3rd Air Division, had spent three hours outlining the strategy for today's mission, and Partridge himself had been to one of the very confidential meetings at 8th Air Force headquarters only the day before. The very aura of secrecy and urgency had in itself all but confirmed today's mission—Daimler-Benz.

"Attention!" The 100th's A-3 officer barked sharply. The men rose from their benches, stopped their chattering, and stood at attention as Sutterlin straightened.

The colonel leaned over the podium and gestured to his airmen. "At ease."

Sutterlin waited until his 500 airmen had settled on their benches. Then he began with a grin. "I feel a little foolish about today's mission. Even the lassies at the local pubs knew we're going to Daimler-Benz." An eruption of laughter radiated through the quonset hut and the colonel waited until the guffaws subsided before he continued— seriously this time. "But that means the Germans also knew we're coming. Daimler-Benz represents Germany's last chance for better peace terms, so the last thing they want is destruction of those factories."

The crowd of airmen mumbled.

"The Germans have apparently prepared themselves for this one," Colonel Sutterlin said. "Intelligence tells us they've got at least 40 or 50 jet fighter planes around Marienfelde and maybe more. They've also got a couple hundred operational ME-109's and FW-190's. And, we understand they've assigned their best ack-ack gunners to the Dummer Corridor."

Sutterlin paused for a moment, scanned his airmen, and then continued. "We'll be part of a 14-group formation, 550 Forts, with about 400 P-51 escorts. And, we'll probably be the lead group. So if the Germans have any jets waiting, we'll be the first to see them."

A new chain of chatter radiated through the 500

airmen. Lead group! That meant they would bear the brunt of anti-aircraft fire, too.

But the 100th Bomb Group had seemingly been bred for tough strategic bombing assignments over Germany. The 100th had arrived in England in mid-May, 1943, training until 22 June 1943. The group then flew its first combat mission, a diversionary attack in the North Sea. By the end of June, they had joined other B-17 groups of the 13th Bomb Wing for an attack on Bremen, Germany. In July, they had participated in one of the longest bomb runs of the war, a 1900-mile round trip to Trendheim, Norway, to hit German U-boat installations.

The 100th had also participated in the first shuttle mission of the war, when in August of 1943 they bombed ball bearings works at Schweinfurt, Germany, and then flew on to Italy. The mission had been disastrous however, as nine of the group's 22 participating B-17's fell to German fighter planes or to anti-aircraft fire.

The 100th received its name, the Bloody 100th, following a mission to Regensburg, Germany, in the fall of 1943, after one of its B-17 pilots reportedly violated the code of the air. The Flying Fortress had developed engine trouble and had lowered its landing wheels as a sign of surrender. Several ME-109's had pulled alongside to escort the captured bomber to a German airdrome. However, for some reason, the B-17 pilot had raised his landing wheels while the ship's gunners had suddenly opened up on the escorting 109's, shooting down two of them. Within minutes, a swarm of German fighter planes had shot down the B-17.

From that day on, according to legend, the Luftwaffe had marked the 100th for extinction. German fighter pilots reportedly singled out the B-17's with the big D on their tails as principal targets anytime an American air fleet that included the 100th Bomb Group conducted an air raid over Germany.

Legend or not, the Bloody 100th had lived up to its infamous name in a mission to Münster on 10 October 1943. Of thirteen participating planes, only one came back. It had been the worst loss for a single B-17 unit in the war.

And on a mission to Brunswick, Germany, on 3 March 1945, two B-17's of the Bloody 100th became victims of the new German jet fighter plane when several ME-262 Snowbirds struck the formation. In seconds, before B-17 gunners could even react to the streaking jets, the two Flying Fortresses were tumbling to earth in flames.

But the group's devastating experiences in nearly two years of combat had also made the 100th the most knowledgeable of all 8th Air Force bombardment groups. They had learned to bomb with pinpoint accuracy against the worst anti-aircraft batteries and against the most vicious German fighter plane interceptors. Thus, as the most adaptable group against stiff competition, the 100th could encourage other bomb groups to complete their bombing runs.

Colonel Fred Sutterlin allowed the chatter inside the quonset hut to peter out before he continued. He made no comment on the lead position for the mission. Instead, he nodded to his A-3 officer. The lights dimmed and a photo of three large factories emerged on the screen.

"This is the Daimler-Benz complex at the Berlin suburb of Marienfelde," the A-3 officer said, running a billiard cue pointer across the lighted screen. "The complex covers over a thousand acres, employs some 20,000 workers, and includes three main factories, along with several auxiliary structures. Our intelligence tells us that at the present time they're turning out at least 15 to 20 tanks a day. As Colonel Sutterlin pointed out, unless we knock out this complex, Field Marshal Von Rundstedt might get enough tanks for his Army of the West to stop our drive from the Rhine."

The A-3 officer than raised his pointer to the emptiness above the screen. "Somewhere up here they've got a couple hundred ME-109's and FW-190's to challenge any attempt to hit Daimler-Benz. And somewhere down here," the officer lowered his pointer to the emptiness below the screen, "they've got their jets, as many as 50 or more. You can be certain—their best pilots are manning them."

A new chain of chatter radiated through the quonset hut as the airmen remembered the jet attack on the 3 March mission to Brunswick. When the chatter subsided, the A-3 officer continued.

"The 1st Division is hitting marshalling yards north of Berlin, but our target is here, the Daimler-Benz complex. Our group is taking the north half of the main plant. The 95th Group will follow us to hit the south half and the 390th will saturate after us. The other wings will be hitting the other two plants, auxiliary structures, and the marshalling yards of the complex. You'll approach your objective from the northwest," the officer said, again running his pointer across the screen. "Your aiming point is here. As the lead group in the first wave, we'll bomb from pickle-barrel height, 25,000 feet. The 95th will bomb from 26,000 and the 390th from 28,000. The weather is uncertain, so you may have to bomb by H2X radar." He paused. "Colonel?" he nodded to the 100th Bomb Group commander.

Colonel Fred Sutterlin returned the nod and then looked at his audience. "I needn't remind you to stick to formation. Even if you're hit by flak or fighters, stick close. Alone, they'll eat you alive." Pause. "Any questions?"

None.

Colonel Fred Sutterlin looked at his watch. "Please synchronize: 0448." A moment later: "Okay, out to the field. Squadron and flight leaders remain for final briefing."

The horde of airmen left the huge quonset hut and piled into jeeps. Moments later, in the growing dawn, the lines of jeeps bounced towards the Thorpe Abbott runways and the growling wing-tip-to-wing-tip B-17's.

In other bomb groups of the 13th, 45th, 47th, and 93rd Bomb Wings, other B-17 commanders also briefed hordes of airmen in equally huge quonset huts. Here, too, A-3 officers acquainted airmen with their targets and pointed out their areas of responsibility. And here too, group commanders warned their airmen to stick to formation.

At the P-51 fighter group base in Debden, England, the commanders of the 4th, 55th, and 354th Fighter Groups also briefed their pilots. At Boxted, England, Colonel Duncan Dade, CO of the famed Wolfpack 56th Fighter Group, briefed his pilots for escort duty on this mission, and he warned them they would probably run into German jet fighter planes. And in ten other fighter groups scattered across the English countryside, more P-51 group commanders briefed fighter pilots on Field Order #613.

At 0515, the B-17's of the Bloody 100th began roaring down the Thorpe Abbott runways at thirty-second intervals. By 0545, the last of the group's 48 Flying Forts were airborne and had rendezvoused in their V patterns. By 0555, the 48-plane patterns of the 95th Group and the 390th Group of the 13th Wing had fallen in behind the 100th over the English Channel. A few minutes later, the other eleven B-17 groups, from the 47th, 93rd, and 45th Bomb Wings, had joined the long line of B-17's now stretching for nearly a mile. By 0605, the 550 Flying Fortresses, soaring at 5,000 feet and cruising at 225 mph, were rumbling over the North Sea. In the early morning English fishermen watched for half an hour as the mile-long line of Fortresses roared across the sky.

Before the B-17's had reached the coast of Holland, whining P-51 Mustangs, 400 of them, from the 64th and 67th Fighter Wings, were hovering above and alongside the B-17's, with the 55th and 56th Fighter Groups settling next to the 13th Wing aircraft. At 0635, the nearly one thousand planes of the 8th Air Force crossed into Holland just above The Hague.

In three hours, if all went well, the huge air fleet would be over Marienfelde to destroy Daimler-Benz and thus end the last threat to General Omar Bradley's continued ground offensive east of the Rhine River.

"Achtung, Feindliche Flugzeuge!" Enemy aircraft. At 0645, the cry of approaching planes came from the warning controller of Jagdführer Holland at Croningen, one of the still unconquered sections of Holland. The controller of this jagdführer unit had caught the location of the American air fleet as it streaked over Holland towards Germany. But the warning operator could do little more than report the enemy formation. The German Air Force had a mere handful of planes still operating in Holland. At best, they could lift a half dozen FW-190's to observe the nearly thousand-plane armada. And far below, the few anti-aircraft batteries still operating in Holland could do no more than spit sporadic flak at the mile-long formation.

"Achtung, Americanische!" A warning of American bombers. Now the cry came from Jagdführer Northwest Germany at Wilhelmshaven, just across the border from Holland. But again, this second jagdführer warning unit could offer no more than token anti-aircraft fire and a few 190 reconnaissance fighter planes to observe. So, by 0810, the long line of 8th Air Force aircraft had crossed into Germany unmolested.

Soon Jagdführer Bremen was tracing the enemy planes on its screen. As with the other jagdführers, controllers of Jagdführer Bremen could offer little resistance to the formations of American bombers and fighters. But now, the Germans were able to compute a fix on the route of the American air armada and determine its probable target. When the armada, now at 12,000 feet, passed over Bremen and continued on a straight easterly course, Jagdführer Reich at Wittenberg offered a final computation on the probable target area—Berlin.

At 0950, General Deitrich Peltz at his air ministry office in the German capital studied the tracking reports from Jagdführer Reich. He then gestured to an aide. "They can be flying to only one target—Marienfelde. Get me General Galland at once."

The aide nodded.

"The American bombers are on the way," Peltz told the JV 44 commander. "Our batteries of Flaknachtrich 1-9 and 1-13 are waiting to blacken the skies with anti-aircraft along the Dummer Corridor. 200 conventional aircraft fighter planes will rise to meet them around Invue. But our most important defense is yourself and the jet fighter planes. Are you prepared?"

"JV 44 is on full alert," General Adolf Galland answered General Peltz. "We will meet the enemy bombers before they reach Daimler-Benz."

After he spoke to General Peltz, Galland rose from his desk at the small one-story JV 44 frame headquarters at the München-Riem field. He looked beyond his office window to the patch of dark forests east of Berlin. He could see the silhouettes of his half-hidden ME-262 Snowbirds coming into focus during the brightening daylight. And he could see the hordes of ground crews moving about the aircraft like obscure shadows as they finished up their work. They had been fueling and readying the 60 jet fighters of JV 44 since yesterday, for everyone at this half-hidden airfield suspected that an American air armada would be heading towards Daimler-Benz.

The seasoned German Luftwaffe commander now looked at his watch: 0915. The sun had risen far above the low-planed ridges to the south by this mid-morning. He could now see the lorries that had carried ammo crates to the waiting jets. And he could see the ground crews hauling back the empty rocket trailers pulled by small loading trucks.

Then an aide suddenly poked his head into Galland's office. "Mein General, the kommodores are waiting."

Galland nodded. "Send them in."

Within a few minutes several officers had seated themselves around an oval table and waited for Galland to speak. Galland had called his staffel leaders the moment the JV 44 commander had heard from General Peltz.

Among Galland's four staffel kommodores of JV 44 were Major Erich Rudolpher, Colonel Josef Kammhuber, Major Erich Hartmann, and Colonel Gunther Lutzow. Goering and Hitler had called these four men the riffraff of the Third Reich, mutineers who deserved execution. But as pressure mounted on Germany for a fighter plane defense against Allied bombing raids, Hitler in a rage had told Galland to do whatever he wanted with the jet plane and to take these mutineers with him.

"They are misfits like yourself," Hitler had ranted at Galland, "the most dispicable rebels in Germany. Just get yourselves out of my sight!"

And now, ironically, the misfits of the Third Reich would be the last hope for Nazi Germany. These four men, though snubbed and criticized by the Nazi leadership, had backgrounds on a par with Galland himself. When Hitler gave Galland permission to form a jet fighter jagdverband, he quickly called on these disparaged officers and others like them to join JV 44.

Major Erich Rudolpher had commanded JV 2 in Eastern Europe and JG 14 in Italy. He had won two Iron Crosses, plus clusters. The major had shot down 222 enemy planes since he first stepped into an ME-109 in 1940. He had risen quickly to fighter geschwader kommodore. No doubt his promotion to colonel had been squashed because he had vehemently defended General Adolf Galland during Galland's row with Goering and Hitler over the proper use of jet aircraft.

Goering had relieved Rudolpher of command and had sent him to a rest area outside of Berlin to recuperate from battle fatigue—such was Goering's report to the press when the German air ace lost his JG 14 command. Rudolpher had needed little encouragement to join JV 44. As soon as Galland asked him, Rudolpher, without any permission or orders, left his "rest area" and joined Galland at München-Riem. And now, the major sat before the JV 44 commander waiting for instructions for this most critical day in his long Luftwaffe combat career.

Colonel Josef Kammhuber had shot down more than 200 enemy aircraft during his airborne career in World War II. Ironically, Kammhuber had replaced Galland as commander of Luftflotte II in January of 1945 when the irascible Hitler had stripped Galland of the fighter command. Galland had been a highly decorated flier, with a wide popularity in Germany and Kammhuber held the utmost respect for Galland. Kammhuber had only accepted the command after Galland urged him to do so. Perhaps, in this new capacity, Kammhuber could wield enough influence to sway the German hierarchy into mass-producing ME-262 fighter planes on a crash basis.

However, before Kammhuber's temporary promotion to general became permanent, he had a run-in with Goering. Kammhuber not only failed to get promoted, but he was also relieved of Luftflotte II command. When Galland formed his JV 44 and asked Kammhuber to join, the short-lived commander of Luftflotte II eagerly left his demoted desk job and enthusiastically joined Galland.

Major Erich Hartmann, narrow-faced and lean, could have doubled for a thin statue in his stiff, almost motionless stance. Hartmann, for most of his combat career, had been a day fighter pilot and he held the record for the most kills of any flier in World War II—352. When Galland asked him to join JV 44, Hartmann at first balked. Despite his respect for General Galland, Hartmann had always flown an ME-109 and he had sworn he would never fly anything else.

"You will be enthralled with the jet aircraft," Galland said.

"I don't think so," the major had answered.

"Try it just once; try a flight in this new jet," Galland had insisted.

Hartmann had shrugged and then taken a ride in the new, highly maneuverable 600 mph plane. When he landed, a wide grin had almost cut his narrow face in half. "Where shall I report?"

"München-Riem."

Thus, in mid-February of 1945, Hartmann had given up the comfortable, non-hazardous command of a coastal patrol unit to join Galland at München-Riem.

Galland's fourth staffel commander, Colonel Gunther Lutzow, was unique. For months, Lutzow had bragged that his greatest achievement of World War II had been his ouster from Italy by General Albert Kesselring.

Lutzow had begun his career as a JU 88 bomber pilot in France, rising rapidly to first a staffel and then a geschwader leader. But, late in 1944, when many bomber units were dissolved in favor of fighter units, Lutzow took over a fighter unit. His troubles began shortly after he took command of JG 47, a 109 unit in Italy. The unit had few planes and little gasoline to fly them. For the most part, JG 47 had simply kept its ME-109's parked under Italian trees in northern Italy to escape destruction from prying low level American attack bombers. So, JG 47 had accomplished very little on the Italian boot. When Goering relieved Galland of his Luftflotte II command and criticized German fighter pilots in general, Colonel Gunther Lutzow had screamed in anger. Against the orders of Kesselring, the angry Gunther Lutzow had come to Germany in early 1945 to protest Goering's ouster of Galland and the air chief's continued defamation of the fighter command service.

Lutzow, the holder of two prestigious oak leaf gallantry awards, had enjoyed renown in Germany and the Nazis could not easily brush him aside. The colonel had almost wheedled himself into Hitler's own sanctuary to submit a formal oral complaint, but at the last moment Hitler had refused to see him. Still, Lutzow managed to win an audience with Herman Goering.

With a reckless courage, Lutzow had denounced Goering to his face. The colonel had demanded that Goering place fighter command ahead of bomber command, that Goering no longer allow bomber command to exercise authority over fighter command, that all ME-262's must be produced as fighter planes and none as bombers, and finally, that Goering must desist from his insults of fighter pilots.

Hermann Goering had been infuriated. "Do you dare to come before me with such charges?"

"Yes," Lutzow had answered boldly.

"And am I to understand that you left your post in Italy, without the permission of your commander in chief, to heap insults like this on me?"

"Yes."

"This is mutiny!" Goering yelled, angrily waving a fat finger. "I'll have you shot!"

Of course, Lutzow did not suffer execution or even demotion in rank. However, Goering had banished the outspoken Lutzow from German soil. And, when Kesselring heard of Lutzow's insult, the field marshal had also banished the colonel from Italy. So, without orders from anyone and with nowhere to go, Lutzow had simply wandered into the headquarters of Major Erich Hartmann at the coastal command station in Holland.

Hartmann had laughed for a full minute when he heard of Lutzow's plight. "I understood you were a refugee. Fine, you can stay with us. But," he said, leaning closer to Lutzow with a grin still simmering on his face, "what happens if the Allies chase us across the border into Germany? Where will you go?"

Lutzow could only return the grin.

When, in late January, Galland had asked Hartmann to join JV 44, Hartmann had asked Galland if the exiled Gunther Lutzow could also join JV 44.

"I know of few fighter pilots in the Luftwaffe who could better serve me in JV 44," Galland had answered. "After all, the hierarchy chooses to call us a rabble of misfits and Colonel Lutzow will certainly fit right in."

When the four staffel commanders had settled themselves about the table, Galland addressed them. "A huge American bomber fleet, with several hundred fighter plane escorts, is on the way to Marienfelde. If we act wisely and follow our established strategy, we can succeed in stopping them. There is no need for a physical victory, only a psychological one. I ask that Major Hartmann and Colonel Lutzow intercept the American escort planes with Staffels III and IV. Staffels I and II will join me to attack the bombers."

"Perhaps the conventional planes can deal with the P-51's," Lutzow said.

Galland grinned. "Should we find ourselves in such a fortunate position, Colonel, you and Major Hartmann may certainly attack the bombers." He paused. "We have already prepared our strategy to meet this Allied air challenge. Are there any questions?"

None.

Galland nodded. "Return to your staffels and prepare for battle." When the four staffel leaders were gone, Galland looked out of his window again at the half-hidden ME-262 jets.

And, while Galland's ground crews readied the 60 jets of JV 44 at München-Riem, Colonel Johannes Steinhoff readied his 12 ME-163 Komets of JG 7 at Lagar-Lechfield, about 120 miles to the west. Up to now, the jets had enjoyed a measure of success against Allied air assaults, but Steinhoff was not certain they could do much against the huge 3rd Division air fleet and its escorting P-51's.

Seated with Steinhoff at Lagar-Lechfield were his two staffel leaders, Captain Ulrich von Brauchitsch and Major Heinz-Wolfgang Schnaufer. The two men had been with Steinhoff when the original JG 7 unit was organized in the fall of 1944 under Major Walter Nowotny, Germany's great air ace with over 300 kills as a fighter pilot. Both the colonel and the two staffel leaders had been delighted to join Nowotny in a 262-jet fighter plane unit.

Steinhoff had felt severe guilt when Nowotny was killed because he thought he had used poor judgment in the air battle that had claimed Nowotny's life. Then, like the Ancient Mariner, Steinhoff had repeated again and again the story of that last day for Major Walter Nowotny.

"So well I remember," Steinhoff would say in a soft, sad tone to anyone who would listen. "We had no real organization then. But during these first weeks with Major Nowotny we shot down no less than 133 of those new American P-51's with a loss of only seven jet aircraft. We were certain the new jet would regain for us the superiority over the skies of Europe. It was after a fight with a gruppen of P-51's on the eighth day of October that tragedy struck Major Nowotny. The major had not landed with us and I wondered why. Then we heard the whistle of the major's jet plane. He had suddenly emerged from a cloud and we could see that one of the engine pods of his aircraft was burning furiously. An enemy aircraft had no doubt inflicted a lucky hit.

"The Major's aircraft dove vertically towards the ground and then crashed in a heavy explosion and thick cloud of smoke. It had been the last flight for this first kommodore of a jet fighter unit. Others told me it was not my fault, but somehow I feel I had failed the gallant major."

After Steinhoff had taken over JG 7, he had received a dozen of the newer, lighter ME-163 Komet jets. He had then reorganized the unit and developed a team attack plan for his unit.

Colonel Steinhoff had not been an outspoken critic of Goering or Hitler, although he had sympathized with Galland. So in early February, he had agreed to train the disparaged and homeless pilots who filtered into JV 44. Steinhoff gave these men instructions in the use of the ME-262. Goering had been disappointed in Steinhoff's accommodating cooperation with Galland and he had scolded the colonel of JG 7.

"They are mutineers who endanger the Third Reich," Goering told Steinhoff.

"But Galland is correct," Steinhoff had answered. "A trained Luftflotte of jet fighter pilots is the last hope for Germany."

"If you feel that way, join this misfit, but expect no help from me."

So the colonel of JG 7 found himself on the same blacklist as Galland and the others.

Steinhoff's two staffel leaders had also agreed enthusiastically to join Galland in the defense efforts for Daimler-Benz and Ruhland. Captain Kurt von Brauchitsch held a personal sentiment for Daimler-Benz. Before the war, von Brauchitsch had been a race car driver, racing his Daimler-Benz cars in Grand Prix's all over Europe and culminating with his win of 1938. When war broke out, von Brauchitsch had transferred his daring and ability as a race car driver to the Luftwaffe, and he had been among the first to seek enlistment in Major Nowotny's JG 7, Germany's first jet fighter unit. Now, von Brauchitsch could think of nothing more appropriate than to rise in defense of Daimler-Benz, the company responsible for his success in the auto racing field.

Major Heinz-Wolfgang Schnaufer, a former kommodore of NJG 4, had been a night fighter pilot for most of his combat career. He had shot down 121 British bombers in the RAF fight strikes over Germany, the highest score ever recorded by a night fighter pilot. The British had called him the "Night Ghost of Saint Trond." By late 1944, the Allies had begun to use the Black Widow night fighter for escort duty and NJG 4 could not cope with the overwhelming odds. Schnaufer lost more and more of his pilots and he became badly discouraged. So he had listened carefully in the fall of 1944 when Major Walter Nowotny told him of the great possibilities with the new jet fighter plane. Schnaufer had joined JG 7 and by mid-February of 1945 he had risen to a staffel leader.

Now the misfits of the German Air Force prepared themselves to defend the Reich for those who had called them mutineers and traitors.

Chapter Four

Meanwhile, the American air fleet, with Colonel Fred Sutterlin's B-17 in the lead, droned unmolested towards the Daimler-Benz target. The 100th as well as the other American air groups had thus far met only token opposition from both anti-aircraft batteries and enemy fighter planes, and Colonel Sutterlin didn't like it. Generally, enemy interceptors rose to meet them as soon as they crossed into Germany. And, after the renewed sorties at the Rhine bridgeheads because of Germany's new oil supplies, Sutterlin was certain the Luftwaffe could offer substantial opposition. The 100th Bomb Group commander drew an ominous conclusion: The Luftwaffe was holding everything for the target area.

Colonel Sutterlin reacted instinctively. "All gunners, stay alert," he barked into his intercom. "We're 35 minutes from target and you can expect bandits soon."

By 1030 hours, 200 FW-190's and ME-109's had zoomed skyward from their air fields somewhere north of Berlin. Only a few minutes later, 60 jet fighter planes from General Adolf Galland's JV 44 taxied out to their runways somewhere east of Berlin. The whistling, high-pitched whines of the jet engines numbed the eardrums of the jagdverband ground crews as they flagged the jets onward and skyward.

General Galland radioed his staffel chiefs. "Our conventional aircraft will engage the enemy aircraft to the rear. We will engage the lead formations. Your superiority lies in your speed. Use this speed to full advantage. I will take Staffels I and II to strike the lead gruppens of enemy bombers. Staffels III and IV will strike enemy escorts who attempt to interfere with us."

The Bloody 100th was in for it again.

Within 20 minutes of target, Colonel Fred Sutterlin saw cirrus clouds to the east. The target would be closed in. He ordered his bombardiers to check their H2X equipment for probable radar bombing.

A moment later, Colonel Sutterlin saw the lead squadron of the Wolfpack 56th Fighter Group zoom away from the formation. The Mustangs whined upwards and eastward and within moments the speedy P-51's were out of sight. Colonel Duncan Dade, CO of the 56th Fighter Group, had no doubt sighted the first German interceptors and he had broken his P-51 escorts away from the bomber formations to meet the challenge. Sutterlin squeezed his face in anxious anticipation, but he was glad the 56th were his protectors.

The Wolfpack group had been in England since January of 1943, destroying over 800 German aircraft in the air and on the ground. They had also produced more than a dozen air aces with five or more kills. Further, the Wolfpack, on long range escort missions, had shown a record of fewer losses among its bomber charges than any other fighter group in the 8th Air Force. So, if anyone could protect Colonel Sutterlin's 100th Group, it would be Duncan Dade's Wolfpack pilots.

Then, high in the blue, the 100th Group CO saw a swarm of dots streaking across the sky. From the long white wakes of smoke and the screaming whines, he knew they were German jet fighter planes.

"Bandits! 11:00 high!" Sutterlin cried into his intercom.

But Colonel Sutterlin felt his nerves tingle. He had flown 21 missions, most of them over Germany. He had weathered anti-aircraft attacks and heavy German interceptor attacks. Such attacks had almost become routine. However, he could not dispel the fear of the dreaded German jet since the 3 March raid over Brunswick where 50 or 60 jets had pounced on the 3rd Division formations. He remembered too clearly the sudden silver streaks coming out of nowhere; then the sudden pops of 30mm cannon. And, before he had seen the sleek planes flash by, two of his Flying Fortresses had tumbled from the formation in flaming death. Other units of the division had also suffered losses and damage from jets on that Magdeberg raid. The ME-262's were too fast, too maneuverable, and too heavily armed for the B-17 gunners and P-51 pilots.

The 100th Bomb Group commander licked his dry lips and waited for the worst.

It was not long in coming.

The nightmare of the 18 March 1945 raid over Marienfelde began with the staccato boom of box pattern anti-aircraft fire some 15 minutes from target area. Thick, heavy flak began exploding like black snowflakes amidst the mile-long B-17 bomber formations. Dozens of B-17's felt the impact of the heavy flak. Some of the aircraft suffered gaping holes in the wings, fusillages, or tails. Some had navigation, radio, or gunnery stations blown away and a few exploded before they tumbled dizzily to earth.

The P-51's themselves were soon locked in high-altitude dogfights with 109's and 190's. The Mustang pilots found the German fighter pilots extremely aggressive. While the superior P-51's shot down two dozen of the attacking German fighters, they lost several Mustangs of their own to the determined Luftwaffe airmen.

Neither B-17 bomber crews nor P-51 fighter pilots could recall the last time they had met such belligerent German opposition from conventional Luftwaffe fighter pilots and German ack-ack gunners. For the past several months, German fighter pilots had shown a strange timidity in the face of far superior numbers of aircraft. But now, the American airmen had suddenly understood the morale value of the Hungarian oil fields. The Germans had obviously intended to defend this unexpected gain with relentless tenacity. But worse, the heavy flak and fighter plane response was a mere prelude to the main attraction—the jet fighter planes.

General Adolf Galland stared down at the B-17's of the Bloody 100th before he picked up his radio. "Zieg Jagdverband!" Then, Galland and his wingman, in perfect unison, broke away from his formation and zoomed towards the B-17's. Long streams of white smoke whooshed out of the twin pods under their glistening wings, and their high-pitched whines whistled across the blue sky like the hums of distant dynamos. While Staffels III and IV successfully lured away many of the P-51 squadrons, Galland's Staffels I and II headed for the Flying Forts. Within minutes of the Daimler-Benz target, the German jet fighter planes had quickly broken away from the pursuing P-51's and swarmed into the bomber formations.

Throughout the ETO, radio shacks of Allied air units had been monitoring the air battle of the 18 March fight over Marienfelde. Allied airmen had been crowded around hundreds of squadron radio shacks to listen, hoping for the best, but fearing the worst.

They heard the worst.

The jets of Jagdverband 44 pounced on the Bloody 100th with such speed that neither P-51 pilots nor B-17 gunners could slow them down. After the first jet walloped a bomber with blistering 30mm cannon shots, its partner quickly followed the first and sent two more whooshing R4M rockets into the fort. Before the screaming jets had vanished, the B-17 victim was dizzily cartwheeling to earth in flames. The pattern was repeated time and time again by more pairs of ME-262's. In moments, a dozen B-17's had been shot down while P-51's chased the jets in futile hopelessness.

After the first assault, the JV 44 jets streaked into the wild blue, reorganized, and dove again on the B-17 bomber formations. Once more they sent a dozen B-17's tumbling to earth with their 30mm cannon fire and R4M rockets. The jet assault had scattered the B-17's of the 13th Wing and the trailing 45th Wing. Disoriented B-17 groups went off in wrong directions, fell in behind other bomb groups, or dropped their bombs too late and too early.

Colonel Duncan Dade and his 56th Group fighter pilots endeavored to meet the ME-262's head on, but the job proved futile. General Galland had needed only Major Hartmann's Staffel III to keep the P-51's at bay. The 15 ME-262's zoomed and climbed and fired almost at will, easily scooting away from superior numbers of pursuing P-51's. Occasionally, a jet came from nowhere to slam a burst of 30mm shots into a Mustang, and then zoomed out of sight before other P-51's could respond. For the first time, the Wolfpack could not contain enemy interceptors.

Colonel Dade could only curse. "Goddam it! Goddam it!"

As other P-51's came in to chase the pesky jets of JV 44, they were suddenly jumped by a dozen Komet jets. The speedy planes of Colonel Johannes Steinhoff's JG 7 had zoomed into the fray from Lagar-Lechfield to help out JV 44. Steinhoff's Komets scattered most of the B-17's from the tail 47th and 93rd Bomb Wings, while knocking down four of the B-17's and damaging a couple dozen more.

Colonel Fred Sutterlin of the battered 100th lead group veered northward to hit secondary targets at the Noabit Power Station. Other 13th Wing groups followed him. The 45th Wing struck the railroad yards, already hit earlier by the 1st Division. Only some of the B-17's from the tail 47th and 93rd Bomb Wings got near the Daimler-Benz complex, but the aggressive defense by

German jets had disrupted any chance of accuracy. As later American reconnaissance photos showed, B-17 bombs, dropped by H2X radar, fell far short of the target: 3.3 miles short, six miles short, two miles short, and one group dropped its bombs in a forest, 14 miles away from target. Only the 93rd Group came anywhere near the objective and they were .2 miles short. By the time the battered 3rd Air Division had left the target, they had lost 28 B-17's to German jet fighter planes and 20 more to ack-ack fire. Half of the other 3rd Division B-17's had suffered damage, from light to very heavy.

By noon of 18 March 1945, when General Galland and his pilots touched down on their runways, ground crews swarmed over them enthusiastically. General Peltz waited eagerly to congratulate the German fighter pilots.

"Excellent, excellent," Peltz praised Galland. "For the first time in over a year we have forced an attacking Allied air fleet to retreat. As we train more jet pilots, we will reconquer the skies over Germany. A mere 60 ME-262's and a dozen Komets have disrupted this huge Allied air fleet. What if we send 200 or 300 or even 400 jet fighter planes to meet future Allied strategic bombing attacks over Germany? The skies will be ours."

In London, the monitored reports from the aerial fight over Marienfelde stunned the 8th Air Force staff. Only grim disbelief radiated from the faces of General Richard Todd and his headquarters subordinates. From a field headquarters near Cologne on the Rhine, General Omar Bradley listened to the reports in astonishment as he waited to push his troops eastward from the Rhine River. Tanks would continue to roll out of Daimler-Benz for the wily Field Marshal Gerd Von Rundstedt, Bradley's adversary. The 12th American Army Group commander cursed this possibility.

Nor was the disastrous 18 March raid a pleasant thought for Colonel Ben Davis, the commander of the 332nd Fighter Group in Cattólica, Italy. Only this morning, a rumor had spread up and down the length of Italy: the 15th Air Force would hit Ruhland as the 8th Air

Force had attempted to hit Marienfelde today. All long-range fighter planes, such as the P-51's of the 332nd, would likely draw escort duty for the 15th's B-17's. Davis suspected that his own 332nd Fighter Group might see these same, awesome ME-262 Snowbirds and ME-163 Komets on the rumored mission against the oil refinery at Ruhland.

Surely, the Luftwaffe would defend the refinery at Ruhland with the same aggressiveness the planes had shown on this disastrous raid to Marienfelde. Davis pursed his lips to stem a tinge of apprehension. How would he and his fighter pilots perform in a confrontation with those 600 mph German jet fighter planes? Any better than the famed Wolfpack pilots of the 56th Fighter Group? Ben Davis, the first black group commander in the history of the Army Air Corps, wasn't sure he and his pilots could cope with jets. He did not relish the idea at all.

On the evening of 20 March, General Omar Bradley sat with his staff in the advanced headquarters of his 12th Army Group, just south of the battered city of Cologne. The American field general on the western front paced the floor anxiously while an array of subordinates followed Bradley's movements in silence. Among those present were General James Hodges of the 1st Army, General William Simpson of the 9th Army, General George Patton of the 3rd Army, and General Alexander Patch of the 7th Army. Also present was General Bob Webster of the tactical 9th Air Force based in France.

These men had assembled in Bradley's headquarters to plan Operation Overtone, the American offensive to drive across Germany from their Rhine bridgeheads. Although the Arado jets had been stinging the Rhine bridgeheads, they presented more of a psychological problem than a physical problem. But the news of the 3rd Air Division debacle over Marienfelde had stunned General Bradley and his army group commanders.

"Those goddamn jets," Bradley finally spoke. "How the hell could a handful of them do that kind of damage to a thousand planes? Our dogfaces will tremble now when they hear those high-pitched whines and see those flashing streaks in the sky. Now they'll believe for certain that our P-51's can't handle them."

"We've been hitting their airfields wherever we find them," General Bob Webster said. "Our 9th Air Force planes had hit their fields at Lippe, Ettinghausen, Kirthorf, Wurzburg, Neustadt, and anyplace else we've found airfields. We must have destroyed 15 or 20 German airfields in the last few weeks."

"But those jets still keep coming," General Omar Bradley said.

"We don't know where the hell those Arados and Comets are holed up," Webster shook his head. "We've tried to follow them several times, but they're too fast. They lose our pursuit planes before we find their airfields."

"With your hundreds of goddam planes, you can't find their airfields?" General Bradley barked.

The embarrassed CO of the 9th Air Force did not answer.

"Well?" Bradley finally asked.

"We're doing our best," Webster said again. "I can assure you, every available fighter-bomber and fighter plane of the 9th will be at your disposal when your armies come out of their Rhine pockets and drive eastward."

Omar Bradley nodded and then sighed. It was time to get down to business—Operation Overtone. General Patton's 3rd Army had reached Wessel and he was ready to drive towards Frankfurt. General Hodges was set to push his 1st Army from the Remagen bridgehead towards Leipzig. General Patch hoped the Arado jet attack at Oppenheim would not shake up his dogfaces too badly, for Patch was ready to send his 7th Army towards Munich. And here in Cologne itself, General Simpson's 9th Army prepared to drive towards Berlin itself. But if German jets interfered with these new offensives, the jets could disrupt the Allied moves and give Von Runstedt time to prepare better defenses. Bradley wanted no such respite for the German field marshal.

"The Germans have gasoline now," Bradley said. "Not much, but enough to make things rough if Von Rundstedt gets more tanks from their Daimler-Benz plants. If they can stall us, they'll have an opportunity to throw more tanks against us."

General Webster promised again to scour western Germany to find the jet airfields. He would send out dozens of reconnaissance planes around the clock until they located these fields and destroyed them. He also promised Bradley again that the 9th Air Force would use every available plane to support Operation Overtone.

General Bradley now turned to his field commanders to discuss Operation Overtone. The plan would include a drive by the 1st and 9th Armies in the north, with French elements to thrust towards east Germany. Patton's 3rd Army would chew its way from Wessel through the battered Saarbrücken defenses and capture the rail junction at Oberwurzban before pushing on to Frankfurt. In the south, the 7th Army, already across the Moselle River, would streak eastward with its armor divisions to link up with the French and destroy German Army Group B and then rush on towards Munich. Hopefully, the operation would totally decimate the German Army of the West, open a path to the Autobahn, and allow Allied armored units to roll across Germany to link up with the Russians at the Elbe River.

The 9th Tactical Air Force arm of B-25's, A-20's, A-26's, P-47's, and P-38's—light bombers and fighter-bombers—would support Operation Overtone. The tactical air assaults would include some 12,000 sorties during the expected week-long offensive. The 9th Air Force would especially attack German strongpoints, enemy held villages, and troop concentrations to open a path for advancing Allied infantry and tank units. Finally, elements of the 9th Air Force would destroy rail and road escape routes in the Saar region and force the

Germans to jam the few roads left that funnelled into central Germany.

Once the retreating Germans found themselves in these untenable positions, Allied air units would chop them to pieces, making them easy prey for Allied ground forces. The decimated German Army of the West must then either surrender or face annihilation.

On paper, the combined Operation Overtone appeared invincible since the Allies enjoyed immeasurable superiority in men, equipment, and aircraft. Bradley simply needed assurances from the 9th Tactical Air Force that the German Air Force could not interfere with jet bombers and jet fighters.

"You've got to find those airfields," Bradley told General Webster.

"We'll spare no effort," the 9th Air Force commander promised.

Still, the army commanders in Bradley's headquarters were not impressed with General Webster's assurances. The disaster at Marienfelde two days ago still clung ominously in their minds.

Chapter Five

At his Army of the West headquarters in Osnabrück, less than 30 miles from the Allies' most advanced position in Münster, Field Marshal Von Rundstedt had also met with his field leaders: General Fritz von Klüge of the 7th Army, General Hasso von Maunteufel of the 5th Panzer Army, and Colonel Joseph Dietrich of the 6th Panzer Army whose temporary assignment to Hungary had won the Lake Balaton oil fields.

Despite heavy German losses in their unsuccessful attempts to hold the east bank of the Rhine, Von Rundstedt had avoided disaster by wisely pulling back his infantry and tank units in the face of imminent Allied pincer movements from their Rhine bridgeheads. Thus, the field marshal still had a formidable army on the western front. Hitler had severely admonished Von Rundstedt for these troop withdrawals.

"I should find a true patriot to replace this coward in the west such as the patriots who fought to the end in the east," Hitler had ranted.

Yet, Hitler had merely rambled, for he inwardly knew that Von Rundstedt had saved the Army of the West to fight another day. The field marshal's tactics had avoided another Stalingrad, where the Germans had suffered the loss of 300,000 men. In fact, because of his crafty maneuvers, Von Rundstedt still had 15 armored divisions and 25 infantry divisions scattered up and down the length of west Germany between Cleve and Cologne. They were established in various defense positions between Münster and Frankfurt. He needed only fuel and tanks to release this huge force against the Allies.

A tinge of optimism radiated from Von Rundstedt's usually sober face as he stood before his army commanders. He was satisfied by the performance of the jet planes on the western front and he expressed delight when news reached him of Galland's aerial victory over Marienfelde. Sorties by the flashing 163 Komets and the Arado 234 bombers had shaken the Allies here in the west. The news from Marienfelde would no doubt shake the Allies even more.

Von Rundstedt was satisfied with the jet bomber attack at Oppenheim that had stalled the American ground forces long enough to enable the Germans to open the Roer River dams and flood the path of the Allied advance. The KG 51 Arado jets had also thwarted American efforts on the west bank of the Rhine at Wessel, Diusburg, Coblenz, and several others points where Allied units were massing for further advances. Finally, on 17 March, the day before the Daimler-Benz raid, a staffel of Arado 234 jet bombers, escorted by a staffel of Komet 163 jet fighter planes, had successfully knocked out the Remagen Bridge and dropped its spans into the Rhine River. The Arados had carried R4M rockets along with explosives to wreak devastation on the bridge. Intercepting American fighter planes had been unable to deal with the speedy 163 jet escorts or with the 550 mph Arado jet bombers.

Now, here at the Osnabrück headquarters, amidst the VIP's, were the two oberstleutnants responsible for the KG 51 jet aircraft successes at the Rhine Bridgeheads: Hans Kowaleski, who commanded the 40 bombers, and Wilhelm Hertzel, son of Germany's best aircraft designer, who commanded the 40 Komets. The generals here at Osnabrück knew that during the first three weeks of March, the Arado jet bombers had been conducting 300 to 400 sorties a day, weather permitting. Hertzel's light, speedy 163's had foiled Allied interceptors so the Arados could carry out their strikes with devastating effects. One spread of R4M rockets alone could knock out half a tank column and the Arado bomber carried 24 of these rockets.

During these weeks Kowaleski had lost only ten jet bombers, and half of these had been lost because of aircraft malfunction and not enemy aircraft interception or enemy ack-ack fire. Hertzel had lost none of his 163's, although many Luftwaffe experts had called the lightly armored Komet a cheaply built, suicide plane that would fall apart from a single burst of P-51 20mm fire.

When the officers had settled down at Osnabrück headquarters, Field Marshal Von Rundstedt turned to Oberstleutnant Kowaleski. "You must excuse my curiosity, Lieutenant, but we know the B-17 air attack on Daimler-Benz resulted in a near disaster for the American air fleet. You and Oberstleutnant Hertzel have thus far done well with your Arado bombers and Komet fighters on this western front. But," the field marshal pointed, "the Allied air fleets will surely attempt again to destroy Daimler-Benz, will they not? And will they not attempt to destroy the Ruhland refinery?"

The Luftwaffe officer nodded. "I have been in touch with pilots of Geschwader 7 at Lagar-Lechfield," Kowaleski answered Von Rundstedt. "Our units are ready to defend Ruhland just as they defended Daimler-Benz. I am told that two to three hundred conventional 109's and 190's will also be ready. General Peltz has spared no effort to make certain that you get not only tanks, but fuel for these tanks."

"Your confidence is quite strong," Von Rundstedt said.

"We know what our jet aircraft can do, Herr Field Marshal," Kowaleski said. "We have seen nothing but success against the enemy. Why shouldn't we be confident in our endeavors?"

"I suppose you are right," Von Rundstedt nodded, softening his face, the closest he could come to bringing a smile to his sober face. Then the field marshal spread a map on a long, oblong table. He pointed a finger on a particular area. "Here the American 1st Army is poised at Remagen. They have been building up supplies of material and men for the past several days according to our intelligence. There is little doubt the Americans intend to strike out soon, perhaps within a few days. Their target would no doubt be Mannheim and then Leipzig. Regretfully, the enemy will have a great superiority in men, equipment, and air power."

The staff members listened in silence.

Realistically, Von Rundstedt told his generals, and despite the opinions of the Führer, the war was lost. Germany's only hope was to inflict such severe losses on the enemy that the Allies would listen to a proposal for a favorable peace instead of unconditioned surrender. Von Rundstedt's hopes rested on the assumption that new tanks and adequate fuel supplies soon arrived on the western front, before the American 1st Army could launch its drive towards Mannheim. So, Von Rundstedt told his staff, a heavy burden would fall on oberstleutnants Kowaleski and Hertzel. The jets would need to support German Panzer and infantry divisions in the unenviable task of scattering the American 1st Army drive that was certain to come. Could the Arados and Komets do this in the face of frightening air superiority?

Lt. Hans Kowaleski again expressed confidence. He again reminded Von Rundstedt that his jets had already done well against Allied efforts along the Rhine, despite the hundreds of P-51 fighter planes that had tried to stop him. Kowaleski promised that he and Hertzel would spare no effort to stop any new Allied offensive into Germany. They had 30 Arados and 25 Komets in serviceable condition and General Peltz had promised Kowaleski another 20 Arados within a few days. Fifty jet bombers did not seem like much in the face of hundreds of Allied fighter planes, but Kowaleski believed that one jet, with its superior speed, armament, and maneuverability, was worth a dozen P-51's in aerial operations.

Von Rundstedt nodded and then looked at his ground troop commanders. "Have we taken all precautions for the movement of troops and supplies against Allied aircraft?"

General von Klüge handed Von Rundstedt a circular he had put out some days ago. The circular had been distributed to all German units, from field commanders to squad corporals. The field order had urged all units to follow instructions carefully, since Allied tactical air units of the 9th Air Force were on daily prowls, looking for targets of opportunity, especially supply trucks, supply trains, and troop carriers. The circular read: "To all passengers and drivers: Whoever camouflages lives longer. Be cautious or fall victim to enemy strafing planes. Ten days furlough, special, for shooting down an enemy strafer. The Anglo-American ground attack aircraft are the modern highwaymen. They are searching not only for columns of traffic, but they are hunting down every gasoline truck and every ammunition truck. Our fighters and anti-aircraft have had considerable success during the days of the great spring battles, especially our jet aircraft. But fighters and anti-aircraft cannot be everywhere. Every soldier can and must join the fight against ground attackers. Special favors will be shown successful gunnery units. Each soldier who knocks down an enemy strafer with his infantry weapon receives ten days special furlough. Units which have been particularly successful in shooting down enemy ground attacking planes with infantry weapons will receive special ration allowances. Therefore, seek cover first, then fire away!"

The circular had had its effect on the German ground forces of the western front, General von Klüge assured Von Rundstedt. The ground troops had done a better job of keeping themselves hidden from the aerial hunters of the Allied tactical air command. The Germans now moved only at night and they traveled cautiously over little known roads and lanes.

After Von Rundstedt read the circular with a tinge of amusement, he got down to the serious business of preparing a strategy against any new Allied drives into Germany. Actually, the Germans were quite familiar with the secret Allied plan, Operation Overtone. The plan was the worst-kept secret of World War II, probably because too many people knew about it.

To oppose Operation Overtone, Von Rundstedt offered these suggestions. In the north, outside of his own field headquarters at Osnabrück, he would station two Panzer divisions and three infantry divisions of von Klüge's 7th Army. In the center, beyond Cologne, the field marshal would station several more infantry divisions, along with the 5th Panzer Army. To the south, before Mannheim, he would entrench Dietrich's 6th Panzer Army and the remaining infantry divisions of his Army of the West.

"The Allied offensive will surely begin with a drive towards Mannheim," the German field marshal told Lt. Kowaleski. "Are your jet aircraft prepared to stop them in this sector?"

"We will make every effort," Lt. Kowaleski promised. "And, as I said earlier, General Peltz had promised to muster more than 600 109's and 190's here in the west to further support your efforts, Herr Field Marshal. These new geschwaders will be fully active as soon as fuel arrives in a week or so."

"Excellent," Von Rundstedt nodded.

Thus, by midnight, 20 March 1945, both sides were poised for new fighting. General Omar Bradley called a final meeting of his staff at his field headquarters south of Cologne.

"All of our units are on go, with the 7th Army kicking off a drive towards Mannheim in a couple of days. By the end of the week, all units should be on the offensive. The 9th Tactical Air Force will offer full support. Brief your commanders thoroughly, and hopefully Operation Overtone will be our last European campaign."

"What about the jets, General? And the tanks?" somebody asked.

"What about them?" Bradley answered brusquely.

The aide did not answer. Like his general, he would hope for the best. Perhaps General Webster's 9th Air Force could find their airfields or learn to cope with these jet aircraft.

And at Osnabrück, Von Rundstedt received an encouraging message from Berlin. "I have received word that new tanks have already left Daimler-Benz," he told his Army of the West commanders. "The Allies will need at least several days before they can launch their offensive on all fronts. By then, our Panzer divisions should be materially strengthened to meet the enemy challenge. And, of course, Oberstleutnants Kowaleski and Hertzel will have their jet aircraft at your disposal whenever the need arises. So," he gestured emphatically, "take this message back to your field commanders: we are not yet beaten."

Strange words from a man who only a few weeks ago had said: "As far as I am concerned, the war is over."

And thus, on the eve of the Battle for Germany, every Allied and German commander knew the stakes. If the Allied air forces could somehow knock out Daimler-Benz and Ruhland, the ground offensive through Germany would be little more than a milk run. But, if the Allied air forces could not stop the twenty-four-hour-a-day Tiger tank production and the fuel pouring out of the Ruhland refinery, the Battle of Germany could be an Allied nightmare.

The first target, Daimler-Benz, had survived an American attempt to destroy it. Now, the Americans would try to destroy the second target—Ruhland.

On 21 March 1945, General Charles Lawrence, commander of the 5th Bomb Wing, 15th Air Force, met with eleven group commanders in his headquarters at Foggia, Italy. Wing personnel had seen the colonels filtering into the converted Foggia Hotel all during the early morning and he suspected the rumors were true—the 15th Air Force would hit Ruhland. Generally, General Lawrence merely sent out instructions to group leaders for bomb runs against German targets north and east of the Alps that had become routine during the past year. The 15th Air Force did not enjoy the glory and publicity of the much larger 8th Air Force based in England, despite the 15th's sometimes wicked blows against enemy targets in southern Germany, Czechoslovakia, and Romania. But now, it appeared to the airmen at Foggia that the 15th would soon gain notoriety themselves.

Inside the hotel ballroom, now a headquarters conference room, General Lawrence scanned the group commanders and their A-3 officers who sat around a huge, oblong table. Behind the general a huge screen lay against the wall, a screen that would soon flash the target and strategy for an upcoming mission.

Seated at the long table were the commanders of six heavy bomb groups—the 97th, 99th, 2nd, 301st, 463rd, and 483rd. These groups had been in continuous operation out of Italy for at least a year or more. Some of them had served in the MTO since 1942, occupying new air bases in the wake of General Mark Clark's infantry and tank unit advances through Tunisia, Sicily, and finally, Italy.

In the fall of 1942, the 97th, 99th, and 301st began operating from heavy bomb group airfields in North Africa, harassing enemy targets as the Germans retreated into Tunisia. The 2nd Bomb Group had seen action in France in World War I and had now returned for a second tour after two decades. Only the 463rd and 483rd were newcomers, having arrived in Italy about a year ago. But these two groups had been involved in almost daily bombing missions since their arrival in the ETO.

Among the fighter group colonels were the commanders of the 31st and 52nd Fighter Groups, and two P-51 units, which had served in the ETO since the North African invasion in November of 1942. The 82nd, a P-38 group, and the 325th, another P-51 group, had been in the Mediterranean theatre since January of 1943, over two years. Only the all-Negro P-51 332nd Fighter Group had served less time, having arrived in Italy in the fall of 1943. But like the other 5th Wing fighter groups, the 332nd had also flown almost daily missions as fighter bombers or as escorts for long-range bombers hitting strategic targets.

As usual, Colonel Ben Davis sat at a far corner of the oblong table. Despite the dozens of briefings at 15th Air Force or 5th Wing headquarters, Davis had not quite overcome his uneasiness among the other 5th Wing officers. He was black and he sometimes felt out of place among the all-white 15th Air Force airmen. Most of the 15th Air Force personnel by this time saw the 332nd Fighter Group as just another air unit, but a few people still agreed with a USAC staff officer in Washington who said: "No country in the world has been able to organize a satisfactory air unit with colored personnel." And, if these disparaging words from an air corps VIP were not enough, a second high-ranking officer had bluntly told General Hap Arnold, commander of the Army Air Corps: "Colored officers do not possess the necessary background to qualify them for supervisory positions now filled by white officers." Within a week, however, this would be disproved.

Still, Davis could not help feeling uncomfortable at this oblong table. But he looked up with everyone else when, at 1051 hours on this morning of 21 March 1945, Brigadier General Charles Lawrence called to order the six bomb-group and five fighter-group commanders.

"Gentlemen," Lawrence began, "we've rescinded Field Order 77A and replaced the order with FO 78A. Tomorrow, the 5th Wing will conduct the longest bombing mission ever run out of the MTO. We'll be hitting the Ruhland oil refinery deep inside Germany."

An eruption of chatter exploded among the officers in the Foggia Hotel ballroom. The defeat over Daimler-Benz lay clearly in the minds of these group commanders and they knew they too could suffer the same fate at Ruhland. Lawrence waited for the chatter to subside before he continued.

"Yes, the rumor is true," General Lawrence said. "We're going to Ruhland. It's no secret that the Allied high command is quite concerned about the German acquisition of new oil supplies. They consider the refinery at Ruhland an important target, as important as the tank factories at Daimler-Benz. We can guess that the Germans think so too and they'll probably defend Ruhland with the same viciousness as they defended Daimler-Benz."

"Isn't Ruhland an 8th Air Force target?" somebody asked.

"Usually," Lawrence answered, "but the Germans have set up usually heavy anti-aircraft and fighter protection along the Dummer Corridor in Western Europe. It's been quite costly for the 8th to hit Ruhland, so General Todd has asked us to hit Ruhland."

The colonels mumbled again. They suspected that 8th Air Force, because they had failed so miserably at Daimler-Benz, wanted the 15th Air Force to suffer through any similar disaster at Ruhland. However, none of the colonels said anything. When the mumbling subsided, General Lawrence nodded to Colonel Fred Eaton, the 5th Wing's A-3 officer. Eaton darkened the ballroom lights and lit up the screen.

"Here's your target," Colonel Eaton said, indicating a glob of stacks, refineries, and buildings with a pointer. "The target is located at 51.29 degrees north by 13.53 degrees east. The complex lies about 1½ miles east of the small village of Schwarzheide and about 65 miles east of Leipzig. The refineries are not in Ruhland itself, but some two miles north by northeast of the city.

"These refinery stacks," Eaton said, pointing to some chimneys in the photograph on the screen, "are about 125 feet high. The target is roughly a rectangle about 1700 yards by 1000 yards square with the axis on a northeast-southwest direction. The target is fairly compact, as you can see, with all vital areas grouped closely together. You'll also notice that the target itself is V-shaped, lying between two branch rails that swing off the main railroad line from the city of Cottbus." Eaton paused and then flashed a map on the screen.

"You'll be following this route," the 5th Wing A-3 officer said, "straight up the boot, over the Alps, across Austria, over eastern Czechoslovakia, and then into Germany. We'll go into the target in two waves. The 97th, 483rd, and 463rd in the first; the 301st, 99th and 2nd in the second. The first wave will rendezvous over Termoli about 0830 and the second wave will rendezvous over Lake Lessio, Italy, at 0825 hours. The two waves will join at Vrogodi, Austria, about 0915 hours and then proceed to target.

"The escort," the A-3 officer said, now looking at the fighter group commanders, "will pick up the B-17's at Konigswarha, Austria, at about 1000 hours and then take the Forts in and out of the target."

"We know that the 8th Air Force hit Ruhland on 15 March with minimal results," General Lawrence pointed out. "The plant is still 75% active, with a probable monthly capacity of 22,000 tons of fuel, half gasoline for aircraft and half diesel for tanks. With the capture of the Hungarian oil fields, the Germans might easily double this capacity. So it's vital that we knock out Ruhland."

Colonel Fred Eaton continued. "Our plan is to get the four remaining active refineries. The first wave will hit the plants at the northeast tangent and the second wave will hit the refineries at the southwest tangent. You should approach the target area between 1224 and 1302 hours. With any luck, you should be on your way back by 1320 hours. Colonel Niles Ohman of the 97th Bomb Group will command this mission."

"What about defenses?" one of the group colonels asked.

"How about fighters?" somebody asked.

"We do know they have about fifty anti-aircraft guns around Ruhland and you can expect a few 109's and 190's to intercept around Vienna and Prague," General Lawrence said. "But your escort should easily take care of them. There may be as many as 100 or 150 fighters near the target area. But again, escorts should be able to handle these."

"How about jets?" another bomb group commander asked ominously.

General Lawrence did not answer immediately, and the group leaders around the table looked intently at the 5th Wing commander.

"We're not sure about jets," Lawrence finally spoke. "Intelligence reports fifty or sixty ME-262's and ME-163's active near Berlin and Leipzig. We do know they've been keeping every available jet in eastern Germany in reserve to defend Daimler-Benz. Whether or not they sent these jets to Ruhland is anybody's guess. Anyway, the prospects of a few jet interceptors should not cause panic."

However, Colonel Ben Davis and the others scoffed. The Ruhland refineries were no less important than the Daimler-Benz plants. The Germans could surely send their jets to intercept from a mere 100 miles away. Colonel Ben Davis stroked his chin. His pilots had never tangled with ME-262's and he wondered if his 332nd pilots could cope with jets. In fact, could any of the 15th Air Force's P-51 or P-38 groups cope with the zooming, heavily armed planes?

When the 5th Wing briefing ended, Colonel Ben Davis carried this uncertainty back to his airfield at Cattólica, Italy.

Chapter Six

Nearly 600 miles away, another conference opened in the München-Riem headquarters of General Adolf Galland, commander of JV 44. Besides the staffel officers of JV 44, Colonel Johannes Steinhoff and his two JG 7 staffel commanders also sat around an oval table to listen to Galland.

Galland opened the meeting with his Luftwaffe officers. "A toast to our first real success against a massive enemy air fleet," Galland said. As General Peltz pointed out, we accomplished this victory with a mere 70 aircraft. What might we do with several hundred of them?"

The men in the room, the jet fighter leaders of JV 44 and JG 7, nodded in agreement. They felt elated, not for General Peltz, not for the Führer, not for the Third Reich, but for themselves. These seven flying officers were outcasts in the eyes of the Nazi leadership, but they along with Galland had proven the effectiveness of the jet fighter plane. These mavericks could not help wondering how the 18 March victory had affected Hitler and Goering.

Ever since the Battle of Britain, Goering had berated the German fighter command for its alleged lack of aggressiveness and even cowardice. In the autumn of 1944, after heavily outnumbered German pilots had failed to stop an Allied air raid, Goering had accused the fighter pilots of receiving too many decorations they did not deserve. In a fury, Adolf Galland had wrenched his Knight's Cross from his neck and flung the medal at Goering. In subsequent weeks, other courageous, experienced fighter pilots like Rudolpher and Lutzow had severely criticized the Nazi leaders, especially after they dismissed Galland as commander of Luftflotte II. In turn, these men, the cream of the Luftwaffe, had lost their own commands.

Possibly, the Führer had allowed Galland to form the jet fighter unit in the hope that vastly superior Allied air units would quickly decimate JV 44, and the Führer could then rid himself of these mavericks once and for all. Certainly, Hitler never expected the results at Daimler-Benz on 18 March 1945—a mere 72 jets warding off a thousand American planes. And now, the Führer could only pout in silence at the success of jet fighter pilots and allow Galland a free reign.

The exploits of these men on that recent air fight over Daimler-Benz had not only silenced Nazi critics, but had made these pilots overnight heroes in Germany. It had not taken long for the thousands of awed employees at the Marienfelde plants to spread the news of this success all over Germany. Still, General Adolf Galland was very uneasy. He did not want this 18 March victory to bring a smugness to his jet fighter pilots. He had called these jet staffel leaders together to warn them about overconfidence as well as to discuss strategy.

"Enemy bombers will surely return again—today, tomorrow, or the next day," Galland said. "The failure at Daimler-Benz will only whet their determination. We do not know where they will strike next, but we must be prepared to meet them wherever they strike. We cannot wallow in our recent victory, for the Americans have a knack for devising new strategies to overcome failure." Galland now looked at Colonel Steinhoff. "What is the status of your JG 7 at Lager-Lechfield at the moment?"

"Our aircraft are ready and our pilots are on full alert," Steinhoff said.

"Should the Americans strike again," Galland said, "I suspect they will attempt to destroy the oil refineries at Ruhland, or they will make another attempt to destroy Daimler-Benz. In any event, we will come to your aid if they attempt to attack Ruhland and you must come to our aid again if they make a new attempt to attack Daimler-Benz."

"My pilots will be ready," Steinhoff said.

Now Galland squeezed his face, looked out of his headquarters window and then turned. "It is possible the Americans may attempt to destroy the oil trains coming from Hungary or the Laubitzer rail lines and bridges. For this task, the Americans will probably use air units from Italy. In that event, Colonel Steinhoff, your JG 7 must be the first line of defense. If you can both alert us and delay them, we will join you with Jagdverband 44."

"We will not hesitate," Steinhoff said.

Galland looked at some papers on his desk. "With only six staffels at our disposal, we are badly understaffed. I have asked General Peltz again to bring our units to full complement. However, he said no, he was having problems getting trained jet pilots. He hopes to assign new jet aircraft and pilots to us within the next few weeks, but that does not help us for the moment, so we must do what we can with what we have. I ask that each of you return to your staffels and make certain that both your pilots and aircraft are fully ready for any emergency."

The meeting in Galland's headquarters broke up and his staffel leaders returned to their units with a new resolve.

At 0500 hours, 22 March 1945, Colonel Ben Davis met with his squadron commanders in the 332nd Fighter Group's operation tent at the Remitelli drome in Italy. As usual, Davis addressed his commanders soberly and they responded with the same sobriety. The group had a strong esprit de corps despite their isolation at Cattólica, where they remained segregated from other 15th Air Force units. They had long ago accepted Colonel Ben Davis's warning: "The future of the colored man in the air corps depends on the manner in which we carry out our mission. The work done by every man in this group, be he ground crewman or pilot, will allow us very little pleasure until the experiment with an all-colored air unit is deemed an unqualified success. Every man in the 332nd will go through an ordeal; he will find that pleasures and relaxations available to men of other organizations will not be available to him because his task will be far greater and his responsibility much heavier. However, the reward will be the advancement of our people."

The Lonely Eagles were indeed proving to other 15th Air Force people that they were capable of carrying out their mission with as much success as any other unit in the MTO. Each day and each new success for the 332nd had lessened the bias among the white personnel of the 15th.

Captain Kenneth Smith, CO of the group's 99th Squadron, had already flown forty missions. Captain Bill Mattison of the 100th Squadron was on his second tour of duty, having completed a year with the old 99th Squadron before joining the 332nd last February. Major Al Turner of the 101st Squadron would be flying his 47th mission today. Among the squadron commanders, only Captain Ed Gleed of the 102nd Squadron had less combat time, but Gleed had been wounded twice and had willingly returned to combat after his hospital discharge.

"Today, we'll be flying our longest mission to date," Davis told his squadron leaders, "over 700 miles one way to the Ruhland oil refineries."

"Ruhland!" Captain Gleed hissed. "I thought the 8th Air Force took those northern targets."

"The 8th hit the place earlier this month," Davis said, "but heavy anti-aircraft and heavy fighter interception spoiled the chance for good results. The 8th only knocked out one refinery, so the place is still operating at 75% capacity."

"Colonel," Major Turner spoke up, "we can handle 109's and 190's, but what about jets?"

"Jets?"

"It's no secret, Ben," Turned said, "the 8th got the shit kicked out of them a few days ago when they tried to hit the Daimler-Benz tank factories. They had more than a dozen P-51 groups escorting the bombers, but they still fouled up. We hear that less than a 100 jets disoriented a thousand planes. That right, Colonel?"

"I don't have a full report."

"Like hell, you don't,". Turner huffed. "Won't we meet these jets over Ruhland? Is that why they're sending us up instead of the prima donnas from the 8th Air Force? Do they figure that a few niggers are expendable?"

"That's enough, Major," Ben Davis barked. "I might remind you that four other fighter groups and six B-17 groups are going with us. If you want out of today's mission, just say so. If anybody wants out, speak up. I'll personally call General Lawrence and tell him the Red Tails can't make this one."

Silence.

"Well?" Davis barked.

Silence.

"Then get your asses out of here and bring your pilots back for briefing—on the double."

An hour later, 30 pilots had joined Colonel Davis in the group briefing tent for instructions on today's mission. Then came breakfast and at 0900 hours, 31 P-51's of the 332nd Fighter Group left the Remitelli drome and headed northward. A few minutes later, 17 P-51's from the 31st Fighter Group left Mondolfo drome 30 miles away. Subsequently, P-51's from the 52nd and 325th left airdromes in Italy as did 28 P-38's of the 82nd Fighter Group. By 1000 hours, the five fighter groups, over a hundred and twenty-five planes, had crossed the Alps and rendezvoused with the B-17's over Konigswarha, Austria—right on schedule.

Colonel Niles Ohman of the 9th Bomb Group, designated attack commander, squinted through the port window of his lead Flying Fort and then picked up his intercom. He said: "Escorts at rendezvous. Tighten formations. Tighten formations." Then the colonel of the 97th Group watched the P-51's and P-38's move close to the bombers and settle next to the B-17's like suspended spiders. Only a small flight of P-38's streaked forward to search the pathways to Ruhland.

By 1100 hours, Jagdführer Knittlefield in Austria had alerted Luftwaffe headquarters in Berlin. Enemy bombers streaking northward across Austria. General Peltz stared at the huge map in his Fleigerkorps Reich office. But where? What target? Meanwhile, anti-aircraft batteries along the southern corridor in Austria and Czechoslovakia threw intermittent, ineffective flak at the passing armada, now flying at 30,000 feet. Occasionally, a flight of 109's or 190's took the air, but they dared not attack head-on against 125 enemy fighter planes. The German fighter pilots could only hope for stragglers. However, the German pilots did report the altitude, strength, speed, and direction of the American air fleet.

When the report of the approaching American bombers reached München-Riem, General Galland charted the route of the enemy air fleet. If the Americans were coming from Italy, the bombers were obviously seeking a target in Czechoslovakia, Austria, or Hungary. But, as more jagdführer warning reports came in, they reported the planes soaring high over these occupied countries without dropping bombs. The B-17's flew past the Libon works, the Kralupy works, and other usual targets in Czechoslovakia. Surely, these American aircarft would soon be out of range from their bases in Italy.

But then, as the enemy air fleet passed over Prague without attacking one of their favorite targets, the Skoda Works, General Adolf Galland suddenly punched a spot on his map. The Allied air fleet was heading for the Laubitzer rail line that ran from the Czech-Austrian border into Germany. They would try to hit the oil trains, rip up roadbed and destroy the Laubitzer bridges to prevent the movement of oil from the Hungarian oil fields into Germany.

"Fliegerkorps! Americanische aut Cesky Brod!" When this last jagdführer alert reached General Galland, he called Johannes Steinhoff at Lagar-Lechfield. "The enemy is no doubt pointing for the Laubitzer bridges. Proceed at once with JG 7."

"At once," Steinhoff answered.

Then, Galland alerted his JV 44, and within ten minutes his sixty jets had taken off from München-Riem to zoom southward. Conventional ME-109's and FW-190's also zoomed from scattered airfields in eastern Germany to intercept the American air fleet around the Laubitzer rail lines.

But General Galland had guessed wrong.

The 5th Wing armada continued straight northward, passing northwest of the JG 7 jets streaking eastward. The U.S. 5th Wing armada also passed west of the JV 44 jets streaking southeast. At 1138 hours, P-51's of the 52nd and 325th groups streaked outwards to meet German interceptors, but the fighter pilots expressed amazement. They found no German fighter planes. The American pilots were unaware that the Germans had guessed wrong, sending both conventional and jet fighter planes towards the Czech-Austrian border.

Soon the P-38's of the 82nd Fighter Group had also banked away from the 150 B-17's to meet the challenge of German fighter planes. But like those before them, the 82nd pilots also failed to find interceptors. Colonel Niles Ohman could not understand. They were almost near the target. Surely, the Germans would send something after them.

"Stay alert, stay alert," Ohman warned his B-17 gunners.

But the bombers droned on until noon, still without sight of German fighter planes. Suddenly, the sound of anti-aircraft fire echoed from the north. The pops of black flak exploded amid the bomber formations, rattling some of them, punching holes in the fusilages of others, but knocking down none of them.

At 1230 hours, Colonel Ohman could see the V-shaped complex of the Ruhland refineries. "Bombs away in one minute," the colonel's lead bombardier cried over the intercom. Then out of the east, at 28,000 feet, came a screaming, unfamiliar whine. Swift-moving aircraft, silver with black bands around their fusilages, came streaking towards the American air fleet. Colonel

Ohman knew instinctively that German jet fighter planes had arrived. His mind whirled with an image of horror: his B-17's falling out of the sky from hits by the speeding jets.

"Jets at three o'clock! Jets at three o'clock!"

The colonel's warning alerted both Colonel Ben Davis of the 332nd and Colonel Bill Daniels of the 31st Fighter Group. Both group commanders scanned the skies and then expressed surprise. There were only three jet planes in sight. Ben Davis reacted first. He ordered three of his squadrons to remain with the B-17's while he led the 99th Squadron towards the jets. A moment later, Colonel Daniels of the 31st followed the same pattern.

At 1232 hours, Colonel Daniels and six P-51's of his 31st Group reached the formation of three jets and opened fire on the speedy aircraft from 600 yards. The jets, heavily outnumbered as other P-51's joined the chase, broke off and zoomed upwards and out of sight. Colonel Ben Davis suddenly saw another formation of ME-163's but again, there were only three of them. Davis led the squadron of P-51's aggressively after them. However, the jets once more scattered and streaked out of range as the P-51's opened with 20mm bursts.

While the P-51's of the 31st and 332nd sought to engage the jets, the bombers, without molestation, soared over Ruhland in steady waves, dropping their 500-pound RDX bombs. Within moments, billowing smoke rose from the staccato explosions. Within minutes, the Forts had turned the Ruhland works into an inferno.

Colonel Johannes Steinhoff stared at the burning refinery.

Steinhoff had guessed the enemy's true target only when his jets had reached the Laubitzer bridges to find no sign and no reports of the enemy air formations. He had them hurried back to Ruhland to intercept, but he had arrived here too late and with too few Komets. Only six of his ME-163's had arrived during the bomb run. The other 163's had not arrived until the bombers had completed their mission. Steinhoff, with his twelve Komets, could do very little against 125 enemy fighter planes. As for Galland, the general had simply gone too far to the southeast and none of his Snowbirds would even see the 5th Wing Armada before the American planes left the area.

Still, despite the successful bomb run, Steinhoff mustered his twelve Komets at 40,000 feet. "Heil Geschwader!" he cried into his radio. Then his jets dove downward, but a flight of P-51's from the 31st Group successfully crossed the ME-163 formation. The P-51's opened up with chattering, strafing fire and thumping 20mm cannon fire. One shell struck an ME-163 and the jet burst into flames before spinning dizzily downward. The fighter group had scored!

But before the bombers had left the target area, the remaining eleven jets from JG 7 struck viciously, knocking three of the B-17's out of the air and damaging a dozen others. The jets had also knocked two P-51's out of the sky, which was quite a score against 125 fighter planes and 150 bombers. Further, the jets had made their score with no help from conventional 109's or 190's because these planes, like the JV 44 jets, were too far south to help Steinhoff.

By 1300 hours, the 5th Wing attackers were heading home. Most of the crews rode back gleefully—they had defeated the jets! Defeated jets! Only three bombers lost and a dozen damaged. A P-51 pilot had even shot down a jet.

Three hours later, at about 1600 hours, the B-17's touched down one-by-one on their bases in Italy. Ground crews met them with elated excitement. Their B-17's had conquered the dreaded jets and successfully carried out field order 78A. By 1630 hours, the fighter groups had also touched down at their Italian bases, where ground crews greeted the fighter pilots with the same elation.

The severity of the Ruhland raid had been confirmed by reconnaissance planes the next day. Only one refinery was still in operation. The news spread throughout 15th Air Force and then up to London and General Todd. The

5th Wing had overcome jets to knock out most of Ruhland, a sharp contrast to the disastrous Daimler-Benz mission of 18 March.

General Richard Todd gleefully informed his staff of the results. "Today, 250 aircraft of the 15th Air Force foiled jet interceptors and destroyed Ruhland. The strategy to send the 15th today was as correct as the strategy to send the 3rd Air Division on 18 March was wrong." Todd leaned over his desk and grinned. "I believe this same 15th Air Force 5th Wing can repeat today's performance over Daimler-Benz."

Nobody answered the air corps general.

Then Todd turned to an aide. "Get me General Lawrence."

In München-Riem, General Adolf Galland expressed disappointment at today's failure. When reports of the vast destruction at Ruhland reached him, he blamed himself for his misjudgment. But General Dietrich Peltz consoled him.

"We were not prepared for an Allied attack from the south," Peltz said. "Never before did the American 15th Air Force send their bombers this far north. We might all have guessed as you did. The raiders from Italy would attempt to destroy the Laubitzer bridges and Laubitzer rail lines. Take heart, Adolf. A mere dozen Komets that engaged the enemy air fleet did considerable damage against preposterous odds."

"But we lost one aircraft."

"Console yourself," Peltz sympathized. "Think what might have happened if Jagdverband 44 as well as JG 7 had been waiting for these B-17's over Ruhland, while two or three hundred conventional interceptors had engaged their escorts. We would surely have gained a victory like the one a few days ago."

"Perhaps," General Galland said. "In any event, the next time, we will be airborne and waiting for them as soon as they are beyond Prague."

Peltz tapped Galland on the shoulder. "Remember, you were only twelve today. Let the Allies foolishly fantasize in their belief that they have overcome our jet aircraft defense. The shock will be that much more devastating when they come again."

But, at the Remitelli drome, Colonel Ben Davis had not been fooled. He had shown little enthusiasm for the festive air prevailing throughout Italy after today's raid on Ruhland. Davis knew that several groups of P-51's had met a mere handful of jets and even so, the jets had knocked five planes out of the air and damaged a dozen others. He knew that today's mission to the oil refinery had not been a real test against the 60 to 100 jets and 200 to 300 conventional German fighter planes that had met the 3rd Air Division at Daimler-Benz.

And, as Davis stared into the growing dusk over the Apennine Mountains, he also suspected the Germans would not be caught offguard twice. He did not appreciate the prospect of another vital target, such as Daimler-Benz, where a skyful of German jets might be waiting for them.

And, in fact, by late evening General Charles Lawrence had flown north from Foggia to talk with Colonel Ben Davis of the 332nd and Colonel Bill Daniels of the 31st Fighter Group. Davis had driven from Remitelli to the 31st's field at Mondolfo. Now he sat in Colonel Daniels' office, drinking coffee with General Lawrence and Daniels while they discussed today's raid.

"I don't mind telling you," General Lawrence said to the two fighter group commanders, "the entire Italian boot is in ecstasy, everybody from the MTO commander to a campsite yardbird." He nodded at the 31st Group commander. "But Colonel Daniels told me the celebration was premature. He said if we didn't believe him, we should ask you, Ben. Well?"

"General," Davis answered, "we were goddam lucky. They just didn't expect us. The 15th never flew that far north before. It's my guess they thought we were going somewhere else."

"Like the Pilson or Skoda works?"

"I don't think so," Davis shook his head. "Maybe they thought we were going to hit their communications systems out of Hungary, like rail lines or bridges, to stop their tankers from carrying fuel from Lake Balaton. Maybe they thought we might even hit the Balaton oil fields themselves."

"That's what I think, too, Ben," Colonel Bill Daniels said.

Charles Lawrence nodded. "But you did run into jets and one of our pilots did knock one of those Komets out of the air."

"Like I said, Charlie," Colonel Daniels answered, "they didn't expect us over Ruhland because the 8th always hit the place before. Only a few jets got back in time to attack us, not the 60 or 70 that waited at Marienfelde for the 3rd Air Division."

Lawrence now looked at Ben Davis. "Daniels thinks we should make clear to the MTO commander and all the other air corps brass that we should not interpret this raid as something the 15th could do better than the 8th."

"I would agree," Davis said.

"Still," Lawrence said, "we did knock out one of those jets."

"I've got an idea how that happened," Ben Davis said, "and if we fly a mission where we're likely to run into jets, I'll explain my theory."

General Charles Lawrence nodded.

Soon the conference ended. Lawrence flew immediately back to Foggia, while Ben Davis drove back to Cattólica. The 332nd CO was not certain that he and Bill Daniels had sold Lawrence at all. So much elation had swept the air corps brass that they couldn't see the truth. So if they were not cautious, a lot of good 15th Air Force airmen would die, just as a lot of 8th Air Force airmen had died on 18 March 1945.

Chapter Seven

At 2200 hours, on the evening of 22 March 1945, General Nathan Twining, commander in chief of the 15th Air Force, received the following coded cable from General Carl Spaatz, commander in chief for all European air forces: "Cancel any 5th Wing strategic bombing missions for tomorrow, 23 March 1945. Bomber and fighter groups of this wing will use the day to service all bomber and fighter aircraft and to rest all combat crews. You, your staff, and the 5th Wing commander will be at 15th Air Force headquarters in Foggia at 0800 hours, 23 March 1945, for an important briefing.

The next morning before dawn, General Carl Spaatz, 8th Air Force Chief of Staff Richard Todd, the 8th Air Force A-3 Officer, Colonel Fred Sutterlin of the 100th Bomb Group, and Colonel Duncan Dade of the 56th Fighter Group boarded a plane in England for a flight to Foggia, Italy. In a second B-17 flew General Earl Partridge of the 3rd Air Division, General William Kepner of the 8th Fighter Command, and several other officers of the 8th Air Force. The 8th Air Force officers were flying in two planes so that the possible loss of one of the planes would not cause the loss of all 8th Air Force leaders.

At 0900 hours the two B-17's landed at Foggia, where General Nathan Twining and General Charles Lawrence greeted the visitors at the airfield. Then, jeeps whisked the array of air corps brass away from foreign correspondents who tried to corner them for questions.

Both these reporters at Foggia and base personnel stared curiously as the jeepfuls of VIP's disappeared from the airstrip and headed towards 15th Air Force Headquarters in the old Foggia Hotel. General Carl Spaatz and the top 8th Air Force brass had not made the long trip to Italy from England for a mere visit. Something big was in the wind and the men around Foggia could only conjecture. Would there be a new invasion? If so, where? The Allies had already hemmed in Germany and they were pressing the enemy on three fronts. Would they plan some kind of monstrous, coordinated air campaign that combined the 15th and 8th Air Forces in some major air operation? The men could only wait anxiously for answers.

At 15th Air Force headquarters, General Carl Spaatz called the meeting to order at about 1000 hours, with General Todd on one side of him and the 8th Air Force A-3 officer on the other side of the air corps commander in chief. General Twining, General Lawrence, Colonel Duncan Dade, Colonel Sutterlin, and Colonel George McGregor of the 5th Wing's 463rd Bomb Group sat around the table.

"We've seen a unique situation in the past few days," General Spaatz began. "Within four days we've suffered a total disaster and a total victory against similar enemy opposition. We know that all combat missions run into heavy anti-aircraft fire, whether the raiders come from England, Italy, or even from the tactical 9th Air Force in France. Of course, we usually meet fighter opposition from 109's and 190's, sometimes heavy and sometimes light. We've learned to overcome these types of defenses.

"However," the air chief emphasized, "the jet fighter interceptor has been something else. We've seen them on and off over Germany since last October, but they've generally been too few and too disorganized to represent any serious problem. However, the Luftwaffe has come a long way. They now have a well organized combined jet bomber-fighter unit on the western front that has been giving General Bradley trouble on the Rhine bridgeheads. And around Berlin, they've got a couple of other well organized jet fighter plane interceptors. The ME-262 unit is about group strength and the ME-163 unit is about squadron strength. These two units have been devastating. They gave our units an awful time over Magdeberg and Brunswick earlier this month. And recently, over Daimler-Benz, these jets caused a shock, to say the least.

"We have a good theory to account for the 3rd Division failure while the 5th surprised everybody with their success against these jet fighter units over Ruhland." Spaatz nodded at the 3rd Air Division commander. "Earl."

General Earl Partridge rose from his chair. The 3rd Division commander pointed out that the Dummer Corridor into Berlin had been getting worse in recent months with more anti-aircraft fire that was heavy and accurate. Further, the German interceptor pilots had become more brazen, despite the overwhelming numerical superiority of P-51 escort fighter planes. Partridge attributed at least some of this new aggressiveness to the fact that Germany was now pressed within her shrinking borders so they could concentrate more anti-aircraft guns and fighter planes into a smaller area.

Now General Todd spoke. He said that Allied intelligence had indicated that the Germans had placed first priority on the defense of Daimler-Benz and Ruhland during the current lull in the western front ground war. The Germans were working desperately to produce more tanks for Von Rundstedt and more fuel for their tanks and planes so they could stall Operation Overtone, the Allied onslaught from the Rhine. The Germans had placed their best flaknachtrich anti-aircraft gunners and hundreds of conventional fighter planes along the Dummer Corridor. By the time the 3rd Air Division reached Daimler-Benz the airmen were already quite shaken. They were also psychologically drained and in no condition to deal with these well organized ME-262 and ME-163 jet fighter units. Disaster followed.

"General Todd is correct," the 8th Air Force A-3 officer now spoke. He referred to some papers in his hand. "We've learned that no less a man than General Adolf Galland himself has organized and trained these new jet fighter units. His jet pilots include dozens of Germany's most experienced and renowned fighter aces. We understand that Galland has about 60 or 70 of these jets in his command. He may soon have a hundred."

General Richard Todd shuffled through some papers in front of him and then spoke again. "This is a report on yesterday's mission by the 5th Wing of the 15th Air Force, Field Order 78A. The strike force consisted of a mere 150 bombers with a 125-fighter escort, with one fighter group including the more inferior P-38. The Ruhland refinery must certainly fall into the category of vital for the German hierachy. While no one doubts that Von Rundstedt needs tanks, how could anyone deny the German's desperate need for fuel? In fact, maybe fuel is even more important than tanks. With the captured oil fields in Hungary, Ruhland becomes indispensible to refine fuel for both German tanks and German planes, including fuel for the jet aircraft. Yet," General Todd pointed, "the 5th Wing P-51 escorts easily handled these jets while the wing's bombers made a good run over the refineries. The question, then, is how could 125 fighter planes ward off the enemy when 400 fighter planes could not do the same thing over Daimler-Benz?"

"Yes, how?" General Carl Spaatz asked.

General Todd leaned over the table and spoke somberly. "The reason, gentlemen, is that the Germans do not possess the heavy anti-aircraft and fighter plane defenses to the south that the Germans maintain in the Dummer Corridor. When the 5th Wing reached Ruhland, their fliers had not suffered the kind of opposition found in the Dummer Corridor, so they were better prepared to cope with the jet fighter planes. In contrast, since the Comets and Snowbirds are far superior to our Mustangs, and since they're manned by experienced Luftwaffe pilots, you can imagine their effectiveness against a group of airmen already drained from a run through the Dummer Corridor."

"That wasn't the reason at all, General Todd," Charles Lawrence suddenly said.

"No?" Todd asked. "Then what?"

"We were goddam lucky," General Charles Lawrence said bluntly.

Lawrence told General Todd that he had spoken to Colonels Bill Daniels and Ben Davis on the previous evenings, and their personal reports had been quite different from the official reports sent to 15th Air Force headquarters.

"We caught them off-guard," Lawrence said. "After I spoke to Davis and Daniels, I spoke to some of the others, including Colonel McGregor," he said, gesturing towards the 463rd Bomb Group commander. "McGregor and the other group leaders of both B-17 and P-51 groups agree with the theory of Colonels Davis and Daniels: the Luftwaffe never expected aircraft from the 15th, based in Italy, to fly so far into Germany. For two years, the 15th had consistently flown to targets in Yugoslavia, Austria, and Czechoslovakia, as well as the Balkans and southern Germany. And, in fact, some of these targets had been so far away, we even flew shuttle missions to Russian airfields. No," Lawrence continued, shaking his head, "they just didn't expect us that far north into Germany."

General Todd grinned. "Come on, Charlie, you are trying to say the Germans didn't know you were coming? They've got the best damn alert systems in the world. You guys didn't get hurt before you reached Ruhland because the Germans have few defenses to the south."

"No," Lawrence said. "They thought we were going someplace else and they apparently sent their interceptors to the wrong place. We only ran into a dozen Komets and there wasn't a damn 109 or 190 in the sky. Yet your own intelligence told you they had at least 50 or 60 of those jets in the Ruhland-Marienfelde area, along with two or three hundred conventional fighter planes. Those planes went somewhere else, someplace in southern Germany or

Austria, or somewhere they expected to find our bombers. They apparently realized their mistake, but too late. No jets reached Ruhland until after our B-17's had already made their bomb runs on the refineries. In fact, the B-17 crews didn't even see a jet until they were on the way home. Does that make sense? Wouldn't those jets have been waiting for our Forts if they knew we were coming to Ruhland?"

"But one of your pilots even knocked down one of those jets."

"Sure," Lawrence scowled, "a dozen jets against 125 fighter planes. Even with the superiority of their jets, those German fighter pilots weren't going to take on those kinds of odds with much enthusiasm. Still, even with those few jets that arrived late on the scene, the jet pilots did shoot down three B-17's and riddle a dozen more. Frankly, I think we might have suffered the same disaster as the 3rd Air Division if a full jagdverband of jets along with a couple hundred 109's and 190's were waiting for us. I've got to go along with the reports of the group leaders; we were simply lucky. They were able to get in and out of Ruhland before those jets came after them."

"That may be the point, Charlie," General Todd said. "Your pilots ran into minimal opposition because they weren't prepared for an air strike from Italy. What you're telling us may be exactly what we're telling you."

"Maybe," Lawrence conceded grudgingly.

"Anyway," Todd said, "the facts as we see them—and they may not really be different for yours—is what prompted us to come up with a theory. We think we can make a wise decision based on these facts."

The 8th Air Force A-3 officer leafed through some papers in front of him and then addressed the group, and more specifically, General Lawrence. "The JCS of European Air Forces has carefully studied the circumstances after the two missions, the one to Daimler-Benz on 18 March and the one to Ruhland on 22 March. While there appeared to be some inferred critism of 8th Air Force, JCS would hardly suggest that the 8th Air Force flyers were any less courageous or conpetent than 15th

Air Force flyers. No, the JCS concluded realistically that the Germans were less prepared for an air strike from the south than they were from the west, because air strikes deep inside Germany had traditionally come from English airfields. In view of these facts, perhaps the 15th Air Force has a better chance for success against a target in eastern Germany than does the 8th Air Force."

"But after yesterday's surprise at Ruhland," General Lawrence said, "can we really expect to fool the Germans again?"

"Not likely," General Todd said, "and that's why we've got to move fast. After the air attack on Ruhland, the Germans will now consider seriously the possibility of more air strikes from Italy. We must therefore hit them before they can set up a real defense along the southern route as they've set up along the Dummer Corridor. JCS proposes, Charlie, that your 5th Wing conduct the next strike against Daimler-Benz."

The 5th Wing commander did not answer.

Todd looked hard at General Charles Lawrence. "Can your 5th Wing do it?"

"I guess we can," Lawrence answered. "The 5th went as far as Ruhland and I suppose we can go a little further to Berlin." The 5th Wing commander shook his head. "I can't promise the same success as they had yesterday in Ruhland."

Todd merely shrugged. "We want this raid immediately—tomorrow, before the Germans can recover from the 15th Air Force strike yesterday at Ruhland."

"I don't know if we can be ready that soon," General Lawrence balked.

"Didn't you get a cancellation order for the 5th Wing to stay home today?" General Spaatz suddenly barked irritably.

"Those orders did come in last night," General Lawrence admitted.

"Then your groups should be fresh enough to go tomorrow," Spaatz said brusquely. "I purposely brought General Partridge and some of his 3rd Air Division commanders to Italy to brief you on this important Berlin target."

"Yes, sir," the 5th Bomb Wing commander said.

"Good," Spaatz answered. "I suggest you contact your 5th Wing group leaders immediately and call them to wing headquarters for a briefing this afternoon at the latest. Meanwhile, General Partridge, General Todd, Colonel Sutterlin and Colonel Dade will fill you in on Daimler-Benz."

The group commanders of the 5th Wing hardly hardly expressed surprise at the sudden call on the late morning of 23 March to attend an immediate briefing at Foggia. The air corps brass had not scratched all missions today out of sympathy for overworked combat crews. They had not been told to spend the day readying all aircraft for a mere inspection. By 1130 hours, eleven group commanders had received word from the 5th Wing to report to Foggia by 1430, bringing with them their squadron leaders and A-3 officers. This allowed the group leaders about three hours to reach 5th Bomb Wing headquarters. When the bomber and fighter group leaders received their coded cables, all of them knew that something unusual was in the works, probably for tomorrow, 24 March.

At the Remitelli base in northern Italy, Colonel Ben Davis called his squadron leaders to group headquarters immediately for a 1145 meeting.

"Don't ask me what it's all about," Davis said, "but we're hopping down to Foggia right away for a briefing with General Lawrence. It has to be something big for a quick call like this and I suspect we'll go on some mission in the morning. I've already called the field to preflight three P-51's so we can fly piggyback, two in a plane. We'll miss noon mess here, but guess they'll feed us in Foggia."

"What's up, Colonel?" Captain Bill Mattison asked.

"Your guess is as good as mine," Davis answered. He looked at his watch. "I want all of you on the field by 1200 hours, 15 minutes. Dismissed!"

That ended any more questions. Both the squadron

leaders and the group A-3 officer, Captain Ray Ware, hurried out of group headquarters. Within a few minutes they had boarded jeeps for the short ride to the airstrip.

In ten other groups, group leaders followed the same pattern as Colonel Ben Davis. At Mondolfo, Colonel Bill Daniels hustled together his squadron leaders and his A-3 officer of the 31st Fighter Group. At Vincenzo Field, Colonel Joe Holtroder corralled his squadron leaders for a ride in the 82nd Group's P-38's. At Rimini Field, a mere 30 miles from the 332nd, Colonel Wyatt Exum and his squadron leaders of the 325th Fighter Group took off. In central Italy, from Piagiolino airfield, Colonel Marion Malcolm of the 52nd Group called his squadron leaders and A-3 officers for a flight to Foggia.

At the various fields of the 5th Wing's heavy bomber units, group commanders reserved single B-17's for flights to Foggia: the 463rd Group at Celone Field, the 483rd Group at Sterparone Field, the 301st Group at Lucina, the 99th Group at Torforcella Field, the 2nd Bomb Group at Amendola, and the 97th Group, also at Amendola. Colonel Niles Ohman appeared most anxious, for he was likely to be the mission commander again, as he had been on the Ruhland mission. Ohman did not know that, for some reason, General Lawrence would assign Colonel George McGregor of the 463rd Bomb Group as the mission commander for this next strike.

As P-51's and B-17's landed at Foggia, waiting jeeps hauled off the colonels, majors, and captains to the 5th Wing campsite in Foggia that included a clump of commandeered buildings in the occupied Italian city. The officers were first hustled through the 5th Wing officers' messhall for a noon meal and then driven to the ballroom of the old Foggia Hotel. Here, the visitors from the various 5th Wing groups found General Charles Lawrence and the wing A-3 officer, Colonel Fred Eaton, waiting for them.

The arrival of the various group leaders at Foggia between 1300 and 1400 hours again aroused a curiosity among the airmen at Foggia: first the VIPs in the morning and now the group and squadron leaders in the afternoon. Rumors quickly spread through Foggia: another important air attack was in the works. These men would not be called here in the middle of the day for a routine sortie. These Foggia airmen surmised that the mission would probably come off tomorrow morning, but they had no idea where.

For some time, the array of group officers loitering inside the Foggia Hotel ballroom mingled among themselves, conjecturing and guessing. What could be so important to bring them here on the double from eleven air bases around northern and central Italy? Even to the point of missing noon mess in their own unit messhalls?

But the conjecture of these 5th Wing group and squadron leaders heightened when they saw General Richard Todd of the 8th Air Force, General Earl Partridge of the 3rd Air Division, and the 8th Air Force A-3 officer come into the ballroom. What were these men from London doing here?

General Charles Lawrence waited a full fifteen minutes before the array of combat officers and A-3 officers quieted down. Lawrence then scanned the group of 70 or 80 men carefully.

"You must have felt a double shock today," Lawrence began. "First, we pulled you away from your posts to report here immediately, and then you find General Todd and some members of his 8th Air Force units here. Well," he grinned, "we're not going on a combined operation with 8th Air Force. Actually, General Todd, General Partridge, and the A-3 officer of 8th Air Force have been briefing us for the past couple of hours so that we'd be ready to brief you when you got here."

General Lawrence shuffled some papers in his hand. "We had planned some strikes tomorrow in Austria and Czechoslovakia, Field Orders #79A and 79B. But these orders have been rescinded. In its place, we've been preparing Field Order #80A, perhaps the most important order this wing ever had." He paused. "Gentlemen," he said, waving a new sheaf of paper in his hand, "this wing will leave Italy at first light tomorrow for the longest 15th Air Force bombing mission of the war."

"Farther than Ruhland?" one of the officers asked.

"Farther than Ruhland," Lawrence answered. "We're going after a target that has generally been a target for 8th Air Force. That's why General Todd and his staff are here—to acquaint us with this target and to help us present a strategy for their strike."

"Where, sir?" another group officer asked.

"Berlin," General Lawrence answered, "the Daimler-Benz tank assembly plants at Marienfelde."

The usual eruption of chatter that followed the target revelation at a briefing never materialized. Only a sober silence and an array of stunned looks answered the 5th Bomb Wing commander. 800 miles away, one way! And right through the most heavily defended areas of northeast Germany. The flyers of the 15th Air Force had never psyched themselves, either physically or emotionally, for any air strikes in northeast Germany. True, they had luckily come off the strike at Ruhland with minimal damage—but Berlin! Somebody was crazy to think the 15th Air Force could pull off a raid this deep into Germany, when everything north of the Remitelli airfield was still in German hands.

Colonel Bob Bivro of the 2nd Bomb Group broke the silence. "I don't get it, sir. We thought the 8th Air Force handled targets that far into Germany."

"Normally they do," Lawrence said. "However, we've had quite a conference with the 8th and 15th Air Forces' staffs and we believe the 5th Wing has a better chance of hitting Damler-Benz than the 8th. The JCS has concluded that the Germans were not as well prepared for an air assault from the south as they were from the west. So our wing will hit this Daimler-Benz target."

The group leaders sensed the finality in the voice of General Lawrence and there were no further protests. Every group and squadron leader here suspected that Lawrence had already committed the 5th Wing to an attack on Daimler-Benz and nothing would change that fact. The airmen of the 5th Wing would strike Marienfelde, or fall out of the sky in the attempt.

"Relax, Gentlemen," General Lawrence said, forcing a grin, "it may not be as bad as it appears." His voice echoed through an eerie silence that still hung heavily in the huge Foggia Hotel ballroom.

Chapter Eight

The briefing at 15th Air Force headquarters in Foggia began when General Charles Lawrence spoke from the podium of the huge ballroom. "We've had a full and accurate report on the target area from General Todd and the group leaders of the 3rd Air Division. We'll pass this information on to you during this briefing." He paused and gestured towards his 5th Wing A-3 officer. "I'm turning the briefing over to Colonel Eaton. He'll acquaint you with the target and strategy."

Colonel Fred Eaton stepped to the podium next to Lawrence and gestured to an aide who darkened the huge ballroom and then flashed a photograph on the screen behind the podium.

"This is a reconnaissance photo taken of the Daimler-Benz complex about a year ago by 8th Air Force," Colonel Eaton began. "The shots were taken from 20,000 feet and you can see the full rectangular site—about a thousand acres. We've made a designation for the three main buildings and the large railroad yard." Eaton tapped his pointer on the screen. "The big structure at the top is 2A, with the railroad yards below 2A. 9A is in the center and the large building at the bottom of the photograph is designated 10A. One problem encountered by the 3rd Air Division was the necessity to make a wide 90-degree turn before coming into the IP. However, since you'll be flying in from the south, you can come directly over the target!"

Colonel Eaton then told the array of 5th Wing group and squadron leaders that the 8th Air Force had offered no excuse for the 18 March foul-up except that the Germans had apparently moved unusually heavy ack-ack units into the Dummer Corridor, and the German interceptor fighter pilots had shown more aggression than they had for many months.

"But," Colonel Fred Eaton gestured, "General Spaatz is quite convinced that the major problem was the new jet fighter plane that forced most of the 3rd Air Division bomb groups to abort Daimler-Benz and hit secondary targets. The 3rd Air Division has given us some excellent current photos of the target and its defenses and that should help." Eaton then gestured to his aide, who flashed a series of new photos on the screen, showing the location of the major anti-aircraft defenses around Daimler-Benz.

There were countless batteries of flaknachtrichs strung for 30 miles in the Dummer Corrider leading into Daimler-Benz from the west. There were a few batteries stretching outward to the north, but only three batteries lined the approaches to the Daimler-Benz complex from the south. The corridor from the Alps northward showed one battery at Komatau on the German-Czech border, another heavy battery around Kumenz, and the worst battery at IP. Neither 8th Air Force combat crews nor 8th Air Force reconn fliers had seen any anti-aircraft batteries east of Daimler-Benz. Lawrence had considered the option of coming into the complex from the east, but the B-17's could not carry enough fuel to make such a long detour. So the air fleet would need to simply stay alert for ack-ack fire from these three areas.

Colonel Eaton now showed the group commanders several photos of ME-109's and FW-190's. "You're all familiar with these. We know the Luftwaffe may have two or three hundred of these conventional planes around Daimler-Benz, but nobody knows how many they can use because of a fuel and pilot shortage. Your escorts can handle them all right. But," he said, gesturing to an aide who flashed a new image on the screen, "you'll surely need to worry about these jets, the twin-podded ME-262's. And you may also see some of these lighter jets, such as the smaller German jet, the ME-163 Komet."

Colonel Eaton explained to the 5th Wing commanders that the 8th Air Force had seen these new German jet planes on and off since last fall. However, only lately had the Allies seen the first well organized geschwaders of jets. An Arado bomber unit with Komet escorts had been harassing the Allied bridgeheads at the Rhine. Despite overwhelming P-38 and P-51 superiority, the German jets had still managed to hamper American operations on the western front, including the destruction of the Ludendorff Bridge at Remagen.

Allied intelligence guessed that no more than 30 or 40 AR-234 bombers, with an equal number of ME-163's, had appeared over the front. Yet the speed and maneuverability of these new aircraft had frustrated American fighter pilots.

"The 8th Air Force ran into its first heavy jet fighter plane oppositon earlier this month at Magdeburg with considerable loss," Eaton said. "And, of course, these same well organized jet units met the 3rd Air Division on the 18 March air attack at Daimler-Benz. No American air fleet had ever met anything like it in the countless raids over Germany. There's no doubt the jets hurt the 3rd Air Division crews psychologically as well as physically. You must therefore make every effort to make your pilots and crews aware of the superior performance of these enemy planes.

"Intelligence tells us," Eaton continued, "that these jets come out of a deep sky from as high as forty or even fifty thousand feet. They carry devastating armament of a half dozen 4RM rockets, the equivilent of a 37mm shell. One of these rockets can knock a B-17 out of the air. Our sources tell us that Galland's unit is supposed to get more jets, so there may be up to a 100 of these planes in northeast Germany in the near future. If your flyers expect an awesome sight," Eaton said, "you can minimize the psychological factor."

"We hope you don't meet any of these jet fighter planes on the mission tomorrow," General Lawrence suddenly spoke, "but you must be prepared." Then he nodded to an aide who passed out mimeographed sheets to the 5th Wing group and squadron commanders. "You're getting a copy of Field Order #80A, which Colonel Eaton will explain to you."

"On this strategic bombing mission into Germany," Colonel Eaton said, "the wing will form into two close columns. The west column will include the 463rd, 97th, and 483rd Bomb Groups. The east column will include the 2nd, 301st, and 99th Bomb Groups. Each group will contribute a minimum of 28 B-17's for a striking force of at least 168 bombers. Colonel Roger McGregor of the 463rd Bomb Group will lead the first wave, the west column, with Captain Perry Ford as the bombadier IP leader. Colonel McGregor will also be the mission commander. Colonel Bob Bivro of the 2nd Group will lead the east column, with Captain Ed Kearns as the lead IP bombardier of the east column."

Some of the 5th Wing group leaders raised eyebrows in surprise when Eaton told them McGregor would lead Mission 80A. They had expected Colonel Ohman to lead the mission as he had led the Ruhland air strike, but no one commented. Further, neither General Lawrence nor Colonel Eaton offered any explanations for McGregor's command designation. Eaton simply continued the briefing.

"The 5th Wing will use the same fighter group escort for the six bomb groups as were used on the mission to Ruhland. Each fighter group will furnish a minimum of 30 aircraft, although we would like to see at least 50 from each fighter group."

Colonel Eaton now suggested that the 31st and 332nd Fighter Groups escort the west column of bombers. The 52nd and the 325th Fighter Groups would escort the east column of B-17's, with the P-38's of the 82nd Group acting as roving scouts. The 82nd's squadrons would scan the forward and flanks of the aerial armada, reporting any potential German fighter plane interceptors. If the

P-38's needed help, they would radio the escort groups, who would furnish whatever they could to help out the 82nd. The escorts, of course, would provide cover all the way: on penetration, over target, and on withdrawal from target.

Colonel Eaton now discussed the physical target itself, flashing a new photo on the screen. "The Daimler-Benz assembly plants at Marienfelde, on the fringe of Berlin, includes three main buildings, a railroad yard, and several auxiliary structures, as pointed out earlier. As we said, we've designated these sites as 2A, 9A, and 10A. The first two groups of the west column will attack the 9A complex and the third group of the west column will hit the railroad yards. The lead group of the east column will attack the 9A complex and the other groups of the east column will attack the 10A segments of the target.

"All aircraft will carry two 1,000 pound RDX fused bombs, with a 1/10-of-a-second nose fuse and a 1/80-of-a-second tail fuse. The double fuse will lessen the possibility of duds, since the bombs can be ignited by either nose or tail impacts. For visual release, we'll use the intervolemeter set up on the bombs, with a minimum PPF of 200 feet. So bombardiers should set their Norden sights for 200 feet."

The A-3 colonel then explained the altitude and bomb run. The lead 463rd Group of the west column would bomb at 26,000 feet, the 483rd at 25,000 feet, and the 97th at 28,000 feet. The lead 2nd Group of the east column would bomb at 26,000 feet, the 99th at 25,000 and the 301st at 28,000. Eaton also reminded the group leaders not to drop any bombs through contrails of preceding squadrons. In fact, the squadrons should release bombs at a minimum of one minute intervals. Thus, the entire bomb run should take about 20 minutes.

"We hope to surprise them again as we did at Ruhland," General Lawrence said, "but the escort must be extremely careful. Gunners aboard the bombers should also be alert during the 20 minutes over target. It was our understanding that many bomb crew gunners of the 3rd Air Division had slackened off during the 18

March raid, and the lapse enabled too many of the German interceptors to penetrate the bomber formations." Lawrence nodded at his A-3 officer. "Continue, Colonel."

Colonel Fred Eaton gestured to an aide who flashed a map of central Europe on the screen. The colonel followed the map with a pointer as he continued the briefing. "The first wave of bombers will rendezvous over Termoli in northern Italy at about 0840 hours, and the three groups will proceed towards IP in formations at 5500, 7,000, and 4,000 feet respectively. The second wave of bombers will rendezvous at Lake Lesina, and then proceed to target also at 5500, 7,000, and 4,000 feet respectively. The key points will be Brbinj, Yugoslavia, where the formations will rise to 13,000 feet.

"At about 1210 hours, the control point should be the small town of Lambach, Germany, about ten minutes from IP. At Lambach the formations will rise to about 21,000 feet. About one minute from IP the formations should assume bombing height. First wave should be over IP at about 1220 hours, and the second wave should be over target at about 1230 hours.

"As for the fighter escort," Colonel Eaton continued, "the 51st and 332nd Groups will rendezvous with the west column at Herzberg, Germany, no later than 1135 hours. The 51st and 325th Groups will rendezvous with the east column of bombers over Torgau, Germany, no later than 1125 hours. The P-38 group should leave for search positions at Herzberg no later than 1115 hours. Fighters should find the bomber units at about 13,000 feet at the rendezvous points and then follow the established pattern: at least one squadron at 1,000 feet above the bombers, one squadron at port lateral, and one squadron at starboard lateral. Each escort group should follow this pattern so that each bomber column will have two squadrons overhead and two squadrons on both the port and lateral positions."

"Colonel Eaton will now familiarize you with your call signals," General Lawrence spoke once more. "Be sure to use only these signals. Copy them on your pads and remember them carefully. Also, make sure your pilots and air crews understand them thoroughly." He nodded again to his A-3 officer. "Colonel."

Eaton read from a sheet of paper. "The bomber calls will be designated Shapely: Shapely leader for the lead 463rd Group, Shapely 2 for the 97th, Shapely 3 for the 483rd, Shapely 4 for the 2nd, Shapely 5 for the 301st, and Shapely 6 for the 99th. Squadrons will be designated a, b, c, or d. Colonel McGregor will be the TO leader and designated Shapely Leader. The escort call signals will be Jetblack: Jetblack 1 for the 31st, Jetblack 2 for the 332nd, Jetblack 3 for the 51st, Jetblack 4 for the 325th, and Jetblack 5 for the 82nd. Colonel Bill Daniels will be the fighter escort leader and designated Jetblack Leader."

"Recall code is Tearoom. Route out call is Pixy 1 and route back call is Pixy 2. If any of you need to fly on to Russian territory because of damage or enemy pursuit, the Russian landing code is Firtree. We've already notified our Russian Allies in Hungary, Czechoslovakia, and Poland. Be sure to use the Firtree call word should you decide to make any emergency landings in Russian held territories."

The A-3 officer gestured for another photo on the screen and then continued. "Rally point after IP," Eaton pointed with his pointer, "will be at Drebskau, Germany, and rally rendezvous should be no later than 1400 hours. Bombers, with escorts, will then proceed south to Cesky Brod, then to Knittlefield at about 1450 hours and then back to base.

"And finally," the A-3 officer continued, "if you look at your FO sheet, you'll see your alternate targets: the Prague marshalling yards in northwest Czechoslovakia, with the IP at Hintring, and a rally left to Cesky Brod; or, the Prague/Ligen AFV works, area three, with IP at Patate, and also with a rally left to Cesky Brod; or, the Pilson/Skoda works with the IP at Rakoneik, and again with a rally left to Cesky Brod." Then, the A-3 officer paused. "Hopefully, we'll drop all our bombs at the Daimler-Benz target, using H2X technique if we find a heavy cloud cover."

Colonel Eaton's comments on three alternate targets drew sober frowns from the flying officers in the Foggia Hotel ballroom. A strike order usually designated one or at most two secondary targets. But FO 80A listed three. Many of these colonels and majors wondered if perhaps 15th Air Force brass harbored doubts about the 5th Wing's ability to hit Daimler-Benz. Maybe they would get no nearer to the vital tank assembly plants than did the 3rd Air Division. Perhaps they would need to expend their bomb loads on the Czechoslovakian targets.

"Any questions so far?" General Lawrence asked.

The answer was a low chatter among the array of group and squadron leaders.

"I hope you carefully study your copy of FO 80A," General Lawrence continued. "The FO pretty well covers the discussion at this briefing. Any questions?" he asked again.

When no one responded, General Lawrence leaned over the podium and scanned the 5th Wing airmen for a full minute before he spoke. "We hope we're as lucky tomorrow as we were yesterday. In fact, our luck yesterday had much to do with designating the 5th Wing for the attack tomorrow. But we cannot discount the possibility of running into a jet jagdverband. True, you only ran into a few jets yesterday on the mission to Ruhland, but they did not interfere with the bomb run and one of them was shot down. Why?"

Nobody answered.

Lawrence then told the assembly that he had spoken to the 31st Fighter Group's captain, John Dillard, who had knocked the Komet out of the air on the mission to Ruhland. The 31st pilot could not really explain how he had managed to shoot down the speedy jet. However, in talking to group commanders, Colonel Ben Davis of the 332nd Fighter Group had offered a reasonable theory. Davis, leading a flight from one of his squadrons, had been in the same area as Captain Dillard, and Davis had seen the kill.

"From studying the circumstances of the kill," Lawrence said, "Colonel Davis concluded that Dillard's squadron was, in fact, still in formation when the several ME-163's streaked down from high altitude. And, as the jets flew past, this line of P-51's took shots at the German fighter planes. Not only did Captain Dillard knock out one of the Komets, but the 163's were not able to reach the bombers during the bomb run. The jets, in reality, had actually flown past a gauntlet of P-51's with the inevitable result of getting hit by at least one of the Mustangs. The gauntlet of fire had also kept the other Komets away from the bombers. Now," Lawrence pointed, "This was a sharp contrast to the circumstances after the bomb run. Later, our P-51's were scattered all over the sky, chasing after these Komets, unable to catch them, and allowing some of them to get some good shots at the bombers, knocking down three of them.

"Perhaps," General Lawrence gestured, "our escorts should create a deliberate diagonal gauntlet. In such formations, perhaps some of the P-51's will get hits on these jets if the planes streak down towards the bomber formations."

Now, Colonel Fred Eaton intervened. "I'm inclined to agree with General Lawrence," the A-3 officer said. "If we keep our fighter escorts in elongated, single formations, and close to the bombers, we might have considerable success against these jet aircraft. I would guess," Eaton gestured, "that not even a jet fighter pilot would relish the idea of running a gauntlet to reach the bomber formations. We've listened carefully to Colonel Davis's suggestion, and he has an excellent theory on how to deal with these jets."

"Colonel Davis will explain his theory," General Lawrence suddenly spoke. "I'm sure you'll find it interesting."

Another chain of low mumbles radiated through the officers about the huge oblong table and they stared at Ben Davis. Few of these men questioned the ability of the 332nd Group commander, for he and his black pilots had certainly proven themselves over the past year. Still, some of the squadron leaders of the 332nd felt uncomfortable. Captain Bill Mattison, one of the Lonely Eagle squadron leaders who had accompanied Davis to Foggia, lowered his head with a tinge of embarrassment as those around the table stared at his CO. However, Colonel Davis remained calm and sober. When the mumbling subsided, Ben Davis rose from his chair and scanned the faces around him. Although many of the officers eyed him curiously, Davis maintained his poise and spoke confidently. He nodded towards the podium and one of the 5th Wing aides flashed a chart on the screen.

"On the screen you can see the diagonal pattern of six P-51's," Davis began. "When we learned formation flying, we learned the diagonal pattern as well as the V, box, and other formations. During the strike at Ruhland, we noted a peculiar circumstance with a flight from the 31st Fighter Group. After peel-off, most of the P-51's simply scattered to chase after the jets. However, Captain Dillard's flight was still more or less in a straight, diagonal line. The six P-51's almost froze in this position when the ME-163's came flashing down. Almost instinctively, I would guess, Dillard and his pilots fired at the passing jets. One ME-163 was damaged and Captain Dillard shot down a second one. But," Davis emphasized, "it might have easily been one of the other pilots in this flight who scored the fatal hit on the jet."

"What are you suggesting, Ben?" Colonel Bill Daniels of the 31st Group asked.

"I suggest that if we see jet interceptors, we peel off by flights of six and deliberately set ourselves in a single diagonal formation to meet these interceptors. They'll come from above and they'll need to get by us to reach the bombers. We'll force these jets to run a gauntlet and we can knock a lot of them out of the air and scatter a good deal more so they can't make effective attacks on the Flying Forts."

"We know," General Lawrence said, "that any attempt to tackle a jet one-on-one or even two or three-on-one is quite futile. These planes simply outrun, outclimb, and outmaneuver our P-51's. They deliberately get us to chase after them. Then they circle back to hit the exposed bombers and scoot away before the P-51's can catch up to them."

"If each group can muster fifty P-51's," Colonel Davis said, "it means we can offer several or more gauntlets from each group against these jets. We'll certainly outnumber them, and our problem will simply be to get into the proper position to meet them."

"It is our belief," General Lawrence said, "that these jet fighter plane pilots know our usual technique of chasing after interceptors after we see them. This has been one of the reasons the jets have been so successful. They allow us to chase after them and then, with their superior speed, they can come back and hit our bombers before our P-51's can catch up to them. If we should run into jet interceptors tomorrow, their pilots will no doubt expect our escort planes to do the same thing. It will be the obligation of escort pilots to control their emotions and anxieties and follow the suggestion of Colonel Davis. You should peel off in flights of six, not too far from the bomber formations, and wait for the jet planes to come to you. Hold your pattern and wait," Lawrence emphasized. "This will no doubt require patience on the part of your fighter pilots, but you must stick faithfully to the pattern and restrain the urge to scoot after a jet plane."

Ben Davis now suggested to the fighter group commanders that they organize their pilots at their own local briefings into flights of six, not in terms of one's, two's, or squadrons. Each flight leader must calculate the probable route of the jet interceptors and then line up his flight in the proper area for a relay volley of fire at the passing jet. In effect, the aircraft would be using a spray of fire, some of which fire must necessarily hit some of the jet aircraft.

A subdued chatter erupted from a few of the fighter group commanders while staid looks beamed from two or three of the bomber group leaders. While most of them had respect for Davis, they did not believe the technique could work. A few simply opposed any suggestions from a black colonel. However, General Lawrence, who noticed the lack of enthusiasm from some of these commanders, squelched any chance of protest.

"Let me conclude," the 5th Wing commander began soberly, "that the diagonal pattern of defense against jet interceptors will be an order from this wing. We all know that chasing after those jets has not done any good and caused harm to bomber formations, so we have nothing to lose in trying something new. All fighter group commanders, therefore, will instruct their flight leaders to follow this technique and all fighter escort groups will sortie and use this technique against any jet interceptors."

Lawrence paused before he spoke again. "I'll expect all escort units to be at rendezvous points at 1125 and 1135 hours respectively. All bomber groups will be at the key point of Brbinj by 1015 hours. Bomb Group commanders should hold briefings by 0500 hours tomorrow morning and leave base no later than 0630 hours. Fighter group commanders may brief and leave their bases at the group commanders' discretion. But," he pointed, "be sure you're at rendezvous on time. Any questions?"

None.

"Okay," General Lawrence nodded, "you can return to your bases for your own local briefing."

An eruption of chatter came from the seated colonels and majors before the flying leaders ambled out of the huge ballroom of the Foggia Hotel.

On the flight back to Remitelli, Captain Bill Mattison and Colonel Ben Davis said nothing to each other for nearly two hours. But as they approached the field, Mattison finally spoke. "Colonel, do you think this technique of diagonal patterns will really work?"

"Colonel Daniels and I made the same observation yesterday against those few jets we met over Ruhland," Davis answered, "and that's that the observations suggest we do make them run a gauntlet. General Lawrence is satisfied."

"If the jets don't knock out the gauntlets," Captain Mattison said.

Davis squeezed his face. Mattison was right. Neither he nor General Lawrence nor anyone else in the ballroom, had considered this aspect, and Ben Davis suddenly remembered that they had only run into a few of these jets yesterday. Tomorrow they might meet sixty or more of them, since Allied intelligence indicated that a full jet jagdverband was defending Daimler-Benz. Perhaps as many as a hundred of these jets would be waiting for them. And if General Galland was leading the jet units, then these jet pilots would have a man who was adept at dealing with enemy fighter planes. Galland might quickly come up with a means to thwart the diagonal defense pattern—like breaking up the six plane flights first, as Captain Mattison suggested.

Davis now felt an uncertainty. It would not take a man like Galland long to figure a way out. The wily Luftwaffe commander might quickly alter his own tactics to scatter the mustangs. Then Galland and his pilots could streak into the bomber formations with minimum difficulty.

Darkness had settled over the Apennine ridges beyond Remitelli Field by the time Colonel Ben Davis came in for a landing. The trip back from Foggia had intensified his uncertainty. The idea that had seemed so optimistic a few hours ago had now soured. He had forced the gauntlet idea on the other fighter group commanders of the 5th Wing. Suppose the technique failed tomorrow? Such a failure would only encourage the few bigots who still prevailed in the 15th Air Force to reinforce their claims that black pilots were too inferior for important combat missions.

Chapter Nine

Darkness still hung over the Foggia Plains on the morning of 24 March 1945. The 31 B-17's of the 463rd Bomb Group sat wing-tip to wing-tip on the Celone airfield, with engines roaring in blaring drones. The Forts of the 463rd sat in the morning darkness. The 463rd ground crews had spent fifteen to twenty hours on 23 March to hone and tune the Flying Fortresses. And now the engines turned smoothly; there were no sputters out of the blocks or cowlings, and no vibrations in the wings and fusilages. When the jeeps and trucks brought crews to these aircraft, the airmen would feel at least one consolation—their planes were fit for the long, nearly 1600-mile excursion to Marienfelde.

Still, the B-17's sat heavily, loaded with bomb bays of 1,000-pound RDX bombs, several crates of .50 caliber machine gun belts for the guns, and 2760 gallons of high-octane gasoline in their tanks. The B-17's would need full efficiency to carry such a load on this longest flight into Germany ever made by the 463rd Bomb Group. The heavy loads would force the pilots to lift their planes in a slow, gradual assent to their maximum 27,000 feet altitude to conserve fuel. Also, the aircraft would need to follow a direct, hazardous route to Berlin as a further conservation measure. The direct route could bring the aircraft through heavy anti-aircraft fire, despite the assurance of air corps brass that the Germans maintained few flak units between the Alps and Berlin. Yet few of the 463rd airmen doubted Colonel McGregor's statement: "This could be the most important mission of the war."

On this Saturday morning, H hour had come at 0430 hours when charge-of-quarters crews began their rounds to awaken 300-odd airmen who would participate in today's mission. In the morning darkness, the airmen first cleaned and dressed and then ate a hearty breakfast in the huge group quonset hut messhall. For many, this morning's fare of sausages, coffee, eggs, and rolls might be their final meal.

After breakfast the men shuffled off to the 500-seat Celone movie theatre that the 463rd used as its briefing quarters. Here, the crews heard the group operations chief and Colonel George McGregor outline today's target and point out the job of each man in the overall 5th Bomb Wing plan. The men reacted in stunned silence when the A-3 officer told them that the Foggia-based 5th Wing would fly all the way to Berlin. And their awe intensified when McGregor explained to the 310 airmen that he fully expected to meet jet interceptors, despite General Todd's suggestions to the contrary. For all of these airmen, the image of the deadly Snowbirds and Komets struck terror. They had heard too much about the superior performance of those planes, including the destruction suffered by the 8th Air Force at this same Daimler-Benz target on 18 March.

But General Lawrence could not have selected a better man than Colonel George McGregor to lead today's attack. McGregor had been a bomber pilot for nearly ten years, working up from the ranks until he won command of the 463rd on 11 September 1943. Since that time he had led his group on more than thirty missions deep inside Germany's Fortress Europe. He had been a major, commanding one of the 463rd's squadrons in March of 1944, when the group won its first unit citation during the long, dangerous mission to the Ploesti oil fields. Since then, the crews in the 463rd had gained extensive combat experience, including shuttle missions into Russia.

True, the 463rd was among the new groups in the MTO, but the 463rd had compiled an impressive record during its year of service in the Mediterranean: 200 combat missions over twelve enemy occupied countries, over 1200 enemy aircraft shot down, probably shot down, or damaged, and a pair of Distinguished Unit Citations for two of their bombing missions.

The group's A-3 staff of the 463rd had spent most of the night organizing the flight patterns for morning briefing. The group would fly in a huge diamond of four squadrons—Able squadron in the lead, Dog Squadron to the rear, and Charlie and Baker Squadrons on the flanks. Seven to eight planes would comprise each double-V squadron formation. The group navigator and the group bombardier would fly in the lead plane of the lead Able Squadron, with the deputy group navigator and the deputy group bombardier in the rear Dog Squadorn.

The wing had asked for 28 B-17's from each group, but Colonel McGregor had assigned three spare Forts to fly in his 463rd complement of Forts. Thus, in the event of losses or aborts, the spares could fill in any gaps in the squadron formations.

Colonel George McGregor himself would fly in the lead plane of the 463rd, aircraft #725, Big Jenny. At 0620 hours, after briefing, the 463rd group airmen boarded jeeps and trucks on this early morning for the ride to their pre-flighting B-17's. Many of the men suspected that today they would suffer through their most hazardous combat experience. And for some, as was always the case before a dangerous mission, they feared they would never come back.

Colonel McGregor was the last man to leave his jeep. He watched the 31 crews clamber aboard the warmed up B-17's before he left his own jeep and ambled towards Big Jenny, the lead plane of Able Squadron. McGregor did not know it yet, but the 463rd would suffer the brunt of Galland's jet fighter planes.

At 0735 hours, Colonel George McGregor settled into

the co-pilot's seat of the lead B-17. McGregor would spend considerable time directing the huge 5th Wing armada and he could not be saddled with also flying Big Jenny. Captain Roger Ball, a man with twenty combat missions and several squadron leader assignments, took the pilot's seat of aircraft #725. When McGregor nodded, Captain Ball called the control tower. "We're ready."

"All clear, sir."

Ball pulled the throttle and the sudden, intense roar of the Fort's four engines screamed like a quartet of banshees across the open plains of the Celone airdrome. Then, when Captain Ball, peering from his cabin window, whirled his hand, ground crews yanked the chucks away from the wheels of the chafing plane. The Fort jerked forward and then rumbled smoothly down the taxi strip towards the runway. Closely behind Captain Ball came 30 other B-17's and soon the long line of Forts rolled down the taxi strips and rocked to a halt behind the lead plane. Then, on signal from the tower, Big Jenny's pilot whirled the big Fort onto the runway. Once here, he revved the four engines into high-pitched whines. Then Ball released the brakes and the heavily loaded B-17 raced down the long airstrip before the ship soared skyward into the bright morning.

Thirty more heavily laden B-17's waited at the end of the long airstrip to follow the lead plane. At thirty-second intervals, each B-17 pilot revved his engines and then sped his plane down the runway and into the sky. By 0655 hours the last of the thirty-one planes was airborne. The 463rd had gotten off 25 minutes late, but they would easily make up the time for rendezvous over the Adriatic Sea.

At moments, the thirty-one Flying Fortresses had disappeared into the northern sky, leaving a somber quiet over the airbase at Celone. The men in the wooden control tower abandoned their station and clambered down the planked steps. Emergency crews in crash trucks, medics in ambulances, and spectators in an array of vehicles now left the airstrip. By 0710 hours, the Celone airfield appeared totally abandoned. But the ground crews of the 463rd would return in about nine hours, the anticipated TA of their B-17's and combat crews. Most of these ground personnel hurried to the messhall to drink coffee and to eat donuts. They wondered—how many of their comrades and how many of their B-17's would not return this afternoon from Marienfelde?

In five other heavy bomb group units, group leaders directed a similar array of men to waiting B-17's that would join the 463rd in the long flight to Marienfelde.

Just across the small valley from Celone, the B-17's of the 483rd Bomb Group sat wing-tip to wing-tip on their field at Sterperone, Italy. Here, Colonel Paul Barton, the CO of the 483rd, also briefed 300 men in a huge, three-poled tent.

"We'll be in the west column," Barton told his airmen, "and that means we'll be among the first to get hit by interceptors as well as flak. So I must ask all gunners to be especially alert today."

The seated airmen squirmed uneasily. The men of the 483rd, The Pathfinders, did not appreciate the idea of a run-in with German jets any better than did fellow airmen in other bomb groups.

The 483rd had been a relative newcomer to the MTO, arriving in Italy only a year ago. But they had not waited around long. In the spring of 1944, they had joined the long-range bomber groups of the 5th Bomb Wing to hit factories, refineries, marshalling yards, storage areas, airdromes, bridges, gun emplacements, and troop concentrations throughout Italy and Fortress Europe.

On 18 July 1944, the group received its first DUC during an escorted bomb run into southern Germany to the railroad yards at Memington. The group had run into forty or fifty German interceptor planes, but they had still managed to fly through the gauntlet of German fighters to flatten the yards, locomotives, repair shops, and over a hundred pieces of rolling stock. The 483rd had lost eight B-17's on that day, but German troop movements to the eastern front had suffered severe curtailment.

The airmen of the 483rd Bomb Group didn't know it

yet, but they would get their second Distinguished Unit Citation today.

The last group of the west column, the 97th Bomb Group, had sustained its motto, *Veni Hora*, the hour has come, with distinction since the early months of World War II. The 97th had been one of the first American bomb groups to see action in the ETO when they joined the 8th Air Force in England in May of 1942. All during the latter part of 1942 and into 1943, they had attacked German targets in France with devastating effect. When the Army Air Corps created the new 12th Air Force in the MTO, General Spaatz had insisted that the 97th be transferred to the Mediterranean area as an experienced nucleus for the XII Bomber Command. The group's experience was vital, for most of the air groups would be untested newcomers.

The 97th had conducted the usual raids deep into Fortress Europe, along with other 15th Air Force heavy bomb groups. They won their first DUC on 24 February 1944 when the group knocked out a German aircraft plant in southern Germany against heavy flak and interceptor opposition.

Colonel Niles Ohman, who took over the 97th on 22 August 1944, held his briefing at Amendola Field where this group shared the field with the famed 2nd Bomb Group. Ohman warned his men on the morning of 24 March that they were probably going on their most dangerous mission in the history of the 97th. "It might be worse than the Ploesti raid, so stay alert every minute."

The 28 crews of the 97th rode silently to the waiting B-17's. Many of them, like bomb crews in other groups, suspected that some of them would not return to Italy today.

At the Sterperone airfield, north of Foggia, thirty B-17's of the 483rd Pathfinder Group soared upwards and away between 0545 and 0620 hours, well before the 0630 schedule. At the Amendola airbase, also outside Foggia, the 28 B-17's of the 97th Group were up and away by 0635 hours, just about on time. The two bomb groups winged northward to rendezvous with the Flying Fortresses of the 463rd over Termoli. Then the west column would begin its long flight north deep into Germany.

If the three bomb groups that comprised the west column in FO 80A could offer a fine record of accomplishment in the Mediterranean, southern Europe, and eastern Europe, the three bomb groups of the east column could offer their own credentials.

From point of service, the 2nd Bomb Group, based at Amendola, also near Foggia, was the first B-17 group to fly the B-17 for the Army Air Corps. On 5 August 1937, at Langley Field, the group received the initial Fortresses that came off the assembly line, the Y-1 B-17. They had flown these Forts to Brazil and Argentina to test their strength and endurance on a long flight. The Fort proved itself, and the B-17 subsequently became the United States' principal heavy bomber for World War II.

During two years in the MTO, the 2nd Bomb Group had distinguished itself quite well. They had made countless bomb runs over northern Italy, eastern Europe, and southern Germany. They too had won a DUC, this one for a raid on Stayrs, Austria, on 24 February 1944 against a horde of FW-190 interceptors.

General Lawrence had chosen well when he chose Colonel Bob Bivro and his 2nd Group airmen to lead the east column on today's mission. Colonel Bivro had been in the Army Air Corps for more than ten years, tracing his service back to Langley Field. He had already won several medals for gallantry and courage. Bivro, however, was one of those few group commanders who could not quite lose his prejudice against Negroes in the air corps. He did not know it now as he left his briefing tent in Amendola, Italy, at about 0600 hours, but in several hours he would lose his bias against the black fighter pilots.

By 0615 hours, Colonel Bivro was in the cabin of his B-17 at the far end of the 5,000 foot runway, his Fortress engines screaming and his plane straining against the brakes. When the control tower operator blinked "all go," Bivro released the brakes and the B-17 shot down the runway and soared into the northern sky. By 0642 hours,

Lieutenant Benjamin O. Davis at the time of his promotion to Commander of the U.S. Air Force in 1965.

Dr. Fritz Nallinger was the chief engineer for the Daimler-Benz enterprises.

Major Heinz-Wolfgang Schnaufer, one of Germany's greatest air aces, joined the JG 7 jet unit in defense of Daimler-Benz.

General Josef Kammhuber commanded one of Galland's jet staffels.

Dr. Wilhelm Haspel was the director of Daimler-Bcnz.

Captain Ed Gleed briefs his pilots for the 24 March attack on Daimler-Benz.

Field Marshal Von Runstedt commanded the German Army of the West. He needed the Daimler-Benz tanks if he was to stop Operation Overtone, a major Allied assault.

Colonel Ben Davis at a briefing in Remitelli for the 24 March 1945 raid.

General Adolf Galland of JV 44, the German jet fighter unit, had the difficult task of defending the Daimler-Benz tank assembly plants.

the 32 B-17's of the 2nd Bomb Group had become faint dots in the distance. And here, as at Celone and at other bomber fields, ground crews soon abandoned the runway areas to return to their quarters or messhalls. They too would wonder, how many men and how many planes would not return today from the longest flight into Germany ever undertaken by the 2nd Bomb Group?

At Lucina, Italy, across a small river from the 2nd Bomb Group base at Amendola, was the air base of the 301st Bombardment Group. This unit had also been among the first American air units to see combat in Europe. They had first served with the 8th Air Force before the experienced 301st came to the MTO to join the newly created 12th Air Force. The group was immediately committed to operations in the North African campaign, where they made heavy strikes against the Afrika Korps. Later, the 301st conducted continuous sorties in the Italian campaign and over Fortress Europe.

The 301st had won two DUC's, the first on 6 April 1943 when they attacked a German convoy against intense shore batteries, heavy anti-aircraft fire, and a horde of ME-109 interceptors. The group had sunk half of the merchant ships and had damaged most of the rest. As a result, General Rommel had failed to get the needed replacements in men and supplies for the defense of Tunisia.

At the briefing on this pre-dawn March morning, the airmen listened apprehensively to Colonel Bob Allyn, the group CO. Every flyer in the 301st guessed that they would face the toughest mission of the group's combat career.

The third unit of the east column, the 99th Bomb Group at Tortorcella Field outside of Foggia and on the coast of the Adriatic Sea, had joined the 12th Air Force in May of 1943. Like the other groups in the 5th Bomb Wing, the "Mighty Sighters" of the 99th had established a solid record in the MTO: North Africa, Sicily, Italy, southern France, and finally Fortress Europe. The 5th Wing commander, General Charles Lawrence, had been a former group commander of the 99th, and Lawrence had led them with honor in countless combat missions, including the attack on the Ploesti oil fields that earned the group its first DUC.

The 99th's commander now was Colonel Ray Schwanbeck, who took over the group only a few weeks ago. Now, this morning, like other B-17 group commanders, Schwanbeck also conducted a briefing with 300 airmen for the Daimler-Benz raid.

"We go in last," Schwanbeck told his fliers. "That means we might become the patsies for enemy fighter planes. Everybody else will be gone when it's our turn and we'll be the only ones left to hit. So I ask all gunners to be especially alert on the return from IP."

A chain of mumbles radiated through the 99th Bomb Group briefing tent. Then, when the briefing was over, the airmen of the 99th piled into jeeps and trucks for the ride to their waiting B-17's. They rode silently because every man here at the Tortorcella field knew that some of them would not return.

The thirty-two B-17's of the 99th Mighty Sighters left Tortocella by 0635 hours and roared north towards Lake Lesina to rendezvous with the 301st and 2nd Bomb Group at 0840.

A hundred to a hundred and fifty miles to the north of the Foggia area, the fighter groups had not yet taken off, even though the bombers were already winging their way towards the Adriatic Sea. From the 82nd Fighter Group base at Vincenzo, a hundred miles north of Foggia, to the 31st Fighter Group base at Mondolfo, a mere thirty miles behind the German lines in northern Italy, American fighter planes waited on their airdromes like anxious greyhounds, P-51 engines yelping in high-pitched whines and steel fusilages twitching like restless canines.

The Remitelli fighter base at Cattólica, Italy, lay on a broad plain in the San Marino Valley, east of the Appenines. Only the 31st Fighter Group airbase at Mondolfo, six miles farther up, lay closer to the Po River front lines, 35 miles or so to the north. On several occasions, the Remitelli drome had suffered Luftwaffe air attacks from FW-190 fighter-bombers. However, the

Germans had caused minimal damage, because by 1945, the Germans could afford few planes to support their ground forces in the stalled northern Italy campaign. Most of the Luftwaffe aircraft remained at home to meet the daily Allied attacks over Germany.

The 332nd Red Tails operated alone from their Remitelli base as part of the Army Air Corp's policy to keep them segregated from their white counterparts. The Lonely Eagles, despite this segregation and its hindrance to morale, had come a long way in the past two years. Most of the black airmen attributed this progress to their group commander, Colonel Benjamin O. Davis, Jr. On this March morning, the men of the 332nd realized that their colonel had ultimately brought them to the apex of equality with this assignment to escort bombers on the mission to Daimler-Benz, one of the most vital missions of the war. They also realized that their colonel himself had reached the heights of respectability among his white counterparts when the 15th Air Force willingly accepted Ben Davis's suggestion to use a gauntlet technique against any possible jet fighter plane interceptors.

AT 0750 hours, 24 March 1945, Ben Davis and his group A-3 officer, Captain Ray Wade, walked to the podium of the Red Tail's briefing tent. Captain Bill Mattison, who sat among his fellow 332nd pilots in the briefing tent, looked at Davis with a near sense of awe. Mattison now wore a tinge of guilt on his narrow face, for he had been among the loudest critics of Ben Davis when his CO had asked the 332nd airmen to maintain patience, perseverance, determination, and loyalty to duty. Only with these traits, Davis had insisted, could the blacks prove their worthiness in the Army Air Corps. Captain Mattison and the others, though impatient and frustrated, had heeded the words of their staid commander and now, in this Remitelli briefing tent, saw the successful results in their reluctant trust of Ben Davis. They would participate in one of the most important air missions of the European campaign.

Captain Mattison remembered that day in the spring of 1943 when the old 99th Pursuit Squadron had embarked in New York City for combat service in North Africa. When the 99th reached the MTO and found P-40 fighter planes waiting for them, Davis had insisted that the squadron go into combat as soon as possible. Davis knew that the future of Negroes in military aviation might well rest on the success or failure of the 99th in combat. However, General Carl Spaatz, who then headed the 12th Air Force in North Africa, had angrily dressed down Lt. Colonel Ben Davis when the 99th CO asked to go into heavy combat.

Mattison remembered how Spaatz had reprimanded Davis. "Who the hell do you think you are, Colonel?" Spaatz asked him. "Here you'll be treated the same as any other new unit that comes to this stinking hell-hole. I don't give a damn how much publicity you got back in the states, your 99th will start slowly. You'll pull the shit details—patrols, mop-up sorties, and all the rest. You'll get your feet wet first like all the other green bastards who come to this theatre of operations. Is that clear?"

At the time, Bill Mattison had felt that Spaatz had disparaged them because they were black, and Mattison could not understand why Ben Davis had reacted with satisfaction to General Spaatz's biting reply: "...like all other green bastards." Davis had told his pilots that General Spaatz would treat the 99th with the same contempt as he treated any other unit, and this was a good first step in equality.

Mattison and other 99th Squadron pilots had not agreed with Davis, but they had promised to follow the advice of their lieutenant colonel, despite any feelings of inferior treatment. For a long time the 99th Squadron in North Africa and then the 332nd Group in Italy did pull the shit details—patrol duty and ground support. But the patience of Ben Davis had paid off. As the pilots of the 332nd gained more experience, they soon became involved in more important combat roles in the MTO air campaigns.

At 0200 hours, 22 January 1944, the Allies began their biggest operation thus far in the MTO—the Anzio landings in Italy, and Captain Bill Mattison recalled that morning on D-day plus two. The 332nd had been assigned close support duty for the invasion force and at mid-morning their P-47's had struck the German defenses opposing the American landings in the Anzio area. But suddenly, a swarm of ME-109's had emerged from the east. Colonel Davis had called on his pilots to intercept the German attackers. In a fifteen-minute aerial melee, the 332nd had knocked 17 enemy planes out of the sky, with a loss of two of their own. The dogfaces at Anzio that morning had not asked what color the pilots were; they only knew that the P-47's with the red bands on their tails had saved them from a heavy Luftwaffe attack. The Lonely Eagles won their first DUC for this effort.

The 332nd had suddenly became a respectable member of the 15th Fighter Command in the MTO. By mid-1944, the 332nd got the new P-51 Mustangs and they joined other fighter groups of the 5th Bomb Wing to escort B-17's on long bomb runs to eastern Europe. The Red Tails won their next DUC over Romania while escorting B-17 bombers deep inside Fortress Europe. The Forts were attacking an array of enemy tanks, troop concentrations, vehicle columns, and German defense positions. The bombers had been jumped by over 100 ME-109's, but the 332nd pilots had destroyed 30 of the enemy intercepters, with one Red Tail pilot of the 101st Squadron knocking down three enemy planes himself. The effort of the 332nd had enabled the B-17's to destroy their targets and the Red Tails had won their second DUC.

Captain Bill Mattison was shaken from his nostalgic reminiscences when the bark of "Attention!" came from Captain Ware. Mattison looked up at the A-3 officer and Colonel Ben Davis.

"Captain Ware will explain our mission for today," Davis said.

Captain Bill Mattison sighed and then sat back to listen as the A-3 officer dimmed the tent lights and flashed a photo of Daimler-Benz on the screen.

Chapter Ten

Colonel Ben Davis was not the only fighter group commander standing on a podium on this morning of 24 March. In four other fighter units, group commanders were also briefing fighter pilots on the particulars of today's mission against the Daimler-Benz tank assembly plants.

The pilots of the 31st Fighter Group at Mondolfo had enjoyed ample sleep during the night and charge-of-quarter crews did not awaken the flying officers until 0630 hours, for breakfast and then briefing at 0730. However, many of the pilots were already up by 0630, for who could sleep with the prospect of this longest flight to date and a run-in with German jets led by Germany's foremost airman-Adolf Galland? In fact, many of the early-rising pilots had come into the already open enlisted men's messhall for breakfast, since officers' mess would not serve food until about 0630.

The 31st Fighter Group briefing began at 0730 hours, when Colonel Bill Daniels issued instructions to his pilots on the role they would play. The 31st Rednecks, along with the 332nd, would provide cover for the west column of bombers all the way to IP and back. For the most part, the white pilots of the 31st had long ago lost their prejudice for the blacks of the 332nd. They had worked alongside the 332nd for nearly a year and now. The 31st Pilots saw the Red Tail pilots as common partners with a common purpose.

The 31st had been in the MTO for two years, starting out with British Spitfires. They had eventually switched to P-47's and then, like the 332nd, the 31st got the new P-51 Mustangs in mid-1944. Almost immediately the group received its first DUC during a long-range mission to a production center in Romania. Since then, the 31st had escorted bombers to targets throughout Hungary, Bulgaria, Romania, Czechoslovakia, Yugoslavia, and southern Germany. On several occasions, the 31st Fighter Group had flown onto Russia after long-range missions into Poland.

In the fall of 1944, flying out of Russian bases, the 31st had made a spectacular air attack on German tank and motorized columns in Poland. They had decimated the columns so badly that the enemy could no longer pressure Russian troops advancing eastward from the Vistula River. A few days later, flying from the same Russian airfields, the 31st put a Luftwaffe air base in Poland out of business to reduce German air strikes against advancing Russian troops. For their efforts, the Rednecks had not only received their second American Distinguished Unit Citation, but they had also received a citation from the Russians, the only American air group ever so honored by the Soviets.

At Mondolfo, the 31st Fighter Group ground crews did not begin engine warmups until 0830 hours, about the same time the last B-17 for this 24 March mission was long airborne. But then, the P-51's, much faster than the bombers, could easily catch up to their Flying Fortress charges at the rendezvous point deep inside Germany.

The Redneck pilots had followed a heavy work schedule for the past several weeks, conducting escort missions for 15th Air Force bombers into Eastern Europe and supporting American ground troops who made probes into the German defenses in northern Italy. Thus, the group had exerted severe strains on their planes and pilots. Further, the Mondolfo airfield had suffered several Luftwaffe fighter-bomber attacks during the past two months, primarily because Mondolfo lay quite close to the usually meek and hidden German 110 light bombers in northern Italy.

Still, by the morning of 24 March, Colonel Bill Daniels mustered fifty-seven P-51's for the long trip to Marienfelde. Some of the 5th Wing staff had suggested that the 31st be scratched from the mission in favor of a fighter group that had enjoyed more rest. But General Charles Lawrence and Colonel George McGregor of the 463rd Bomb Group had frowned on the idea. McGregor, especially, had enjoyed Redneck escort on a dozen missions, and the 31st pilots had developed a smooth teamwork relationship with the 463rd bomber crews. Therefore, McGregor preferred the 31st planes to a more rested P-51 fighter group that was unfamiliar with Colonel McGregor's operational procedures.

McGregor liked the idea of a 116 fighter planes of the combined 332nd and 31st Fighter Groups as the escort for the 84 bombers of the west column. Besides, Colonel Bill Daniels himself was eager to participate in the mission.

In the 31st Fighter Group briefing tent, on this 24 March, Colonel Bill Daniels warned his pilots that jet fighters might be waiting for them. "I thoroughly agree with Colonel Davis's suggestion for a gauntlet defense disposition," Daniels told his pilots, "and it will be every man's responsibility to use this technique if we run into jet fighter planes. Otherwise, we may suffer the same fate as the 3rd Air Division." Then Daniels briefed his pilots on their position, rendezvous areas, and duties for the Daimler-Benz raid.

The bombers of the west column which would strike at the heavily defended Daimler-Benz plants could thus feel some comfort knowing that the distinguished 31st Rednecks and the capable 332nd Red Tails as their escorts.

Parked in a narrow valley at Rimini airfield in northern Italy were the Liquidators, the P-51's of the 325th Fighter Group. Inside the 325th briefing tent,

Colonel Wyatt Exum explained today's mission to his pilots.

The 325th, activated in 1940 in the United States, had arrived in the MTO in January of 1943, only a few months after the 31st. Since then, the Liquidators had seen combat almost every day. The experienced pilots of this fighter group had escorted bombers on dozens of missions into Eastern Europe, including shuttle missions to Russia.

"I don't know if the gauntlet formation will really work against jets," Colonel Exum told his fighter pilots, "but we know the P-51's of the 3rd Air Division fouled up pretty badly with the conventional method of chasing after enemy interceptors. It's important, therefore, that we stick carefully to his pattern."

The 325th's tandem escort of the east column, the 52nd Fighter Troup, had also served in the MTO for two years. The 52nd, like the 31st, had also entered combat with British Spitfires early in the Mediterranean campaign. They had not arrived here, however, until the Algeria-Morocco phase of the North African campaign had ended. However, the 52nd had then joined other 12th Air Force units in attacks on Axis-held bases in the Mediterranean, Sicily, and Italy, preparatory to the invasion of the European continent. In mid-1944, the 52nd had also been assigned to the 5th Bomb Wing as a longe-range escort unit.

The 52nd Fighter Group, whose motto, "Seek, Attack, and Destroy," had been carried out to the fullest, had won two Distinguished Unit Citations. On 13 August 1944, the group, operating alone as fighter-bombers, destroyed a massed group of Luftwaffe transport and fighter planes on the German's main air base in Romania. The raid had cut short a German attempt to reinforce the eastern front by air. The effort won the group its first DUC.

All during 1944, the 52nd had escorted long-range bombers for heavy attacks in Czechoslovakia, Austria, Hungary, Romania, and finally southern Germany. On 9 January 1945, the 52nd pilots had held off nearly 100 FW-190's and ME-109's, while their bomber charges leveled an aircraft factory in southern Germany. The group's efforts won for the 52nd their second DUC.

The 52nd Fighter Group held its briefing on the morning of 24 March at Piagilolino Airfield in Italy, 60 miles from the Remitelli base at Cattólica. The 52nd had not worked closely with the Red Tails of the 332nd and they knew little about them. They simply assumed that these black pilots, like white pilots, were trying to do the best job they could. The 52nd Group commander, Colonel Marion Malcolm, did not even think about the 332nd as he spoke to his pilots on their escort duties and outlined their part in this vital mission to Daimler-Benz. By 0845 hours, the pilots of the 52nd Fighter Group finished their briefing and headed for the P-51's sitting wing-tip to wing-tip on the field.

The east column of bombers for this dangerous mission to Daimler-Benz could not have asked for a better escort than the pilots of the 325th and 52nd Fighter Groups.

"Up and at 'em!" was the motto of the 82nd Fighter Group, whose parked P-38's lay waiting wing-tip to wing-tip on the taxi strips at Vincenzo Airfield in Italy. The 82nd, with its twin-engine Lightnings, had been up and at 'em on more than 600 missions. They had served as both escort planes and fighter bombers. In fact, the 82nd Fighter Group held the distinction of being the only air group in Europe who had won a DUC on both a fighter escort mission and on a bombing mission. They had won the escort DUC in July of 1944 while holding off German fighter planes while their bomber charges destroyed an iron works in Czechoslovakia. They had won their fighter-bomber DUC while macerating a German armored column that threatened the American bridgehead at Salerno.

Colonel Joe Holtroder, the 82nd Group commander, warned his pilots at the 24 March briefing that they could run into the dreaded jet. After instructions to the 82nd pilots on their deployment as vanguard scouts for this mission, Colonel Holtroder sent his pilots to breakfast before they manned their aircraft.

By 0800 hours on this 24 March 1945 morning, the P-38 pilots had settled themselves into the cockpits of their twin-engine Lightnings. The 82nd would run interference for the 5th Wing. General Charles Lawrence could not have picked a more capable MTO fighter group for this job.

Colonel Bill Daniels, commander of the 31st Fighter Group, had organized his P-51 pilots into the six plane flights for the diagonal defense pattern. After briefing, Daniels and his 56 pilots piled into several jeeps and headed for the whining P-51 Mustangs, the jeeps zigzagging over rough terrain and bouncing over ruts as the vehicles whined towards the taxi strips. By 0930 hours, 56 pilots had settled themselves into their cockpits and ground crews slammed shut the canopies. Then the Redneck group commander, Bill Daniels, climbed into his own P-51. By 0935, he too was settled in his pilot's seat.

"Are guns okay?" Daniels asked his crew chief.

"Yes, sir," the sergeant answered.

"Gas?"

"Full tanks, plus two full 110-gallon auxiliaries, sir. If you release the belly tanks around Brux, just south of the German border, you should have enough gas in your regular tanks for another seven hours."

"Good."

The crew chief paused. "And, sir, good luck."

Daniels nodded. "Thank you, Sergeant."

Then Daniels lowered his goggles and snapped on his oxygen mask. The sergeant snapped shut the canopy and then leaped off the wing of the P-51. Then, when a blinking signal came from the rickety control tower, Daniels gunned the engine of his P-51 and the Mustang screamed, vibrating and straining against the wheel chucks. Then, when the colonel whirled his hand, his crew chief pulled away the wheel blocks. The P-51 lurched forward and slowed down only when Daniels decelerated the engine. He rolled down the taxi way with fifty-six more P-51's trailing behind him. Soon he spun his P-51 into an 180-degree turn until the American fighter plane pointed its nose at the runway. The colonel revved the engine again before he roared down the strip and zoomed upwards at about 45 degrees into the bright morning sky.

At mere fifteen or twenty second intervals, the other P-51's of the 31st Fighter Group also shot down the airstrip and followed Daniels into the clear sky. By 0941 hours, the last of the group's Mustangs were gone. And here, as at the bomber bases, ground crew personnel meandered off from the runway and control tower. Soon the Mondoldo airstrip looked deserted.

Six miles to the south at the Remitelli airstrip in Cattólica, Colonel Benjamin O. Davis, Jr. prepared for the most important day of his military career. He recognized a sober fact. On this cool March morning, at about 0845 hours, as he drank coffee in the officers' mess, he knew the future of the black man in the Army Air Corps might well depend on the performance of the 332nd over the heavily defended Daimler-Benz plants in Marienfelde. Since the day Ben Davis had entered West Point in 1932, nearly thirteen years ago, Davis had been obsessed with a single goal—equality for blacks in the United States armed forces. He remembered well the response of Congressman James DuBois in 1932, when Davis had insisted on an appointment to West Point.

"No black has been there in forty years," the congressman had told young Ben Davis. "Sure, I can get you an appointment, but they'll make your life miserable. I strongly urge you to go to Tuskegee with your own kind. You can get an army commission out of there just as you can from West Point."

"I want West Point," Davis had insisted.

Congressman James DuBois had acquiesced and in the fall of 1932, Ben Davis, Jr. enrolled in West Point. He had taken abuse and ostracism, but Davis had maintained his calm and perseverance. By graduation day in 1936, he had earned the respect of his fellow cadets. Then Davis had refused to settle for an army career in the artillery or in a service unit, the only areas open in the army for blacks. In 1942, he had told his father, Brigadier General Benjamin

Davis, Sr., that he would go into the Army Air Corps.

"You're crazy, Ben," his father had answered him. "They don't use blacks in the air corps and they aren't likely to."

But Davis had persisted and he joined a token black air unit at Tuskegee, a unit that seemingly was going nowhere. Alone and isolated from the rest of the Army Air Corps, the unit had been dubbed the Lonely Eagles. However, Davis had vowed to turn this epithet into a badge of pride. He complained and howled and finally, the Air Corps sent Davis and this first black fighter unit, the 99th Pursuit Squadron, into the MTO. But, the 99th had fouled up on a couple of missions for lack of combat experience, and the foul-up had encouraged the bigots to seek disbandment of the black air unit.

"Based on the performance of the 99th," one colonel said, "it appears that black pilots cannot make it in the Army Air Corps."

Only ardent pleas by Ben Davis and his father before a congressional committee had given the black man another chance. In fact, the Air Corps formed the all-black 332nd Fighter Group and sent them back to the MTO with Lt. Colonel Ben Davis, Jr. in command. The group had remained isolated and relegated to minor shore patrol duties. Still, Ben Davis had continued to encourage his dejected black pilots.

The black pilots and black ground crews, however reluctant, had stood by their group commander. And, by 1945, Ben Davis had become a full colonel and had carried his 332nd Lonely Eagles to a high place in the 15th Air Force. The Lonely Eagles knew they were successful in 1944 when Colonel George McGregor told a group of 15th Air Force brass: "Any time I have to fly deep into the continent on a bomb run, I'll be glad to have Ben Davis and his Smokes along as my escort."

And now, the fortunes of the 332nd had come down to this 24 March 1945 morning. As he drank his coffee, Ben Davis looked at the squadron commanders around him: Captain Ken Smith of the 99th Squadron, Captain Bill Mattison of the 100th, Major Al Turner of the 101st, and

Captain Ed Gleed of the 102nd Squadron. Some of these men would earn DFC's today and one of them would not come back. The four squadron leaders ate their rolls and drank their coffee in silence, occasionally glancing at the clock. Within an hour they would be flying north on the longest mission of their careers.

These men had often complained when JCS sent the 8th Air Force on the most important missions. They had complained the loudest when the 3rd Air Division had drawn the Daimler-Benz assignment, certain they had again taken a back seat to the glory boys out of England. Then, like a sudden thunderbolt, they had received the Field Order 80A—mission to Daimler-Benz. On this 245th combat mission for the 332nd Fighter Group, they would be responsible for staving off attacks on the west column so that beombers could destroy the tank assembly plants. The complaining black pilots had gotten their wish. Of all the dozens of fighter groups in the European Theatre, these black pilots, who had often been relegated to second place, had now been told to put up or shut up. Now that they had the opportunity, Smith and Mattison and Turner and Gleed, and even Ben Davis, were not sure they could put up.

At 0900 hours, Colonel Ben Davis gulped down the last of his coffee. Then he looked at his squadron leaders. "Okay, let's go."

Nobody answered. Almost as one, they rose from the table and walked into the morning sunshine where jeeps waited to carry them to their pre-flighting P-51's.

In the jeep with Ben Davis, Bill Mattison sat next to the colonel. Mattison stared at his group commander with deep respect, for Mattison had been among the loudest critics of the white establishment that controlled everything, including the Army Air Corps. Mattison had often complained that the 15th Air Force, the 5th Wing, the 2nd Bomb Group, or somebody else continually put down black pilots and treated them as inferiors. He had often scoffed at the pleas of his group commander to keep the faith and to maintain patience. And now, inside this jeep,

Mattison had seen his commander's determination pay off.

Yet, ironically, now that the 332nd had been among those picked for this vital Marienfelde mission, Captain Bill Mattison was not so sure he wanted it. Davis could not help but notice the apprehension on Mattison's narrow face.

"Are you okay, Bill?" Davis asked.

"Sure."

"We'll probably run into those jets today. You know that, don't you?"

"I know," Mattison answered.

"You're not letting this thing with the 3rd Air Division on the 18th bother you?"

"No," Mattison shook his head. "Anyway, the bomber crews have to worry more about those jets than I do."

"You've got to protect them, Bill. McGregor and all his guys are depending on us. So are the guys in the 97th and 483rd. If we fail, half of them may not come back today." Davis leaned closer to Mattison. "We've got to keep those jets away from those bombers, far away, and the only way to do that is to put your own lives on the line. McGregor and Lawrence and Todd and all the rest think we can do it. Are you ready to put your life on the line for them, Bill? Are you?"

"What the hell kind of a question is that, Ben?" Mattison growled. "That's my job. I'll do it."

"Well, sometimes I wondered."

"Wondered?"

Davis looked around the quiet San Marino Valley of northern Italy and he then squinted at the rolling hills beyond. "We're alone on this base and you never liked that; neither did some of the others in this group. But today they put their lives in our hands. It might be easier to say the hell with them because we've had a tough time getting as far as we did in the air corps. But they called on us, Bill. If you're not ready to risk your life for them, maybe you shouldn't come along."

Captain Bill Mattison lowered his head and then bit his

lips. "I'm sorry, Ben, I'm sorry as hell. But I promise you, when I get up there today, I'll make sure those guys in the B-17's mean as much to me as I do to myself. I'll do my job, I guarantee it."

"Good." Ben Davis nodded and grinned.

By 0910 hours, only ten minutes later, the loaded jeeps with 59 pilots reached the screaming P-51 Mustangs. None of the other four fighter groups for today's mission could launch 59 aircraft, only five less than a full complement of 64 for four squadrons. Perhaps the 332nd had been lucky, suffering only minimal losses during the past several missions, or perhaps their ground crews had done an exceptional job in the maintenance and repair of aircraft.

Now, the Lonely Eagle pilots spilled out of their jeeps and scrambled towards their waiting P-51's, wincing from the thunderous, high-pitched whines of engines that echoed across the valley floor and richochetted off the rolling hills beyond. Aircraft ground chiefs stood on the wings of planes, cowering against the wash of propellers. They helped the pilots into their cockpits and then helped them with their gear. When the pilots had settled into their seats, checked their instruments, lowered their goggles, and snapped on their oxygen masks, the crew chiefs pulled shut the canopies and then leaped off the wings of the aircraft.

At 0925, Colonel Ben Davis signalled to the control tower who responded with green blinks from a strong flashlight. Then Davis moved his lead aircraft forward and other pilots of the 332nd followed him. At exactly 0930, Colonel Davis zoomed down the runway and hoisted his Mustang above the rolling hills beyond the San Marino Valley. At fifteen-second intervals, other P-51's followed. By 0945, the last of 59 Lonely Eagles had soared northward above the Apennine hills. And, as they did at other Italian airfields, the 332nd ground crews at Remitelli had also dispersed and wandered off to the air group's campsite. Soon, Remitelli Field also appeared deserted. In three other fighter group air bases, the personnel repeated the pattern of the 31st Rednecks and the 332nd Red Tails.

At Piagilolino, 20 miles south of Cattólica, forty-nine P-51's of the 52nd Fighter Group were all airborne by 0930 hours to race towards their rendezvous point with the 5th Wing's east column of bombers. By the same 0930 hours, fifty-three P-51's of the 325th Liquidator Fighter Group had left their field at Rimini, just east of Cattólica, and zoomed northward.

The fifty one P-38's of the 82nd Fighter Group had gotten off first. By 0900 hours they had left their Vincenzo airfield in central Italy and had streaked northward. They would be the last to rendezvous, for they would act as scouts for the 5th Wing air armada. The P-38's would drone forward and report or engage the first of any German aircraft interceptors.

By 1000 hours, an eerie silence settled in the 5th Bomb Wing campsites because their planes were gone: 181 B-17 bombers, 269 fighter planes, and 450 total aircraft, 38 more than the minimum requested by General Lawrence. Now, in Italy, the long wait had begun. For the rest of the morning and for most of the afternoon, the ground crews would wait. Then they would return to their airstrips and count the planes as they circled to land, the men noticing that some were missing—for always some aircraft failed to return. Then would come the conjectures: what planes and which airmen had failed to return? Some of the ground personnel, blessed with an ability to identify their planes even while the aircraft were airborne, would guess at once who had not come back. For the not-so-talented, they would need to wait until evening chow to know the truth, to know which rumors had become fact.

But for the moment, on this mid-morning of 24 March 1945, the airfields were quiet up and down the boot of Italy.

Chapter Eleven

At 0700 hours on the morning of 24 March 1945, General Galland ate his breakfast alone in the small office of his JV 44 headquarters at München-Riem. As the daylight grew more pronounced, he squinted through the window of the small wooden building, looking at the half-hidden ME-262 Snowbirds that gleamed polka-dot white from their widely scattered dispersal areas under the trees. Galland heard soon enough that the Americans were planning a special mission out of Italy, perhaps another attack on Daimler-Benz. If the Allies possessed espionage agents in Germany, the Germans also had their spies in England, France, and Italy. Not long after the 15th Air Force's 5th Wing group and squadron leaders had returned to their bases from the briefing at the Foggia Hotel, spies had notified German intelligence that the 15th Air Force was preparing an important air strike.

German agents in Italy knew the general routine of the 15th Air Force for briefing American air groups on bombing missions into Europe. They also recognized that the VIP meeting in Foggia, followed by the mass meeting of group and squadron commanders in the afternoon, obviously meant something special. Further, the American 5th Wing had remained idle on 23 March, apparently to prepare themselves for some kind of special air mission. The spies did not know where the 5th Wing intended to strike, but Galland had made his own guess. Since the 5th Wing had succeeded at Ruhland after their surprise flight from Italy, the JV 44 commander suspected that the Allied air staff had probably concluded that these same planes from Italy could succeed at Daimler-Benz.

The JV 44 commander saw two advantages on his side. First, he knew that the 15th Air Force wings had adopted the V-X plan of strategic bombing, using small attacking forces of no more than 150 to 200 bombers. The air formations could thus concentrate their bombs on selected zone points, either visually or with radar. If the bomber force was small, so would the number of escort planes be small. So, Galland reasoned, if the German conventional fighter planes could keep the American escort planes at bay, he and his jet fighter pilots could wreak havoc on the B-17 formations. Secondly, the air armada from Italy would be making a long flight and the Italian-based airmen were unaccustomed to them. So they would be tired and tense by the time they reached Berlin and not prepared physically and mentally to meet heavy opposition.

Galland squinted again at the ME-262's in the dispersal areas around München-Riem. The jets were ready enough—checked out and loaded to the last rocket. However, General Peltz had failed to give Galland the promised new jets to bring his combined JV 44 and JG 7 up to a hundred aircraft. He would need to meet any air attack with the 71 jet fighter planes at his disposal.

"I'm sorry, Adolf," Peltz had told him last night, "but we simply do not have the pilots to fly these jets. However, I can assure you that close to 200 FW-190's and ME-109's will come to the aid of any attack on Daimler-Benz or Ruhland. I'm sure these pilots can deal with the enemy's escorting fighter planes, leaving the enemy's bombers to you and the jet fighter pilots."

Galland could not really complain, considering the

shortages in Germany by 1945. The JV 44 commander guessed that the Americans would use no more than five or six P-51 escort groups, if they used the V-X plan of smaller bomber formations. If the conventional Luftwaffe fighters of Fleigerkorps Reich could indeed handle 150 to 200 American fighter planes, Galland's 71 Jet fighter planes would be enough to scatter the enemy bombers.

By 0720 on this March morning, Galland called his jet fighter kommodores into his office for a briefing: Major Erich Rudolpher, Colonel Joseph Kammhuber, Major Erich Hartmann, and Colonel Gunther Lutzow, all the "traitorous misfits" who had suffered derision and contempt by the Nazi leadership. Colonel Johannes Steinhoff and his two staffel kommodores, Captain Ulrich von Brauchitsch and Major Heinz-Wolfgang Schnaufer, were also here. They had flown in from their JG 7 base at Lagar-Lechfield in a JU-88 transport plane so that Galland could conduct a single briefing with both unit leaders against an expected raid from Italy, probably on Daimler-Benz.

"We have received word from our agents in Italy that the American 15th Air Force staff held two important meetings in Foggia yesterday," Galland said. "The staff of the American 8th Air Force was at a morning meeting while group leaders of the American 5th Wing of the 15th Air Force attended an afternoon meeting. What does this mean?" Galland gestured. "It means the 8th Air Force leaders have briefed the 15th Air Force on a target that the 8th Air Force normally attacks itself. And, since the 15th Air Force leaders brought in its group leaders personally from many areas of Italy, it also means they plan to attack a very important target. The most important targets for the Allies at this time can only be Ruhland or Marienfelde."

"Which one?" Major Hartmann asked.

Galland grinned. "We know the 8th Air Force failed in its mission against Daimler-Benz, while the 15th Air Force did quite well against Ruhland because we foolishly went elsewhere to intercept the enemy striking force. As General Peltz pointed out, they mistakenly believed they had overcome jet aircraft opposition at Ruhland, so we can guess that the Allied air leaders now believe a striking force from Italy can also be successful over Marienfelde. I must believe that they intend to attack Daimler-Benz, perhaps today."

"A logical conclusion, Herr General," Major Hartmann said.

"We also know something else," Galland continued, "the Allied air command is quite apprehensive about our jet fighter planes. General Todd himself, the American 8th Air Force chief of staff, has expressed a fear of our jet. He believes the jet aircraft could seriously hamper the Allied efforts."

"Does this General Todd really believe this?" Colonel Lutzow asked.

Galland nodded and then shuffled through a sheet of paper in his hand. "I have here a copy of Todd's very memorandum issued to Wing commanders two days ago. His very words were: 'At the moment, we have at least a five-to-one superiority over the Luftwaffe, and yet, against all our hopes, calculations, wishes, and plans, we have not been able to act on the scale we would like. The new German jet fighter plane has become a serious menace to bringing this war to a quick close. We must give top priority to the destruction of German jet aircraft production and jet fighter plane bases wherever we can find them. We cannot afford another loss such as the one on 18 March."

"Yes," Galland nodded vigorously, "the American air chief speaks the truth." He rattled the sheet of paper. "It is now up to us to prove the truth of General Todd's fears."

Those around the table understood clearly both Galland's optimism and Todd's pessimism. Up to now the German jet had knocked down bomber after bomber despite a sometimes 100-to-1 superiority. And, of course, the 18 March air fight had been the last and most horrifying example of what a well-organized jet fighter unit could do against an Allied air armada, despite the odds.

"If we can succeed again today," Galland told his Luftwaffe jet plane leaders, "we will surely encourage the Minister of Production to accelerate the training of jet fighter plane pilots. Many 163 and 262 jet fighter planes are coming off the assembly lines. Within a month we can have a full jagdverband of ME-163's and another jagdverband of ME-262's. If we can delay the Allies long enough, we may still win an honorable place for our country."

"We will make every effort to thwart them again as we did several days ago," Herr General," Colonel Gunther Lutzow said.

Galland nodded and he then walked to the window of his barracks headquarters to look again at the men bustling around the jet fighter planes. Ground crews had finished leading the R4M rockets under the wings. The aircraft were fully armed and ready.

Galland thought of the Daimler-Benz plants some twenty miles to the northwest, and the hundreds of workers ambling into the plants to relieve those workers on the graveyard shift. The general wondered how many tanks had come off the assembly lines during the eight-hour night shift just completed. He wondered how many tanks would roll out of the assembly plant today and how soon Field Marshal Von Rundstedt would have enough Tigers to offer a real resistance on the western front.

Galland also pondered the American armada he suspected of coming today. If even a few of these American bombers broke through, they could slow down or even halt production for two weeks. If most of the bombers got through they could knock out the plant completely, a total disaster for Germany. Then Galland stiffened for a moment, wondering if the Americans had concocted some new tactic to deal with the jet fighter plane. The Americans were known for their ability to initiate quick, new tactics, for they were creative, imaginative people and they had the resources to turn new ideas into reality.

The Americans had done little up to this point to meet the challenge of the jet, because up to now there had not really been a necessity. But a severe crisis, like the one on 18 March, or like the disruption of the ground war on the Rhine, had a way of spurring on the Americans. Galland could not help but wonder: during the six days since the 18 March aerial defeat, had the Americans come up with some new technique to thwart the jet aircraft defense of Daimler-Benz?

No, Galland told himself, the Americans could not find a successful technique against jets. The Snowbirds and Komets were too fast, much more maneuverable, and too heavily armed to suffer any setbacks from the inferior P-51 propeller-driven fighter planes. JV 44 and JG 7 could stop an American air armada again now, just as they had on 18 March. Galland glanced from his window at the ground crews finishing up their preparations on the jet fighter planes.

"Herr General," Colonel Johannes Steinhoff suddenly interrupted Galland in his meditations, "will there be anything else? We of Geschwader 7 must return to Lagar-Lechfield to brief our own pilots, while your own staffel kommodores of JV 44 must brief their own staffel pilots."

"Of course," Galland nodded. He then motioned to an aide who poured several tumblers of brandy and passed them out to the seven Luftwaffe officers seated about the table. No one touched his tumbler until Galland himself returned to the table and picked up his own glass.

"Gentlemen," Galland raised his tumbler aloft, "I offer you a toast for success. Let this day launch another *Die Grosse Schlag*. The first schlag failed, true. Still, we can dare to dream that now, at this moment, we can bring this war to a new turn for the better with our superior aerial weapon. The word jet has brought doubts and fears to our enemies, despite their overwhelming superiority in numbers. The same magic word has brought us together in a new camaraderie to perhaps begin a new *die grosse fliegerei*." Galland lifted his brandy glass. "Drink."

Within a half hour, the six Luftwaffe jet fighter plane kommodores had left Galland's office. The general, alone now, stared once more out of his office window and craned his neck to stare into the sky where broken clouds moved lazily overhead. Galland was not sure he could repeat the debacle he had caused on 18 March. But the Luftwaffe commander felt a satisfying consolation. The leaders and pilots who would meet the enemy today, probably over Marienfelde, were the best. They were weighted down with medals and awards of all manner and descriptions for their honor and gallantry in battle. They were men of loyalty and resolve, the best in the Luftwaffe.

Ironically, the valor of these men in battle had also been reflected in a valor to criticize their Nazi leaders and thus bring them into disfavor. So, absurdly, the fate of the bungling Nazis themselves now rested on the misfits they had ostracized.

By 0745 General Galland was shaken from his meditations. "Mein General," an aide said, "can I bring you some coffee?"

Galland nodded. Then he slumped into the chair behind his desk and gestured. "Then bring me my flying suit."

"Yes, Herr General."

On the western front, both General Bradley, commander of the American 12th Army Group, and Field Marshal Von Rundstedt, commander of the German Army of the West, took note of the upcoming attack on Daimler-Benz.

On the evening of 23 March, General Bradley had received a secret communication from the Allied JCS in London. The report told him that the 15th Air Force bombing raid on 22 March had knocked out three of the refineries at Ruhland in an attack that had thwarted German jet interceptor planes. Today the same 15th Air Force wing would attack Daimler-Benz. Bradley had expressed delight. The attack yesterday had been quite a turnabout from the 18 March disaster. However, JCS had not told Bradley that the 5th Bomb Wing had reportedly caught the Germans off-guard, so Bradley looked upon the abortive Daimler-Benz raid by the 3rd Air Division as a mere piece of bad luck. The air force was back on the right track and Bradley had no doubt that this second attempt to knock out Daimler-Benz would be a success.

At his headquarters in Cologne, the commander of the 12th American Army Group arose early on the morning of 24 March and peered out of his billet window at the battered city beyond, where an array of birds chirped in a multitude of different octaves. The chattering sounds seemed out of place in the drab, deserted city. The general had just finished breakfast when an aide brought him a new message from JCS.

"The 5th Bomb Wing is on the way," the aide told the general.

Bradley nodded and looked at the communication the aide handed him. An armada of six bomb groups, escorted by five fighter groups, would leave their bases in Italy and attack the Daimler-Benz tank assembly plants. 15th Air Force had every reason to expect to be successful. When Bradley finished reading the communication, he turned to his aide.

"What about our own plans for Operation Overtone?"

"All set, sir. The 7th Army is poised to move as soon as you give the word. Their scouts think the Germans have all but evacuated the Mannheim defenses and our guys expect to reach the rail junction at Oberwurzban in a matter of days. From there, it's just a run across southern Germany to Munich, depending on how much opposition they meet along the way."

"How about the center?"

"Same thing, sir. Patton's 3rd Army is pretty well established in an operational base across the Moselle beyond Wessel. He's realy to move towards the Autobahn. At the moment, the German Army Group B doesn't look very good. They still lack tanks and they can't do much without armor. The sooner we move, the less chance they have of getting tank replacement before we threw a pincer around them."

Bradley looked down at his communication: 15th Air Force's 5th Bomb Wing to bomb Daimler-Benz today. Yes, if the 5th Wing succeeded, the Germans would get no tanks to reinforce Army Group B. Within a week, the 7th Army would easily be in Mannheim and Patton would be at the Autobahn. Bradley then studied the array of maps on a desk in his quarters, the sketches and charts, and the figures and symbols. Everything looked so neat and easy on paper. He glanced again out of his billet window, staring once more at the battered buildings of Cologne. Somewhere beyond this rubbled city was Von Rundstedt, as cagey a field commander as any man who led an army. What was he up to? What did he really have? And what about the jets that had caused serious psychological problems, if not dangerous physical problems, on the Rhine? Could the 9th Air Force stop them?

Bradley looked at his aide. "Send out an order for a meeting of all army and division commanders for 0900 tomorrow morning. We'll hold a final briefing before we set Operation Overtone in motion."

"Why not today, sir? They're waiting to move."

Bradley looked once more at the communication in his hand. "We'll have to wait. We'll have to see what happens on that bombing raid today at Daimler-Benz. If the 5th Wing succeeds, we go at once. If they fail, like the 8th Air Force failed a few days ago, I don't know what the hell we'll do."

The aide did not answer.

"Bring me some more coffee."

"Yes, sir."

And, some one hundred miles to the northeast, at Osnabrück, Field Marshal Gerd von Rundstedt had also arisen early on the 24th March morning. He too looked out the window of his small headquarters building, staring at the still intact peaceful village. For him, the morning chirps were melodious tunes that blended perfectly into the peaceful aura of pretty Osnabrück. From his window, the field marshal could see a few civilians meandering up the narrow cobblestone main street of the village, civilians on the way to the fields to perhaps start spring planting, or on their way to their shops to ready themselves for a day of business. Occasionally, groups of German troops marched briskly up the street, or a motorcycle and side car sputtered up the street.

Von Rundstedt quickly dressed and then looked at his watch: it was 0635 hours. Daylight had come but the sun had not yet risen fully from the east. He yawned and then called his aide.

"Coffee and rolls, please."

"Yes, mein Field Marshal."

Within a few minutes the aide was back with a communication from Berlin. Von Rundstedt read the memo quickly. The Luftwaffe suspected that an American air unit would make a new attempt today to destroy the Daimler-Benz tank assembly plants. General Dietrich Peltz, Obercommandant of Fleigerkorps Reich is confident the attempt will fail. He has taken every precaution to thwart any such air attack, just as his precautionary measures thwarted an American armada over Marienfelde on 18 March.

But the memorandum brought an uneasiness to the field marshal. Despite the optimism from General Peltz, Von Rundstedt felt an air of uncertainty. The jet fighter planes of the Luftwaffe had decimated an enemy air attack over Marienfelde, but they had failed to stop the air attack over the Ruhland refinery. Why? The general turned to his aide.

"Is Oberstleutnant Kowaleski awake?"

"Yes, mein Field Marshal. He is having breakfast."

"Ask him to come in as soon as he is finished."

"Yes, sir."

Within a few minutes, the young Luftwaffe officer arrived at the field marshal's quarters and found Von Rundstedt staring out of his office window at the village.

Kowaleski waited a full minute before he finally spoke.

"You wanted to see me, sir?"

Von Rundstedt turned. "Leutnant, we have received word from Berlin that an enemy air armada will again attempt to destroy Daimler-Benz."

"I have heard the rumor, but nothing official."

"It is true," Von Rundstedt said. He nodded and then glanced again at the slip in his hand. "I have called you here out of curiosity. It seems strange to me that our jet aircraft units could so successfully ward off a huge enemy air fleet over Marienfelde but could not hamper a small enemy air fleet over Ruhland. Do you have any theories about this?"

The Luftwaffe officer grinned. "I have spoken to some of the pilots of Geschwader 7, Herr Field Marshal. According to these pilots, our jet fighter units were unprepared for the attack on Ruhland. General Galland and Colonel Steinhoff had never expected the Allies to attack Ruhland from Italy. They were certain the enemy air armada from the American 15th Air Force had planned to destroy the Laubitzer bridges to stop the flow of oil from our newly won Hungarian oil fields. General Galland had ordered all interceptors to the Laubitzer rail lines area. By the time the Komets of Geschwader 7 had learned the true target, the American air fleet had completed its bombing raid. Even our conventional ME-109's and FW-190's had been duped into flying southeast towards the Laubitzer rail lines."

"Very interesting," Von Rundstedt nodded.

"Be assured, Herr Field Marshal," Lt. Kowaleski said, "General Galland will not make the same mistake twice. He made an unfortunate but quite logical miscalculation concerning the objective of the American air armada out of Italy. But," Kowaleski pointed, "General Galland will be ready the next time, especially since he now knows the Americans will attempt to send an air fleet to attack Ruhland or Daimler-Benz from Italy."

Von Rundstedt looked at the memorandum in his hand and then looked at Lt. Kowaleski. "How does the

Luftwaffe know the Americans are sending an air fleet today to attack Ruhland or Daimler-Benz?"

Lt. Kowaleski grinned. "We have our sources in Italy, Herr Field Marshal."

"Of course," Von Rundstedt nodded again before he once more peered out of his window. "This village is so peaceful, like it was before this terrible war. How nice it would be if we could keep at least this one village of Osnabrück intact."

"We will try." the Luftwaffe lieutenant said. "You can be certain that our jet bomber and jet fighter pilots here on the western front will spare nothing to stop the Allied advance from the Rhine."

"You are a credit to the Luftwaffe, Leutnant. You may return to your quarters."

"Thank you, sir," Kowaleski said. Then he jerked to attention before he spun and left the room.

Now, like Bradley in Cologne, Von Rundstedt also studied an array of maps on his desk. He too looked at the lines and symbols and pictures and pinpointed marks. He knew well enough that Operation Overtone was set to begin soon, perhaps in a few days. With a finger, he traced the probable route of the 3rd Army, which would thrust towards the Autobahn; Hodges' 1st Army, which would come out of Remagen towards Saarbrücken and the rail junction of Oberwürzban beyond; and the American 7th Army, which would drive with armored spearheads towards Mannheim. Von Rundstedt stroked his chin. He could stop 'em with his forces he had deployed in the north, center, and south. He had only one problem—a need for gasoline and tanks.

True, fuel might still come from Ruhland's one operational refinery, but what of the tanks, the Tigers of Daimler-Benz? Thirty or forty were on the way, he was told yesterday, the first consignment of new tanks since the return to full production. Within a few days, if the American 5th Bomb Wing failed in its suspected air mission to Marienfelde today, Von Rundstedt would have another hundred tanks. Yes, he nodded to himself, with another hundred Tigers and a stout crew to man them, he could stop anything.

In the field, in the defense areas up and down the length of the Rhine Valley, the Panzers and Wehrmacht soldiers waited. They waited for more ammunition, and they waited for scouting reports of Allied movements from their Rhine bridgeheads. They waited for the certain air strikes, the softening-up process by American fighter planes and fighter-bombers, before the Allied infantry and armor moved forward. They waited to see their own Arade jet bombers wing swiftly overhead and they waited to see their Komet jet fighter planes zoom like silver meteors across the sky. Finally, they waited for the drums of gasoline from Ruhland and the new tanks from Daimler-Benz.

At 0630 hours, all along the front of the German Army of the West, the German troops were at breakfast. Some felt that inevitable fear of every combat soldier: that this meal might be their last. They said little to each other—these vastly outnumbered, tired Wehrmacht and Panzer soldiers. They could only hope that in the air far to the east, over Marienfelde, the German Luftwaffe would score another victory today to mitigate the suffering of these German troops.

And at the Rhine bridgeheads themselves, the American Infantry dogfaces and gritty tank crews also waited. They waited to break out from their pockets, and they waited for the skyfuls of 9th Air Force planes that would drone eastward to the front to make things easier for the advancing GI's. They, too, ate breakfast at about 0630 hours. They, too, waited for the air battle that rumors said would take place again over Marienfelde today. They wondered if the air corps would suffer another defeat that might encourage the Germans to resist them all the more and encourage the Luftwaffe to strike back with determined aggressiveness. These GI's, too, like their German counterparts, ate their breakfast in near-silence, and they too wondered if this meal might be their last.

Chapter Twelve

By 0840 hours, from the co-pilot seat of the "Big Jenny," Colonel George McGregor stared at the sun to the east. Ahead, the Adriatic loomed before him, a hazy blue mist in the distance. In a few minutes he would reach the sea to begin the long flight northward to Marienfelde. Soon the colonel saw falling behind him the Apennine Mountains that ran like a huge straight caterpillar along the boot of Italy. Then McGregor looked to his right at the B-17 wingman hovering diagonally next to him. The colonel yawned, already bored with the monotonous flight. Then Captain Roger Ball tapped the arm of the 463rd Bomb Group commander.

"Colonel, to the right," the pilot pointed.

McGregor leaned in his seat and squinted into the distance. He could see a misty outline of aircraft approaching the formation.

"It's the 97th," McGregor said, "and the 483rd is right behind them."

Colonel McGregor now looked at his watch and stared below him, where the sleepy village of Termoli sat like a group of white stones on the shoreline of the Adriatic. He grinned at Captain Ball. "They made the rendezvous right on time."

The two men in the cabin of Big Jenny then watched the misty group of planes behind them. The 97th maneuvered to its position behind the lead 463rd Group while the 483rd, misty dots to the rear, fell in behind the 97th to complete the long west column of bombers. McGregor looked at his watch again, then squinted at the emptiness in front of him. For another ten minutes, the B-17 droned on, until McGregor had lost sight of Termoli and the Italian coast. Now, over the wide expanse of the Adriatic Sea, Colonel George McGregor picked up the mike of his TBS, the intership communication system.

"This is Shapely Leader. Come in Shapely 2."

"Shapely 2 responding," came the reply from Colonel Paul Barton, the 97th Group leader.

"Are you in column?"

"Right behind you, Shapely Leader."

Then McGregor called Shapely 3.

"We read you," Colonel Ohman of the 483rd Group answered.

"Are you in column?"

"Right in formation."

"Good. Shapely 2 and Shapely 3, stay alert. We'll be assuming rendezvous pattern in two minutes. Our Shapely 1 will rise to 5,500, Shapely 2 will assume 7,000-foot altitude, and Shapely 3 will drop to 4,000. We'll maintain this pattern all the way to key point. Out."

Within a few minutes, the west column of bombers of the 80A force had settled in their flight positions. The tail gunners of the 463rd's Dog Squadron's rear flights called Colonel McGregor and reported the rise of Shapely 2's B-17's to 7,000-foot altitudes and the drop of the 483rd's squadrons to 4,000 feet. McGregor acknowledged the tail gunner reports. Then the colonel sat back in his co-pilot's seat and once more stared at the open blue sky around him or at the endless expanse of the Adriatic under him.

Soon, however, Colonel George McGregor felt tense. He worried about hundreds of airmen in the 80A mission, especially the men of his own bomb group, and particularly the nine other men aboard his own lead Big

Jenny. McGregor had always been a friendly, understanding group leader, but he also maintained strict discipline in regard to efficiency, promptness, and responsibility. His 463rd airmen had responded to both of these traits. They came to him when they needed him and they carried out his orders with dedication and loyalty. McGregor knew this aircraft and the crew quite well, for he had flown missions aboard Big Jenny several times. The 725. crew was good and the colonel could trust them on this long, dangerous flight. He looked at his pilot as Captain Ball studied the instrument panel.

"Pressure?"

"Okay, sir."

"RPM?"

"2500."

The colonel nodded and then looked out of the starboard window of the cabin. He knew that he'd need to control Big Jenny as well as this mission if something happened to Captain Roger Ball. But if Colonel McGregor was concerned, so too was the crew of aircraft #725.

Captain Roger Ball had been an aircraft commander on many missions, but today was the first time he had operated the lead ship on a mission. He wondered how he'd react if something happened to Colonel McGregor. The captain again checked the instrument panel: speed, altimeter, RPM, pressure. He nodded to himself. The B-17 was droning softly and easily, despite its heavy load, and its engines purred smoothly. Ground crews had done a good job in servicing the plane yesterday. The pilot leaned back in his seat and tried to relax.

In the nose of Big Jenny, the bombardier, Captain Perry Ford, moved about uneasily in his cramped compartment. He stared at the endless expanse of Adriatic sea and the blue sky. Nothing lay in front of him, but he would be the first to see flak when or if it came—and Ford was certain the flak would come. He might also be the first among the 80A airmen to see enemy interceptors, which Ford was certain would also come.

And finally, the bombardier wondered how he'd react if he saw the speedy, heavily armed jets come towards him.

"Perry?" Captain Ball called. "How are the instruments?"

"All okay, Rog," Captain Ford answered.

"Stay alert."

"I will."

Then Captain Perry Ford looked again at his instruments: the bombsight he would use on visual, and his H2X radar he would use in the event the target was closed in. He also checked his smoke flares, for he would be the man to release them when they reached the IP over Marienfelde. His flare trails would be the signal for the bombardiers on the other B-17's to drop their bomb loads of thousand-pound RDX explosives on the sprawling tank assembly plant. Ford licked his lips, but he and Captain Ball needed to make certain they had the correct coordinates, right to the last second, before Ford released the bombs.

The bombardier also checked his twin fifties because he might need to use them after he completed his bomb run. The guns were in good order and Ford had plenty of ammo belts.

In the top turret, just aft of the cabin, Staff Sergeant Marty Walsh, the gunner scanned the empty skies above him. To his left and right, Walsh could see the wing B-17's of this lead flight, and behind him he could see the other 30 B-17's of the 463rd Group. And far to the rear, he saw the planes of the 97th droning in formation at 7,000 feet. However, he could not see the last group in the west column, the 483rd, for the Forts of this group were far behind and hanging at a mere 4,000 feet.

Marty Walsh was also the engineer of this lead B-17. In the event of any malfunctions aboard the aircraft, he would leave his cramped top turret and crawl into the bowels of the plane to make any needed repairs. Luckily, he had thoroughly checked out the equipment with the ground chief and mechanics at Celone, making certain that every last item was in good order.

Below the turret, Captain Dave Karin, the navigator, checked his charts, T-squares, and communications. Not only was Karin responsible for his own plane, but the other 88 Flying Forts of the west column also depended on his calculations. He checked the oxygen regulator because once inside heavily defended Europe, they would climb into high altitudes. He also checked his radio compass to make certain the needles worked accurately. If he miscalculated by a single degree, the armada could wind up in Poland instead of eastern Germany. Captain Karin felt somewhat frustrated, for he had no idea what anything looked like outside of his windowless compartment.

"Dave," Captain Roger Ball suddenly called from his pilot's cabin, "can you give me a reading?"

"Still at .023 bearing. Right on track and right on time."

"Good."

"Keep us posted every thirty minutes," Colonel McGregor now spoke, "and if we fall off track, let us know."

"Will do, Colonel," Captain Karin answered.

In the middle of the fusilage, Sergeant Burl Hancock, the radio man, checked his instruments. He felt isolated in his lonely compartment, with only the array of dials and the nearby .50 caliber machine gun to keep him company. Sergeant Hancock studied the route coordinates and check point in Herzberg, Germany, where the fighter cover would rendezvous with the bombers. Hancock next tuned his radio equipment to make sure his frequencies were accurate. He would need to transmit orders for attack on secondary targets in case they could not make hits on the primary target at Marienfelde. When the sergeant remembered the story of the 3rd Air Division's debacle at Daimler-Benz, he knew there existed the possibility that they would need to hit secondary targets.

Hancock glanced at the plexiglas skylight above him. He was sure he'd leave his radio and dials, and man his gun by the time they reached Marienfelde. He had visited the radio shack at Celone last night to pick up his code sheets and he had learned from radio men that German jets had definitely been reported around Marienfelde. Now, to get his mind off the long flight and the prospects of jet interceptors, Hancock read his code sheets again.

"Sergeant Hancock," a call came from the cabin of #725.

"Yes, sir."

"Are the frequencies okay?"

"Yes, sir, they're all in order."

"Have you got your coordinate sheets to call instructions to the others?"

"Right in front of me, sir."

"Good," Colonel McGregor answered.

To the immediate aft of the radio compartment, the waist gunners, Sergeant Luther Ogle and Sergeant Pete Cody, swung their weapons in 180-degree turns, left and then right. Then they swung the guns up and down in 120-degree arches. Their twin fifties swung smoothly and loose on their fulcrums and the two gunners could move their weapons easily. Both men then stared out the side windows, the lateral openings in the fusilage of the B-17 that offered the best view of any oncoming enemy intercepters. But the mid-fusilage positions also suffered the greatest damage in a B-17 and the greatest casualties among crew members because the elongated length offered German fighter pilots their biggest target. "Like shooting at a barn wall," one Luftwaffe pilot said. "We almost always get a hit if we aim at the fusilage."

The two waist gunners, Ogle and Cody, had already flown 20 and 21 missions respectively, and they needed only a few more to complete their 25 missions for rotation home. But neither gunner felt confident on this long and dangerous mission to Marienfelde. Both men feared the prospect of getting jumped by planes too fast and too maneuverable for their .50 caliber gun sights. And worse, they had no belly gunner below them in the ball turret, because this lead B-17 had eliminated the belly gunner on today's mission in favor of a photographer who could also act as radio man or navigator.

"Waist," Captain Roger Ball called from the cabin, "do you see anything?"

"No, sir," Sergeant Ogle answered.

"Are your guns free and ready?"

"Yes, sir." This time, Sergeant Pete Cody answered.

"Bundle up." Now it was the colonel who spoke. "Within an hour we'll start climbing. We'll be above 25,000 feet by the time we cross into Czechoslovakia. I don't want any frozen fingers and frozen eyelashes on those waist guns."

"Yes, sir," Sergeant Cody answered.

The two waist gunners knew the truth of the colonel's warning. At 25,000 feet, the temperature often dropped to 40 below zero. True, the men wore electrically heated flying gear, but they needed to keep suits, hoods, helmets, and gloves zipped tight to prevent frostbite and thus render the gunners completely useless in the face of enemy fighter planes.

Below the two waist gunners, a Big Jenny stranger sat in the ball turret. He was Lt. Jim Frye who at the moment was checking his K20 cameras, particularly his film and settings. He would take photographs—if a German jet did not shoot them down first. Frye also checked out as a navigator and radio man. Thus, in a pinch, he could take over either of these stations.

Lt. Frye had often flown aboard lead flights on a bombing mission because of his experience in several areas. Today he got a call for perhaps the most dangerous mission of his young life. He had only met Big Jenny's crew briefly last night and again this morning. They had impressed him as capable and friendly airmen and he had welcomed the chance to fly with them. Now, as the young lieutenant looked down at the endless Adriatic Sea below, he hoped he'd see the same Adriatic again this afternoon, because the sight of the blue waters several hours from now would tell him he was safely on the way home.

"Lieutenant Frye," Captain Ball called the ball turret gunner, "are your cameras in order?"

"Everything okay here, Captain," Frye answered.

"Good. Stay alert."

Finally, at the rear of the big Flying Fortress, in the lonely tail cubbyhole, sat Staff Sergeant William Heise, the tail gunner. He could see the swarms of fellow 463rd Group planes around him, rising and falling slightly in their monotonous flight. The B-17's of Dog Squadron behind him appeared to be chasing the young Staff Sergeant as though the planes were trying to overtake him and chew him to pieces with their propellers. Heise could also see the twin V-formations of the 97th Bomb Group diagonally upwards to his rear. They hung like monstrous vultures waiting to pounce on a carcass. And, diagonally below, far to the rear, the tail gunner saw faintly the distant shapes of the 483rd's B-17's. They looked like dragonflies about to alight on the sea below.

Heise licked his lips and then swung his gun bubble that represented the aft extremity of this Flying Fortress. Heise was frightened, even though he had flown fifteen previous missions inside Germany's Fortress Europe. If German interceptors jumped them, he would see nothing from his tail position before he heard the strafing fire or the whooshing rockets from the enemy aircraft. Several times in the past the young tail gunner had seen the rockets from 109's whoosh past him; and several times he had heard the staccato chatter of tracer fire puncture the tail section of his B-17. On 22 March, the mission to Ruhland, Heise had seen something flash past him, something he could not even identify. Only later had he learned that it had been a speeding jet that almost defied visual identification. Heise wondered how he would ever get off a burst against a darting plane like this. A plane that he was sure would come after them today.

"Sergeant Heise, what does the formation look like?"

"Very good, Captain," the tail gunner answered Roger Ball. "They're in perfect double-V's and right in position."

"If you see anybody stray, call me."

"Yes, sir," the tail gunner answered the Big Jenny pilot.

Throughout the long west column, several hundred other airmen felt the same fears and apprehensions as the airmen aboard Big Jenny. In these other B-17's, navigators also studied charts, bombardiers checked bomb sights, radio men tested equipment, co-pilots and pilots checked instrument panels, and gunners swung their .50 caliber weapons. All of them also scanned the vast emptiness around them, the endless sky above and the vast sea below, or they squinted at the droning B-17's next to them, behind them, or in front of them, Flying Fortresses that hung in the sky like suspended tarantulas. Most of these airmen had flown this route before to hit enemy targets in eastern Europe: the German submarine and destroyer bases at Brbinj, Yugoslavia, the iron works at Knittlefield, Hungary, the rail lines and marshalling yards in Czechoslovakia, the steel mills of Lambach, the Skoda and Pilsen works at Prague, and the truck factories in Karez. Some of them had even been on bomb runs to the Laubitzer bridges in Hungary that crossed the Danube River, and on the long, dangerous oil field raid to Ploesti, Romania.

Most of these 5th Bomb Wing crews had been on the flight to Ruhland two days ago, their longest bomb run of the war. They had met anti-aircraft fire along the way, but they had seen few interceptors, so they had come home in the elated belief that the Germans had run out of planes. However, they had sobered quickly when they learned the truth—the 5th Wing had caught the Luftwaffe off-guard. Today they suspected a truth: they would probably meet enemy air opposition, including the dreaded jets.

As the long, monotonous flight continued, the men aboard the B-17's had too much time to consider the terrible ways to die: their plane split apart from an ack-ack burst, their heads splattered by the strafing guns of a German fighter plane, their bodies blown away by a zooming rocket from a German jet. Or when these men looked at the sea below, some of the Americans envisioned themselves tumbling downward in a burning B-17, their flesh hot and black from fire. Or they saw themselves over Germany, where enemy guns had sliced off the wings of their planes, shorn away the tails, or cut the fusilages in half before they tumbled thousands of feet downward and crashed. Most of the airmen worked over and over at their routine tasks to forget the horrifying images that wracked their minds.

Miles to the east, the east column of 80A bombers also kept their rendezvous. Over Lake Lesina on the Montagargano Peninsula, the spur of Italy's boot, the 2nd Bomb Group hovered at 5,000 feet. Colonel Bob Bivro had just looked down at the crescent-shaped lake from his co-pilot's seat when his pilot tapped his shoulder.

"The other groups are coming in, sir."

Bivro nodded and looked at his watch: 0842. He squinted beyond the cabin window at the other B-17's in the distance. By the time he had led his lead plane out of peninsula and over the Adriatic, his fellow east column bomb groups had joined him. He ordered his east column of bombers into the rendezvous flight pattern: the lead 2nd Group at 5,500 feet, the 301st at 7,000 feet, and the 99th at 4,000 feet. By 0850, the east column of the 80A mission was also droning northwards towards Daimler-Benz.

And in this east column, the dozens of bomber crews felt the same tension and fears as the airmen of the west column. Most of these 15th Air Force flyers had also struck targets in Austria, Czechoslovakia, and the Balkans. And some of these men had also participated in the nerve-shattering raid at Ploesti. Here in the east column, men also suffered monotony, apprehension, and the uncertainty of too much free time to meditate on horrifying deaths in this attack over Marienfelde—death from the shrapnel of an ME-262 rocket, an anti-aircraft burst, or a volley of strafing fire.

At 0900 hours, both the west and east columns of bombers had begun their gradual ascent from 5,000 to 13,000 feet. Then the B-17's droned steadily up the length of the Adriatic Sea, the west column over the middle of the sea and the east column skirting the coast of Yugoslavia. Both units, the east lateral to the west, would cross over Brbinj on the Yugoslavian coast at about 0929 hours.

By 1010 hours on 24 March, Colonel Bill Daniels of the Redneck 51st Fighter Group had brought his 57 Mustangs far over the Adriatic Sea. His fellow pilots hung close to him in a box pattern of six V's. Daniels looked at his instrument panel and nodded: 300 mph. He was cruising at the right speed to meet the bombers at the 50.3 latitude, 13.18 longitude rendezvous point. Then Daniels scanned the blue skies around him, searching for the 332nd who would meet the 57 planes of the 31st where the Adriatic Sea hit the northwest coast of Yugoslavia.

The colonel picked up his TDS. "All flight leaders, yellow, blue, and green, this is red leader. Any sign of the Red Tails?"

Within moments, the colonel got four negative responses. The Red Tails of the 332nd were nowhere in sight.

Then, perhaps as an afterthought or perhaps to occupy himself, Colonel Bill Daniels picked up his TDS again. "Stay alert. The Krauts may send a few 109's or 190's out of northern Italy to give us some trouble."

Then Bill Daniels settled back into the cockpit of his Mustang. He again checked his altimeter, his speed, his pressure, and his gyro. The instruments were normal. For another ten minutes Daniels droned on, fifty-six P-51's around and behind him. Then he crossed the Yugoslavian coast and a patch of mountainous sheep country. When he started across a stretch of plains, some fifty miles northeast of Trieste, a call came from the flight leader of the port squadron.

"This is yellow leader," Major Joe Forrester called over the TDS, "a swarm of aircraft at nine o'clock, coming towards us."

"Bandits?"

"No, sir, Colonel. They look like the Red Tails."

Colonel Bill Daniels nodded. Then he squinted to his left and soon recognized the misty shapes closing on him. When he made out clearly the red bands on the tail section of the lead P-51, he picked up his radio phone. "This is

Jetblack Leader. Davis? Is that you?"

Colonel Ben Davis picked up his own TDS. "We're wearing our red tails, aren't we?"

"Where the hell have you been?"

"We were supposed to meet you at 1020 hours. We're only a couple of minutes late. We've got plenty of time to rendezvous with the bombers."

Daniels squinted against the huge flock of oncoming P-51's. "Jesus, I thought we did well with 57 planes. What have you got with you? Every stray Mustang in Italy?"

"Fifty-nine Jetblack Twos," Davis said, "fifty-nine. Our guys keep our birds in good shape." He paused. "How are we going to pick up the bombers?"

Daniels squinted at the 332nd planes again before he answered. "Why don't you take the port with three squadrons and assign your tail squadron as rear topcover. We'll take starboard and send our own tail squadron to forward topcover."

"Very good," Colonel Ben Davis said.

Then, Colonel Davis picked up his TDS and called his own squadron commanders. "This is Jetblack 2 leader. Keep open for instructions." He paused. A moment later, he spoke again. "Jetblack 2A, 2B, and 2C squadrons will assume port positions when we rendezvous with Shapelys. Jetblack 2D will assume rear high cover. Do you read me, Jetblack 2D?"

"I read you," Captain Ed Gleed of the 102nd Squadron said.

"Jetblacks 2B and 2C, you will remain in column behind Jetblack 2A aircraft," Ben Davis continued. "Repeat: we'll assume port escort stations at rendezvous with Shapelys."

"Roger," Captain Mattison of the 100th Squadron answered.

"Roger," Major Al Turner of the 101st Squadron answered.

A few minutes later the swarms of P-51 Mustangs fell into two columns in the clear skies over Yugoslavia. Colonel Ben Davis remained in the van of the lead three aircraft V, with forty-one P-51's of the 99th, 100th, and

101st Squadrons behind him. A few thousand feet above and to the rear, Captain Ed Gleed maneuvered the fifteen Mustangs of his 102nd Squadron to a few thousand feet above the rest of the group. A few miles to the east, Colonel Bill Daniels established the four squadrons of his 31st Fighter Group into a similar pattern. Then the two flocks of P-51's upped their speed to 350 mph and raced north by northeast towards Austria.

Ben Davis occasionally scanned the clear blue sky or the terrain under him. He occasionally looked at his altimeter, his pressure gauge, his gyro compass, or his fuel gauge. He listened to the soft purr of his engine, nodding. His ground crews had done a good job yesterday, putting the Mustangs of the 332nd into excellent shape.

But Ben Davis also felt his nerves tingle. He was sure he'd run into those German jets. Allied agents had definitely told 15th Air Force A-3 that Luftwaffe jet fighter planes had been seen around Marienfelde. Davis prayed that he and his black pilots of the 332nd could meet a jet fighter challenge and win. But suppose they failed? Suppose the German jet fighter pilots broke through the 332nd's P-51 screen and mauled the bombers as they had mauled the 3rd Air Division bombers six days ago. The bigots would scream once more with disparaging criticism: "Black pilots cannot perform."

Strangely, Ben Davis feared a censure in case of failure more than he feared the prospect of death at the hands of the German Luftwaffe aces who flew these superior jet fighter planes. And worse, suppose the diagonal pattern, six planes unleashing a spray of fire, did not stop the jets? Davis knew that many of the fighter pilot commanders had frowned on his suggestion, although these same pilots would carry out this pattern of defense as ordered by General Charles Lawrence himself. If the pattern failed, Davis would get the blame. Further, Davis knew that some fighter pilots acted instinctively when they zoomed away from the bombers to pursue enemy fighters as soon as they saw the interceptors. Davis prayed to the Lord, to let the pattern work.

The 332nd colonel broke his agonizing meditations by

picking up his radio phone again. "All Jetblack 2 leaders, stay alert. There might be some eager beaver Luftwaffe pilots around Trieste who could make a stab at us."

"Roger," Captain Bill Mattison of the 100th Squadron answered.

Ben Davis again scanned the sky around him, but he saw nothing. Then he squinted at the zig-zag patches of earth below. And as he droned on, the first rise of hills in northwest Yugoslavia came into view. Soon, he saw the patch of green forests that would fuse into the distant mountains. Davis looked at his watch: 1045 hours. He checked his reading: 47.2 north and 14.0 west. They would soon reach the Austrian border. The colonel flew only another few minutes when his TDS buzzed.

"This is Jetblack Leader," Colonel Bill Daniels said. "The mountains are just ahead. We're going up to 20,000 feet."

"Roger, Jetblack Leader," Davis answered.

As Ben Davis brought his plane upwards, he snapped the oxygen mask over his face. Then he called his flight leaders. "We're going to 20,000 to clear the Alps. Notify all pilots to check and secure oxygen masks."

"Roger," Major Al Turner of the 101st Squadron answered.

Then Davis continued his climb, with other P-51's following his lead. When Davis reached 20,000 feet, he leveled off and then squinted to his right. But the P-51's of the 31st Fighter Group had vanished somewhere to the east. He could not see them again until they reached the bomber rendezvous point. Then, when Davis saw a snow-capped peak ahead, he shivered. The stark mountain ridges were desolate, cold, and hostile, worse than the Swiss Alps. He picked up his TDS again.

"Maintain V's in column and stay alert. We might hit cloud banks in these mountains and I don't want anybody plowing into a rugged peak. In fact, I think we'll go up another couple thousand feet."

Then Ben Davis banked his P-51 and zoomed upwards and left. His two wing men followed his lead, and within a few minutes the 332nd Fighter Group had settled in the silent, frigid air above the Austrian Alps. Ben Davis shivered again as he peered down. He had crossed these mountains many times before, but he had never gotten over the fear brought on by the sight of this ominous, cold isolation.

Davis squinted ahead, waiting for the broad green plains of central Austria.

Chapter Thirteen

Colonel George McGregor and his long stream of west column Flying Fortresses had bypassed the city of Fiume in northern Yugoslavia before the Forts had risen to 24,000 feet. Now the bombers were crossing the menacing peaks of the Austrian Alps, where the bomber crews felt the same fears as the fighter pilots. They too shuddered at the sight of tall, snow-capped peaks and deep, ragged abysses that snaked through the desolate mountain range. Before McGregor's lead group had passed through the ice-chilled air, and finally cleared the frigid landscape, two B-17's of his 463rd Bomb Group had developed aileron and engine problems from icing on the wings and cowlings. They got permission from McGregor to abort and return to Italy. Spares then filled the gaps in the squadron formations.

As the 463rd and its companion 97th and 483rd Groups continued on, every pilot worried about icing wings that could strain their already heavily loaded planes. But by 1010 hours, the long west column had cleared the ice-chilled air above the Alps and dropped into the moderate atmosphere of the Carinthia plains in Central Austria.

As the column of bombers winged northward, however, a B-17 of the 97th developed mechanical trouble and returned to Italy. Two B-17's of the 483rd developed problems, engine trouble and pressure loss on one and a frozen compass gear on the other. These two Forts also fell out of formation, climbed the Alps, and headed back to Italy. By 1100 near the Czechoslovakian border, only 84 of the west column of B-17's still droned on at a 20,000 feet at a comfortable 240 mph. Colonel George McGregor picked up his TDS.

"This is Shapely Leader to all aircraft commanders. Please check readings and compasses. We should be at 48.5 north and 13.52 east on a .023 bearing. If anybody's off, please correct and call back Shapely Leader in five minutes to confirm."

But ten minutes passed and nobody called McGregor. Thus all planes and navigators had proper readings. Now, as the B-17's droned onward, the crews stared down at the rubble of former targets in northwest Austria: Willach, Steyr, Linz. Then the column sooned crossed into Czechoslovakia, where the Flying Fortresses passed the battered city of Prague whose iron work factories had been long ago demolished by 15th Air Force bombers. The B-17's soon passed the huge marshalling yards at Passau, one of the secondary targets for today's work, in the event the 5th Wing could not drop their bomb loads at Marienfelde. And finally, the lengthy air armada droned over the city of Brux on the Czech-German border. A locomotive factory still operated here, and this factory too was one of today's alternate targets.

As the air armada flew over these battered cities, the Germans set up their usual protective smoke screens, because the B-17's overhead might have singled out their cities as today's objective. Colonel George McGregor pursed his lips when he flew over the smoke-camouflaged Brux. If his only problem over Marienfelde was a smoke screen, he would consider himself fortunate indeed.

The weather was clear, wind turbulence was at a minimum, and up to this point, the monotonous flight was uneventful. No longer did German ack-ack in Austria and Czechoslovakia spit massive flak at passing American aircraft. Bombers and fighter planes of the 15th Air Force had long ago wiped out most of the ack-ack batteries, and only token flak now came from Villach, Steyr, Linz, and Prague as the 5th Wing passed over these destroyed cities. No longer did the Luftwaffe send up its ME-109's and FW190's from bases in these two countries. Even if the Luftwaffe had elected to keep fighter planes here, they had no place to base such planes. American aircraft had long ago demolished the last of the Austrian and Czechoslovakian air fields.

But then, as Colonel George McGregor led his column of B-17's over Brux into Germany, the uneventful flight that began from the Foggia airfields abruptly ended. McGregor had just crossed the inconspicuous hamlet of Komatau in southeast Germany when the Germans reacted with 282 heavy anti-aircraft guns in the Brux-Komatau area.

At 1105 hours, the cry of approaching aircraft came from the warning control center of Jagdführer Erzgerbirge at the village of Komatau. The jagdführer warning prompted no fighter planes to rise against the B-17's, but the warning stirred the flak gunners of the Flaknachtrich 137 battery just inside the German border. The gunners, determined and loyal, understood the importance of Daimler-Benz, and they felt a sense of pride from their personal recruitment by General Dietrich Peltz himself.

Soon the bomber crews would curse General Todd, who said the southern approaches to Berlin did not have the heavy ack-ack defense that 8th Air Force bombers met in the western approach to Berlin through the Dummer Corridor. But Allied agents in Germany had apparently neglected to tell the Allies that General Peltz had moved heavy anti-aircraft guns into the southern corridor as part of the defense for the Daimler-Benz assembly plants.

Heavy, staccato concussions of exploding flak shook the B-17 formations along a twenty-mile route north of

Komatau. Bombardier Perry Ford stiffened in horror when he saw holes on his starboard from a sudden burst of flak that had hit the nose and the underbelly of Colonel George McGregor's lead B-17. Miraculously, none of the penetrating shrapnel had struck the bombardier or damaged his instruments. Captain Ford quickly tied a canvas over the riddled starboard shell and he then gaped at the black puffs still exploding around him.

In the Flying Fort's midsection, Waist Gunners Luther Ogle and Pete Cody hopped about like men avoiding six-shooter blasts from a gunfighter in an Old West saloon. Shrapnel fragments tore through the metal floor under them, leaving an array of holes as well as several dents on the topside of the fusilage. The gunners, like the bombardier, also slapped themselves from head to feet, but they felt no pain or blood. They too had escaped the shrapnel fragments.

In the ball turret, Photographer Jim Frye had cringed in his cramped quarters from the ack-ack bursts. The hit on the nose had only shaken him, but the hit on the underbelly of Big Jenny had jarred him viciously. For an instant, he thought the hit had severed him and the ball turret from the fusilage of the B-17 and plunged him downward to earth. But the horrifying seconds passed quickly and now, although safe, Frye stared anxiously at the bursting black puffs exploding around him.

In the cabin, Captain Ball picked up his intercom. "Crew, report damage! Report damage! We felt a couple of hits up here."

"We got hit in the nose," Bombardier Perry Ford answered, "but I'm okay and so is our gear. I threw a canvas cover over the damage."

"We got hit in the underbelly, sir," Waist Gunner Cody told the pilot. "Shrapnel through the floor. We're putting paste in the holes. No other damage."

"Anybody else?" McGregor now cried into the intercom.

Negative. There had been no other damage at any of the other stations. However, Engineer Marty Walsh crawled out of his top turret to check engine RPM and dropping oil pressure. He quickly found a loose pressure hose and tightened it. Then he called the captain. "Pressure okay again, sir."

"Okay, Sergeant, back to your turret. We may run into bandits."

"Yes, sir."

Then, Captain Ball called the navigator. "Dave, what's the reading?"

Captain Karin squinted at his compass and gyros before he studied his chart. "We're still on course, still on the .023 heading. We just got shook up a little."

"Stay alert. Call me if you have a problem."

"Okay, Captain."

In the radio compartment, Sergeant Burl Hancock sat stiffly, watching the knobs of his radio equipment jerk and vibrate everytime a new flak burst detonated beyond the fusilage of Big Jenny. Hancock felt trapped, like a man inside a locked room caught in a tornado and with no means of escape. He bit his lips with each new burst, waiting for the explosions to stop or waiting for the sudden death from a spray of hot ack-ack shrapnel. Happily, he could report no damage in the radio room.

From his co-pilot's seat, the CO of the 463rd Bomb Group, bouncing in his seat as the plane bounced through the incessant ack-ack barrage, squinted again at the continued puffs of exploding flak that punctured the blue sky with hundreds of black holes. He wondered how the rest of his group and the west column itself had made out. He called the tail gunner.

"Sergeant, what does it look like back there?"

"Bad, sir, bad," Staff Sergeant Heise answered. Heise had been staring at the flak attack like a man witnessing a nightmare. In twenty missions, the tail gunner had never seen such vicious and accurate ack-ack fire. The barrage had already struck at least a dozen planes behind and around him.

The lead plane of the 463rd's Baker Squadron had suffered a direct hit from an ack-ack burst that had torn away the two right engines and most of the right wing.

The big Flying Fort had then careened erratically downward until the plane disappeared into the depths below. Heise had seen no parachutes and he could only conclude that the entire ten-man crew was lost. Less than a moment later, the tail gunner had seen a second B-17 from Baker Squadron become enveloped in smoke and flames from a double dose of ack-ack explosions. Seconds later, the plane had split in half, with both parts of the aircraft plummeting straight down like a pair of misshapen rocks. This plane, too, had disappeared somewhere below.

Next, a Fort from the 97th Bomb Group suddenly lost its tail as a burst of ack-ack ripped away the aft section from the B-17's fusilage and sent the fragments skyward before the pieces had fallen to earth like huge chunks of black confetti. The rest of the aircraft had simply cartwheeled dizzily to earth, following the fragments of its tail.

"How bad, Sergeant?" Colonel McGregor asked anxiously.

"We lost two planes from Baker Squadron, sir, and I saw one from the 97th go down. I don't know how many are damaged, but the whole 463rd is out of formation and scattered all over the sky."

"We've never run into ack this bad and this accurate, Colonel," Captain Ball said.

Colonel George McGregor gaped in horror. If Luftwaffe fighter planes appeared now, they could maul wayward B-17's like wolves pouncing on strays. McGregor had long ago learned that a tight formation, with its heavy concentration of .50 caliber fire, offered the best defense against enemy interceptors. He picked up his TDS. "All Shapely aircraft, all aircraft, get your ass back in formation! On the double! Back in formation and close ranks!" The colonel then called the 2nd Flight leader of Baker Squadron. "Captain, take over the lead position and close ranks. You other squadron leaders, close ranks. On the double!"

Despite the heavy ack-ack fire, the pilots of the 463rd's

B-17's responded. They were soon back in formation. Then, suddenly, McGregor saw only sparodic puffs ahead. He closed his eyes in gratitude. They had come through the full five minute interval of heavy flak. Now the colonel settled in his cabin seat of Big Jenny and picked up his TDS again.

"This Shapely Leader," McGregor said. "All Shapely 1, Shapely 2, and Shapely 3 commanders please report losses and damage."

"This is Shapely 2 leader," Colonel Ohman of the 97th Group answered. "We had one plane down and three damaged. We're in pretty good shape."

"Shapely 3 leader responding," Colonel Barton of the 483rd Group now answered McGregor. "We have two down, four planes damaged. Three of the damaged planes will continue on, but one has to abort. They've lost their bomb release controls."

"Okay," McGregor said. The colonel then learned that two of his own 463rd planes had suffered damage besides the two lost from Baker Squadron. He spoke into his TDS again. "All cripples form to the rear of the column. If any such cripples need to abort, the aircraft commander will call Shapely Leader."

But as the damaged planes fell into the rear of the west column, none of their pilots called Colonel McGregor to abort. Some of the damaged planes carried wounded airmen aboard, but none of the injured flyers had asked to abort. They had settled for shots of morphine to ease their pain, sulfa powder and bandages on their wounds to ward off infection, tourniquets around an injured leg to prevent excessive bleeding, and air mattress beds on the floors of fusilages in the waist gunner compartments to rest their torn bodies.

For another half hour, the west column continued northward, now droning deeper and deeper into Germany. Soon the formations of B-17's hit another ack-ack gun-infested area in Kumenz, northeast of Leipzig, and the west column suffered through another five minutes of intense, vicious, accurate anti-aircraft fire. More B-17's suffered an array of damage, and more airmen suffered shrapnel wounds from bursing ack-ack shells. But the west column suffered no aircraft losses and the column droned on. Soon Colonel George McGregor in the lead B-17 saw the hazy panorama of Ruhland to the east, the target they had hit two days ago in the longest flight they had made into Germany until today.

Then Colonel McGregor felt a new fear. They had not seen a single interceptor, only vicious ack-ack fire. The colonel suspected that enemy fighter planes had concentrated themselves somewhere ahead for massive interception. McGregor remembered the reports from Allied intelligence: a couple of hundred conventional German fighter planes and at least fifty jets were stationed in northeast Germany. The colonel stared auxiously at the sky around him, but he saw no signs of the fighter escorts. He looked at his watch: 1145 hours. He was now about forty-five minutes from target and a couple minutes away from his rendezvous point with fighter escorts at Herzberg. Then a sudden panic stung the colonel's nerve. Suppose the escorts failed to show? Suppose his shaken column of B-17's flew into Daimler-Benz with no fighter plane portection? He licked his dry lips, but then he suddenly relaxed. In 23 missions over Fortress Europe, his escorts had always arrived on time. He should no more fear a rendezvous failure today than he should fear his B-17 suddenly falling out of the sky. He would see his escorts at any moment.

In the east column, 30 miles to the southwest, Colonel Bob Bivro and his airmen in this column had also suffered through the intense flak over Komatau and Kumenz, losing one B-17 from the 2nd, two from the 301st, and one from the 99th. But over the Elbe River, near the German village of Torgau, the P-51's of the 325th and 52nd Fighter Groups began settling themselves alongside and above the B-17's of the east column. The airmen of the east column felt a measure of relief when their escorting Mustangs joined them. These bomber airmen knew that German fighter planes could not be far off now, and they hoped the pilots of the 325th and 52nd would take care of such interceptors.

Up ahead, the west column of the 5th Bomb Wing continued to run into anti-aircraft fire as the planes continued north. But most of the fire was sparodic and did little damage. Only a few guns opened up on the bombers at Spremberg, Grosserbain, and Cottress, a mere 120 miles south of Berlin. The last heavy concentration of Flaknachtrich 137 guns, 394 of around Berlin itself, would open up, on the American bombers as they approached Marienfelde.

Within a hundred miles of target, Colonel George McGregor looked again at his watch: 1153. But as he looked left and right from his cabin seat, he still saw no Mustangs. The colonel squeezed his face and looked at his pilot. "Where the hell are those escorts?"

"I don't know, Colonel." Captain Ball shook his head.

Now, despite his location deep inside Germany, George McGregor called Colonel Bob Bivro of the east column that was flying some 30 miles diagonally behind him. "This is Shapely Leader to Shapely 4 Leader. Please come in."

A garbled response came from Colonel Bob Bivro. "I read you, Shapely Leader."

"How did you make out in that heavy flak?"

"We lost four planes coming through those two blocks of heavy flak and we have a dozen others damaged. How about yourself?"

"We lost five planes and we had five aborts over the Alps. We've got a squadron of cripples to the rear."

"Too bad," Bivro said.

"How about escort? Has your escort picked up the east column yet?"

"Right on time over Torgau."

"We haven't seen a sign of our escort," Colonel McGregor said.

They should have met you by now, George. But don't get shook up. They should be along."

"Yeah," the 463rd commander said. "Roger and out."

McGregor squinted from his cabin, saw nothing, and then sat back. However, Captain Ball suddenly tapped the colonel's shoulder. "Look, at eleven o'clock."

McGregor peered from the cabin of Big Jenny and gaped. A swarm of misty shapes darted and zoomed and arched in the sky ahead. McGregor's eyes widened. "Good God, bandits! A swarm of them!" The colonel was about to alert his bomber column gunners to prepare for fighter interception when his TDS buzzed on.

"Jetblack Leader, Jetblack Leader," the voice of Colonel Bill Daniels came over the intership TDS. "Where the hell have you been?"

"Where have I been?" McGregor huffed. "Where have *you* been?"

"You're late," Daniels answered. "We've been buzzing around this sky like homeless hawks for at least fifteen minutes."

"But you should have met us at least fifteen minutes ago. Did you lose your bearings?"

"We're at the rendezvous point: 50.2 north and 13.13 east. There's the village of Herzberg below."

"What? Hold on." McGregor called his navigator. "Captain Darin, can you give us a our heading and a reading on where we are?"

Karin checked his charts and compasses. "We're still on our .023 heading. Present location—50.2 by 13.13. We should be meeting our escorts just about now." From his enclosed, windowless compartment, the navigator did not know that the P-51's were right in front of them.

Colonel George McGregor grinned sheepishly before he spoke into his TDS. "Sorry, Jetblack Leader, you're right. We're the late ones—we must have slowed down coming through that ack-ack fire. We'll have to increase the speed of our column to reach the IP on schedule."

"We can keep up," Bill Daniels said. "We'll pick you up in two columns. Jetblack I will hang on your starboard with three squadrons while our Jetblack 1D will provide forward topcover. Jetblack 2 will hand on your port, with Jetblack 2's rear squadron as your rear topcover. We'll form up and alongside in about two minutes."

"Roger and out, Jetblack Leader," Colonel McGregor answered.

A moment later, Colonel Ben Davis, in the lead plane of the 332nd Red Tail Fighter Group, dipped his wing, zoomed upwards in a wide arch, and then brought his Mustang down. He slowed up and straightened until the 332nd's lead P-51 hung at 25,000 feet, some 200 yards off the port of Colonel George McGregor's lead Big Jenny. Soon Davis's two wing men came alongside and settled diagonally to the left and right of the Red Tail colonel. Forty-one more aircraft of the 332nd also settled into three V's to the left of the west column, while the fifteen Mustangs of the 102nd Squadron climbed to a thousand feet over the rear of the west bomber column.

On the starboard side, Colonel Bill Daniels settled his own 31st Fighter Group into their escort positions.

Now, as the armada continued on, Colonel Ben Davis felt apprehensive, wondering if the fighter pilots would follow the diagonal pattern of defense he had suggested at the briefing for the 80A mission. The Red Tail colonel felt relieved when he heard Colonel Bill Daniel's voice over the TDS.

"This is Jetblack Leader to all Jetblack pilots: a reminder that all fighter units will follow the diagonal pattern against any jet aircraft interceptors. Repeat: all Jetblack fighter leaders, remind your pilots—they will use diagonal defense pattern against any jet interceptors. You may, however, use standard techniques against conventional enemy aircraft."

Satisfied, Colonel Davis now called his own pilots. "This is Jetblack 2 Leader. You just heard escort leader. Make certain all Jetblack 2 flight leaders follow diagonal defense pattern in the event of enemy jet interceptors. Don't get impatient and dart off after such interceptors." Then Ben Davis settled back in his pilot's seat.

In the cabin of Big Jenny, Colonel George McGregor and Captain Roger Ball also relaxed, looking at the P-51's alongside of them, or at the empty blue skies ahead, or at the sprawling Brandenburg farmlands below. Others aboard Big Jenny also relaxed: Bombardier Ford in the damaged nose again played with his instruments and bomb sights. Navigator Karin, in his isolated compartment, once more studied his charts, compresses, gyros, and clocks. In the radio compartment, Sergeant Burl Hancock checked his dials, volume control, and reostats. In the top turret, Staff Sergeant Marty Walsh wheeled his turret first 90 degrees left and then 90 degrees right, while he scanned the bombers and P-51's around him. In the damaged waist gunner compartment, Sergeants Ogle and Cody had huddled inside their electrically warmed suits while they swung their guns. Inside the ball turret, Lieutenant Jim Frye again checked his K20 cameras and peered downward at the sprawling landscape. He waited uneasily for the east German farmlands to give way to the battered buildings of Berlin. Finally, in Big Jenny's tail, Staff Sergeant Heise manipulated the bubble that held his twin tail guns He squinted at the lines of B-17's behind him or at the P-51's alongside of him. He waited for the first bursts from enemy strafing guns or the first whoosh of a streaming rocket.

And in the long line of bombers behind Heise, the airmen of the 97th and the 483rd Bomb Groups also waited tensely, fidgeting with their guns or their instruments to pass the time and to temper their growing apprehensions as they neared the Daimler-Benz target.

The men of the 5th Wing had reason to fret. The Luftwaffe had not remained idle. As soon as Jagdführer Erzgerbirge reported the approach of the 5th Wing B-17's across the Czech border, General Dietrich Peltz checked with the tracking staff at his Fleigerkorps Reich headquarters in Berlin. He suspected immediately that the enemy armada was heading for Berlin, and more specifically for the Daimler-Benz plants at Marienfelde. Peltz knew well enough that Galland and his jet fighter pilots had thwarted the first attempt to bomb Daimler-Benz on 18 March. He also knew that the 5th Wing American 5th Wing from Italy had successfully assaulted

Ruhland two days ago because Galland had guessed wrong. The Fleigerkorps Reich kommadant guessed that the Allies had ignored the Luftwaffe miscalculation during the Ruhland raid and they preferred to believe they had a better chance against Daimler-Benz with an air strike from Italy. So the Americans had decided to send a 15th Air Force armada to assault the tank assembly plants.

Peltz immediately called General Galland at München-Riem. "An enemy bomber force is now over Komatau. The south battery of Flaknachtrich 137 has engaged them. Quite probably this enemy fleet plans to bombard the tank works at Marienfelde. I have already alerted the Messerschmitt and Fokke-Wolfe geschwaders in the area. They will rise at once and endeavor to lure away the enemy's fighter escort cover. That would leave the American bombers free for your jet aircraft. I suggest you prepare your jagdverband to meet them before they come over Berlin."

"At once, Herr Peltz," Galland answered.

Less than a half hour later, the warning crew of Jagdführer Kumenz reported the enemy bomber fleet. Only moments later, the Flaknichtrich 137 central battery northeast of Leipzig had opened on these same B-17 formations. And when Jagdführer Stremberg reported the northward flight of the B-17's, General Peltz harbored no more doubts. The B-17's were definitely heading for Daimler-Benz.

"There is no question about it," General Peltz now told Galland when he called the JV 44 commander again. "They have come too far north and they can be no more than an hour from Marienfelde."

"I called Colonel Steinhoff as soon as I received your first call, Herr Peltz. The colonel and his pilots of JG 7 are already here at München-Riem. The aircraft of JV 44 and JG 7 will be airborne and waiting at least ten minutes before this enemy air fleet's estimated time of arrival over Marienfelde."

"You are certain, Adolf?"

"I'm certain," Galland promised.

By 1210 hours, when the 5th Wing came within sixty miles of IP, the screaming whines of jet and rocket engines echoed across the landscape of München-Reim. In tree hidden revetments, General Galland, his staffel leaders, and fifty-five other jet pilots had settled themselves into their ME-262's. They waited to roll towards the runway as soon as the tower operator flashed the take-off blinker. The 60 ME-262's had been loaded with 12 R4M rockets and dozen 3O mm shells in their wing cannons. Ground crews, cringing from the deafening whines of jet engines, held wheel chucks in check, waiting to pull the blocks free as soon as Galland gave the signal.

Across the airfield, Colonel Steinhoff, Captain von Brauchitsch, Major Schnaufer, and eight other ME-163 Komet Pilots also sat in their own aircraft, ready to take off in their rocket engine planes, each loaded with 5cm rocket explosives. These JV pilots had arrived here from Lagar-Lechfield about an hour ago. After a quick snack of coffee and biscuits, they had returned to their Komets. Now Steinhoff and his JG 7 pilots waited to follow JV 44 into the sky to meet the American attackers.

Fifty miles southeast of Berlin, only 55 ME-109's and 60 FW-190's had taxied to the runway and taken off on this cloudy March morning. As so often happened, General Peltz had over-estimated the availability of conventional fighter aircraft in Fleigerkorps Reich. The aircraft had been in combat almost daily for the past several months. Many 109's and 190's were badly in need of service, many had damage from air battles, and a shortage of pilots prevailed. So a mere 115 109's and 190's zoomed westward to intercept the nearly 450 bombers and fighters of the 5th Bomb Wing. Hopefully, these 109's and 190's could lure off the escorting American fighter planes, leaving the bombers easy prey for the jet fighter units. The technique had worked well on 18 March and General Peltz hoped the strategy would succeed again today.

Twenty miles northeast of the B-17 bombers, Colonel

Joe Holtroder in his lead P-38 of the 82nd Fighter Group scanned the skies around him. His Lightnings had been banking and arching like restless fledglings looking for anything that might strike their fancy. They would report enemy interceptors, particularly jet planes, and then make initial contact with such Luftwaffe fighter planes. Like the P-51's, these P-38's of the 82nd also carried 110-gallon belly tanks to give them enough fuel for the nearly 1600-mile round trip from Italy. The Lightning pilots would salvo these belly tanks as soon as they saw the first German fighter planes, if the P-38's are encumbered by extra gas tanks, they could not easily engage them.

Shortly after noon on March 24th the whistles blew throughout the Daimler-Benz complex.

Red alert! Enemy air raid!

The thousands of employees quickly left their stations. Maintenance crews shut off electrical equipment and banked fires to minimize damage from high explosives and incendiary bombs. The workers filed out of their plants like a long parade of ants and they hurried through tunnels to air raid shelters in concrete block houses or under huge slag piles. The workers moved efficiently, well trained to seek shelter from an air raid. By 1215 hours, the Daimler-Benz plant became totally quiet and deserted.

At this same 1215 hours, the squadron leader of the 82nd Fighter Group's Baker Squadron spotted aircraft coming from the east. When he reported the bandits to Joe Holtroder, the colonel ordered his pilots after them. At the same time, the kommodore leading the first ME-109 geschwader unit saw the oncoming Lightnings and he picked up his radio. "Americanische!" Then the German fighter plane kommodore gunned his engine and sped westward.

In moments, the clash between these FW-190's and ME-109's against the American P-38's would ignite a furious, nerve-wracking, devastating battle in the skies over Marienfelde. The clash would sap the strength of hundreds of American and German airmen alike.

Chapter Fourteen

The 82nd Fighter Group commander, Colonel Joe Holtroder, called Shapely Leader, Colonel George McGregor. "This is Jetblack 5, Jetblack 5. We've got about a hundred bandits coming in to engage. We're about 30 or 40 miles northeast of your formations. I don't know if we can handle them with fifty-one P-38's. Can you spare a couple of squadrons from your escort to help out?"

"Two squadrons?" McGregor asked.

"That would make the odds about even," Colonel Holtroder said, "and we'd be able to make pretty sure that none of these 109's or 190's reach you."

"I don't know," McGregor balked. The 80A mission commander had 116 P-51's covering his own column of bombers and 102 P-51's of the 325th and 52nd Fighter Groups covering the east column. He expected fifty or more jets in the target area. McGregor guessed he would need at least five-to-one odds to engage these jets successfully in the diagonal defense pattern that required six aircraft per unit. Thus, McGregor was reluctant to release any of his escort.

The 463rd colonel tightened his face, pursed his lips,

and peered out of the Big Jenny cabin window at the escorting P-51's. The obvious uncertainty on his face drew the attention of Captain Roger Ball, who glanced at the colonel but said nothing.

"I'm at a loss, Captain."

Ball didn't answer.

"If we release any of the P-51's, we may run into difficulty over Marienfelde. Still, we probably should help those guys in the 82nd."

Roger Ball still said nothing and McGregor frowned. The captain had his opinions, but the decision lay with the colonel, and the pilot of Big Jenny apparently wanted no oart of the responsibility for such a decision. But McGregor put Ball on the spot.

"What do you think, Captain?"

The pilot now frowned and looked at the formations of aircraft around him. He answered the colonel calmly. "Our B-17 gunners are pretty good against conventional German fighter planes, Colonel, but I don't know about jets."

George McGregor nodded, satisfied that Captain Ball's answer had paralleled his own. Still, McGregor wanted more imput, so he called Colonel Bob Bivro over the TDS. "This is Shapely Leader to Shapely IV."

"I read you," the 2nd Bomb Group commander answered.

"We've got a request from Jetblack 5. They've run into a hundred or so conventional German fighter planes about forty miles northeast of us. They want some of our escort to help out. What do you think?"

Bivro never hesitated. "I think they better do the best they can. If some of those 109's or 190's break through, our gunners can handle them. But hell, we'll need every fighter plane we've got to tangle with any jets."

"I agree," McGregor answered. Now he was satisfied.

The 463rd colonel sighed, stared beyond the B-17 cabin for a moment, and then picked up his TDS. "This is Shapely Leader to Jetblack 5, Shapley Leader to Jetblack 5."

"I read you," Colonel Holtroder answered.

"Sorry, Joe, we can't send anybody. We expect jet fighter plane interceptors over IP. We'll need every P-51 we've got. You'll have to do the best you can. I know that means some of those Messerschmitts will break through, but we'll take our chances."

"Okay, Colonel," Holtroder answered, "it's your show." Then, the 82nd Fighter Group commander called his pilots. "No help from Shapely, boys. We go alone. Get ready for scramble and peel off in pairs."

The 82nd pilots, outnumbered about two-to-one by the oncoming German fighter planes, had two advantages. First, the German pilots were not looking for a dogfight with the 82nd. The Germans preferred to elude the P-38 pilots to get at the bombers. Thus, the Germans were more likely to take evasive action rather than fight. But more significantly, most of the 109 and 190 pilots, hastily trained and inexperienced, would be no match for the skilled American pilots. The Luftwaffe had lost most of their talented pilots over the past two years or more, and these novice pilots closing on the 82nd lacked the ability to really cope on even terms with the P-38 fighter pilots.

As the German fighter planes raced westward, the P-38's zoomed upward to gain altitude for an attack. At 1220 hours, on this 24 March 1945, the P-38 pilots loosed a heavy stream of .50 caliber fire at the ME-109's and FW-190's. The Germans attempted to evade, but they simply could not do so. The Luftwaffe Kommodores decided to leave their complement of 109's—55 planes— to deal with the P-38's, while the 60 FW-190's sped towards the B-17 bombers. However, Colonel Holtroder would not allow the Germans this neat strategy. Holtroder split his group in half, sending 25 Lightings after the 109's and the other 26 Lightnings after the 190's. Within minutes, the first two squadrons of P-38's knocked a half dozen 109's out of the air and damaged a dozen more. The Lightning pilots scattered the rest.

Colonel Joe Holtroder, meanwhile, zoomed down from 27,000 feet with his wing man to lead the other two squadrons against the 190's that were speeding towards the bombers. Holtroder quickly came into the tail of an enemy plane shot a pair of 20mm shells at the surprised German pilot. The first round missed, but the second shell caught the after-fusilage and blew the plane in half. The two pieces dropped to earth in two balls of fire.

"You got 'im, Colonel, you got 'im!" the wing man cried.

"We haven't got time for bows," Holtroder answered. "Keep after them. Those B-17's will have enough trouble with jets and ack-ack, and they don't need these conventionals to give them more trouble." Holtroder paused before speaking into his radio again. "In pairs—keep after them in pairs."

For the next several minutes, the P-38's of the 82nd continued to climb, dive, and zoom after the conventional 109's and 190's, chasing the Germans in a running dogfight as the Luftwaffe aircraft attempted to reach the bombers. The Luftwaffe pilots, however, could not shake off the P-38's. Soon the 109's had been forced to fight back, along with the 190 units. A few of the German pilots did maneuver behind some of the twin-tail Lightnings to unleash streams of chattering .50 caliber bullets from their wing guns. Colonel Holtroder saw the twin tail break off from one of his P-38's before the Lightning disappeared in a huge wad of debris. Other P-38's had also suffered hits from .50 caliber bullets or from exploding rocket fire.

"Hang in pairs, in pairs!" Holtroder warned his pilots. "They'll get you if you don't hang in pairs."

The pilots of the 82nd responded as they continued the aerial brawl with the 109's and 190's. Two pilots came into the tail of a 109, releasing a heavy chatter from .50 machine guns that caught the rear of the Messerschmitt before the 109 exploded and disintegrated in mid-air. Another pair of P-38's came down at a three fighter formation of 190's and released a half dozen 20mm cannon shells. Two shells slammed into the fusilage of one of them and blew the plane in half. The other two 190 pilots, shocked by the sudden demise of their comrade, tried to zoom away, but the two P-38 pilots turned after them and unleashed a heavy chatter of machine gun fire that drew smoke from the tail of one and whooshing fire from the engine and cockpit of the other. The two German planes arched across the sky like a pair of small meteorites before they plunged to earth.

Below, in a small hamlet east of Berlin, German civilians peered up at the aerial battle high in the sky. Even from the ground, they could easily see that most of the falling aircraft were German, because the single-engine 109's and 190's were quite different from the twin-fusilage American Lightnings. The spectators had seen two P-38's drop out of the sky, but they had seen at least a dozen German fighter planes falling in smoke or flames.

The lopsided dogfight in the sky merely confirmed the suspicions of these civilians—the German Air Force was finished. The Luftwaffe could no longer cope with the hordes of aircraft the Allies sent over Germany day after day. Their 109's and 190's, superior fighter planes for most of the war, now showed their inferiority to new American and British aircraft. And finally, the poor showing above these Brandenburg farms verified the most pessimistic rumor of all: the experienced pilots were gone, leaving nervous, inexperienced novices to challenge the thousands of well-trained Allied airmen.

These German civilians merely watched the aerial battle overhead in sober silence, because the dogfight reflected the continuing deterioration of Germany. The war had opened with flushing victories nearly six years ago, and the conflict was now closing with devastating disaster. Few of these rural Germans knew of the desperate, last-ditch strategy by General Peltz and General Galland to save Marienfelde. These civilians knew nothing of the oil coup in Hungary or the hope the coup had brought to the German military. They had not seen fuel in over a year and they were unlikely to see fuel now because one of their armies had won an oil field.

True, these farmers had heard of jet aircraft, but they had rarely seen one and they knew little about their potential.

These rural residents saw no significance in the tank assembly plants at Marienfelde, as did Peltz and Galland and Von Rundstedt. To these civilians, Daimler-Benz was just another factory, another target for the skyful of Allied bombers that came over northeast Germany almost daily.

In this late March of 1945, these farmers knew that the Allies were destroying the last vestige of the Luftwaffe and the Wehrmacht and that nothing could stem the imminent defeat of Germany. They were grateful for one thing: the Allied bombers had concentrated on the German cities like Berlin, and these quaint rural farms and villages had been spared the devastation that had leveled Germany's urban areas.

When the view of the darting, turning, screaming planes faded to the west and out of sight, these German civilians ambled passively back to their rural homes and rural chores.

And high in the sky, the Luftwaffe geschwaders that battled the 82nd Fighter Group had suffered badly—sixteen 109's and 190's down, with another forty or fifty damaged. Colonel Holtroder had lost three P-38's, with several more Lightnings damaged. Still, despite the battering by the 2nd Fighter Group, the German kommodore struggled eastward with whatever fighter planes he could to attack the Flying Fortresses.

"This is Jetblack 5 Leader to Shapely Leader, Jetblack 5 Leader to Shapely Leader," Colonel Holtroder called the commander of the 463rd Bomb Group.

"Shapely Leader," Colonel McGregor responded.

"We got lucky. We mauled those conventional German fighter planes pretty good, but they won't all give up. You can expect some of them to be on your necks in a few minutes."

"Okay," McGregor answered.

But when Colonel George McGregor scanned the skies around him, he had yet to see any signs of enemy aircraft.

He looked at his watch: 1225. He should have been over the target five minutes ago, but he remembered that heavy ack-ack fire along the way had cost him at least ten minutes, so he was still several minutes away from IP. He picked up his TDS.

"This is Shapely Leader. Shapely Leader to all units. Tighten formations. Stay close and tight. Bandits on the way. Gunners, check your weapons and say alert. All Jetblack top cover units will disengage to meet conventional enemy interceptors from the east. Other Jetblack units will assume diagonal pattern in blocks of six to engage possible jet interceptors."

When Colonel McGregor finished, Colonel Bill Daniels spoke into his own TDS. "This is Jetblack Leader. You heard Shapely Leader—bandits expected from three o'clock. Top cover squadrons only will engage these conventional interceptors. All other units will prepare to assume diagonal pattern for expected engagement with jet interceptors."

As the high cover P-51's broke away from the Flying Fortresses, the bomber crews of the B-17's grew tense. They knew they were now moments from the target, more anti-aircraft fire, the 109's and 190's from the east, and the dreaded German jets. All were sure to be waiting somewhere ahead. Gunners tightened their grips on weapons. Bombardiers checked their bombsight during these precious moments of calm. Navigators once more checked bearings, track, altitude, location, and speed. Radio men played with dials. Pilots and co-pilots fumbled with instrument panels. Only the monotonous hum of B-17 engines interrupted the tense silence that now prevailed among the bomber crews.

In their lonely cockpits, the P-51 pilots of the four American fighter groups scanned the skies intently, waiting, holding the buttons of their .50 caliber wing guns or the plungers of their 20mm cannons. These pilots knew the cover squadrons could handle the conventional 109's and 190's that had broken through the 82nd Fighter Group screen, but few of these P-51 pilots relished a fight with German jet fighter pilots, whom intelligence said were an array of experienced Luftwaffe aces.

The American airmen of Mission 80A listened tensely when McGregor spoke into the TDS again. "This Shapely Leader to Shapely 4, Shapely Leader to Shapely 4."

"I read you," Colonel Bob Bivro of the 2nd Bomb Group answered.

"We've got some 109's and 190's coming towards us and I've sent our top cover to intercept."

"If we see any of them back here," Bivro said, "I'll send our top cover after them."

"Okay," McGregor said. "We're only a few minutes from target and you're supposed to follow us in five minutes. Is your east column five minutes behind us?"

"We've been closing for the past half hour," Bivro said. "We'll be over IP on time."

"Good," McGregor answered. "We want to get in and out as fast as possible."

McGregor had barely switched off when the calm skies immediately south of Berlin suddenly shook from massive concussions of anti-aircraft fire. In less than a minute, the sky was a huge field of black and blue polka dots. Hundreds of exploding puffs blossomed under, around, above, and amidst the 80A formations. The groups of B-17's shuddered from heavy, deafening explosions, while the smaller P-51's bounced and jerked from the same barrage of ack-ack. All 394 guns of the Flaknachtrich 137's Berlin batteries had seemingly oPened up at once. Now the incessant, staccato blasts had left a ring in the ears of the airmen, and they could speak to only each other over their intercoms.

In the pilot's cabin of Big Jenny, Colonel George McGregor squinted through the flak at Berlin, endless blocks of battered buildings and countless squares of rubble. McGregor gaped, so awed by the sight that he had momentarily forgotten the dozens of flak bursts exploding around him. He had never been over Berlin before. And, although he had heard of the widespread destruction to Germany's captital city, he could not believe what he saw below him. Not a single structure was without damage. Not a single street was devoid of debris. And nowhere in the sprawling ruins did Colonel McGregor see a vehicle moving through the rubbled streets.

Big Jenny was crossing the southeast corner of the capital city before the lead B-17 of Mission 80A reached the target in the eastern suburb of Marienfelde. McGregor was studying a map in his lap when a flak burst suddenly shook Big Jenny. The colonel jerked instinctively and then spoke into the intercom.

"Damage! Any damage?"

None. Nobody reported damage or injury and McGregor sighed in relief.

But if the 463rd colonel felt relatively at ease, Staff Sergeant Heise did not. With each passing moment, he stared for the second time at the havoc behind him. The day had darkened from the thousands of black ack-ack puffs floating through the air. Two more B-17's of the 463rd Group had become victims of the vicious ack-ack fire. One of the Baker Squadron B-17's caught a twin flak hit under the left wing and the double blast had shorn off the wing like some giant jerking a man's arm from his shoulder. The plane had simply flipped over and then cartwheeled downward like a huge bird falling out of the sky. Then, to his right aft, at about four o'clock, Heise saw a B-17 of Charlie Squadron catch a flak burst in the tail and then another in the belly. The tail gunner saw the guts of the B-17 fall out of the fusilage like a pile of descending debris before the plane fell nose first and spun dizzily to earth.

Next, the tail gunner of Big Jenny gasped when he saw another B-17 of the west column-fall from a symmetrical flight pattern. A plane from the 97th dropped out of formation like an exhausted soldier falling from the ranks of a rigid file-on-parade. Heise did not know where the aircraft got hit; he only knew the hit was fatal because the plane went tumbling downward out of sight. Several parachutes opened in the sky behind the falling plane, so at least some of the crew had escaped.

Finally, Heise saw another B-17 of the 97th Bomb Group totally in flames. A heavy burst of orange flames had smothered the entire right wing and fusilage, and a flak burst had apparently ignited its gas tanks. Its crew had no doubt died instantly from the sudden, engulfing flames. Big Jenny's tail gunner watched in horror as the flaming Fortress simply arched erratically across the sky, out of control. The burning plane soared under Heise's own B-17, sending up an aura of heat as it passed. Heise did not relax until the burning aircraft disintegrated and chunks of flaming debris plummeted downward like the residue of a huge aerial firework display.

And far to the rear, in the 483rd Bomb Group, the tail gunner saw the faint outlines of two more B-17's spinninq to earth, one of them trailing a streamer of smoke from its engines, while the other left a thick billow of smoke from its tail. Heise could not tell if any airmen had escaped from those planes, because the two bombers had been too far away to see any parachutes.

The tail gunner also saw flak bursts chop holes in the frames of other B-17's. He saw an occasional engine sputter and die from an ack-ack hit, and he saw chunks of metal spin away from a wing or a fusilage or a tail section, but he didn't see any more Flying Forts tumble out of the sky.

Suddenly, Heise heard the sudden voice of Captain Roger Ball. "Bandits! Bandits at three o'clock!"

In the cabin of Big Jenny, Colonel George McGregor also reacted to Captain Ball's cry. The colonel squinted off starboard at the oncoming 109's and 190's that had eluded the 82nd Fighter Group. But the thirty or forty Luftwaffe fighter planes moved in gingerly. Their pilots had apparently lost their aggressiveness after the destructive dogfights with the P-38's.

Back in the tail section of Big Jenny, Heise swung his twin fifties to the left and waited for the oncoming German fighters. In the top turret, Staff Sergeant Walsh craned his neck frantically for a glimpse of the German interceptors coming from the starboard quarter. In the fusilage, Waist Gunner Luther Ogle merely peered out the starboard window while his companion, Right Waist Gunner Pete Cody, held tightly to his twin 50's and aimed the barrels to the east.

The first flight of ME-109's, in pairs and flying through their own ack-ack fire, came diving into the bomber formations from three to five o'clock, but the top cover squadrons of the 31st and 332nd Fighter Groups waded into the oncoming Messerschmitts. Similarly, several planes from the east column's 325th and 52nd Fighter Groups also zoomed off to meet the forty or fifty German interceptors. The clash was no contest.

In pairs, the P-51's arched downward in wide curves to attack the German fighter planes. Soon another dogfight ensued only moments from IP. The P-51's, even more swift and maneuverable than the P-38's, had an easier time than the 82nd Group's P-38's. In less than a minute the Mustangs had knocked a dozen of the enemy planes out of the air. The nervous men aboard the B-17's listened with a mixture of excitement and relief at the squawking radio reports from the P-51's.

"You got 'em, Joe. The whole wing's on fire!"

"She's going down! Going down!"

"There goes his tail! Scratch another Messerschmitt!"

"Man, oh man! We shot his goddam wing off!"

"He isn't hanging on your tail anymore, Eddie!"

Despite their euphoria, there were also some anxious moments, because the Mustang pilots could not keep all of these 190's and 109's at bay. Some of the German pilots, aggressively determined, despite the odds and their inexperience, battled the P-51's deftly.

"Watch out! Watch out! He's on your tail! On your tail!"

Too late. A double whoosh of rockets spewed out of the 109 and smashed into the Mustang. A sudden explosion followed with plane and pilot smothered in a sheet of flames.

"One o'clock, one o'clock! Two bandits at one o'clock!"

Again too late. More rocket thumps, and a moment later another shattered Mustang tumbled to earth, a P-51 from the 52nd Fighter Group.

The aerial fight continued for more than a minute or two. However, in this short period, fifteen or twenty German fighter planes broke through the fighter screen to attack the B-17's. But this handful, a far cry from the 115 109's and 190's that had started after the bombers, could do very little against some 160 bombers, and the several hundred guns that spewed .50 caliber fire at the German fighter planes.

Within a minute the B-17 bomber formations, utilizing hundreds of guns, had chopped apart the handful of fighter planes that had managed to clear first the 82nd Group and then the P-51 screens. The Luftwaffe fighter planes had run into a wall of fire. True, many of the B-17's had been hit, some of the flyers suffered wounds, and several men were even killed. But the German fighter planes had not knocked any of the bombers out of the air. The furious machine gun fire from top turrets, waists, bellies, tails, and even bombardier nose guns had cut several German planes to pieces in mid-air. Other German planes had suffered damage from the Flying Fort machine guns. By the time the minute was over, the surviving 109's and 190's had disappeared somewhere to the west.

"Cover squadrons, cover squadrons," Colonel Bill Daniels cried into his TDS, "this is Jetblack leader. You did a good job. Get back in formation. You can break off again if those bandits come back. Then Daniels called the 82nd Fighter Group. "This is Jetblack Leader to Jetblack 5."

"We read you," Colonel Joe Holtroder answered.

"Any more bandits on the way?"

"Maybe a few, but we pretty well scattered them."

"Okay, bring your pixies in and hang tight in front of us."

"What's the score there?"

"Pretty good so far, except for flak. We'll be at IP in a couple of minutes."

"No Jets?" Holtroder asked.

"Not yet, but we're expecting them," Bill Daniels answered.

The 82nd Fighter Group thus returned to its outer screen station, north and east of the 80A formations. The B-17 crews, especially the gunners, felt a momentary relief after the episode with the attacking 109's and 190's. The P-51 pilots brought their diagonal flights closer to the bombers, shortening the ring around the Flying Fortresses. Then the heavy flak that had shuddered the B-17's and P-51's slowly abated and seemingly diminished to silence. The 394 ack guns of Flaknachtrich 137 had ceased firing. Colonel George McGregor frowned and looked at his watch: 1235 hours.

"I wonder why the hell they stopped?"

"I don't know," Captain Ball answered.

Then McGregor suddenly scowled. "I can guess, Captain. Jets! Jets are up ahead and they don't want anything to interfere with them."

A sudden call came from Bombardier Perry Ford. "Target Daimler-Benz ahead! I can see the heavy smoke screen over the tank works at Marienfelde."

McGregor squinted at the smoke screen forward and below, and then picked up his TDS. "Target Daimler-Benz in two minutes. They've got a smoke screen, so we'll have to use radar."

McGregor again scanned the sky, now empty of ack-ack puffs, and saw no jets. He felt a fleeting exhilaration, but then he got a call from Colonel Ben Davis over the TDS. "This is Jetblack 2 Leader, Jetblack 2. Bandits eleven o'clock high, eleven o'clock high. Jets!"

The cry sent a tremor of fear through Colonel George McGregor. Jets were indeed waiting for them only a few miles from target. McGregor wiped the sudden perspiration from his face. During his combat career, the colonel had accustomed himself to piston engine interceptors and heavy German flak. But the uncertainty of jets left him nervous and numb. A macabre image came into his mind: the image of twenty-eight B-17's that had fallen victim to these jets on 18 March 1945. He licked his lips and squinted hard out of his cabin window for a glimpse of the jets. He did not see any. Then he stared again at the smoke-covered Daimler-Benz target looming ahead. He almost relaxed when he now heard the voice of Colonel Bill Daniels.

"This is Jetblack Leader, Jetblack Leader. You guys know what to do—diagonal defense in flights of six, flights of six. Don't chase after them! Repeat: don't chase after them. Make them come to you."

The jets were upon them. A few seconds later, Colonel George McGregor saw the P-51 pilots, alongside his Big Jenny, gunning their engines and tightening their sextet formation.

Chapter Fifteen

High over Marienfelde, at 30,000 feet, General Adolf Galland sat restlessly in the cockpit of his Snowbird. He had a total of seventy-one planes, sixty ME-262 jets and eleven ME-163 rockets. The jet aircraft had been circling over Daimler-Benz in four-plane diamonds for about ten minutes before Galland saw the approaching 5th Bomb Wing armada. The JV 44 Kommodore had disciplined his pilots thoroughly, warning them not to break off prematurely and chase recklessly after the oncoming B-17 formations.

"We will attack only in pairs, and not until the enemy escorts chase after us as they always do. We can easily outdistance these P-51's and then return to attack the bombers before these enemy fighter planes can recover to reach us and interfere. Under no circumstances should we attack the bombers before their jet fighter planes leave the B-17's. We have only one purpose—to defend Daimler-Benz. We must not spend our small resources in aerial engagements with the American P-51's. It is not the enemy's bombers. We must either knock these bombers out of the sky, or we must scatter and disrupt them so badly that they cannot effectively bomb the tank factories."

As the 5th Wing approached Marienfelde, Galland frowned. Swarms of enemy fighter planes hung about the bombers like bees around a hive. Where were the Messerschmitts to draw off the enemy's P-51 escorts? Galland had quickly surmised that the conventional fighter planes had failed, as they had failed repeatedly during the past year. The JV 44 commander sighed. He should have known better. Now Galland was faced not with a few Mustangs that had not gone off to engage the conventional German fighter planes, but with probably the entire American escorting force.

Still, Galland could not dwell on the apparent failure of the 109's and 190's to lure away the Mustangs, for he himself could not waver from his commitment. He told himself it would not matter. His speedier, more maneuverable jets could elude a hundred P-51's as easily as they could elude a dozen P-51's. As long as the Mustangs chased after him, no matter how many, he would succeed in his attack on the bomber formation.

When Galland saw the P-51's move slightly away from the bombers in their six-plane diagonal patterns, the JV 44 commander grinned He was certain the Mustangs were coming out to attack his jets, as the Americans always came out to chase after German interceptors. When he had drawn these P-51's far enough away from the B-17's, Galland would lead his jet pilots back to attack the exposed bombers. Galland signalled to his pilots to feint and parry in the sky to encourage the P-51's to hurry after them.

"All staffel leaders, prepare for pursuit," Galland cried into his radio. "When they have chased us far enough from the bombers, we will make our bid. Do not go after the bombers until I give the signal."

However, the P-51's had gone only far enough from the bombers to establish their six-plane diagonal patterns. Then, the six-plane formations remained immobile, like antennae attached to some giant aerial machine. Galland wrinkled his face in surprise. Why didn't the Mustangs come after them? The Kommodore brought his 262 flight closer, feinting again and hoping to draw the Mustangs. But the P-51's would not move from their established positions.

Now the JV 44 leader felt frustration. Why didn't the Mustangs come out to fight as they usually did? But Galland couldn't wait much longer because the B-17's were moving ever closer to Daimler-Benz. If the P-51's would not come out to fight, Galland would simply drive past the Mustangs and get to the Flying Fortresses. He spoke into his radio.

"They will not engage, so we must take the initiative. We will attack in pairs." He paused. Then said: "Heil Jagdverband!"

Galland dipped the wing of his Snowbird and then dove towards the lead bombers of the 463rd Bomb Group. The general's wing man zoomed alongside of him. The P-51 pilots of the lead 332nd diagonal flight held their positions, checking the urge to attack the jets. Colonel Ben Davis, at the top of this first diagonal flight, felt perspiration dampen his face as he nervously moved his fingers over his .50 caliber machine gun button and his 20mm cannon plunger. What if his strategy failed? What if these ME-262's successfully got by them? They would surely knock a couple of B-17's out of the air.

But Davis did not falter, despite his tightened, rattled nerves. He waited until Galland and his wing man came into the right position. Then as the jets zoomed within range, Davis pressed both his machine gun button and the cannon plunger. The heavy fire signalled the other pilots in the diagonal line and they too sent succeeding bursts of .50 caliber machine gun fire and 20mm cannon shells into the speeding pair of 262's.

Neither Galland nor his wing man reached the bombers. Several of the 20mm shells tore into the wing man and the jet plane disintegrated in mid-air before the pieces cascaded to earth. The same gauntlet of fire ripped holes in Galland's ME-262 and the JV 44 kommodore veered to the left and upwards, away from the P-51's and away from the bombers.

The next pair of ME-262's met the same burst of fire as the speeding 550 mph Snowbirds raced towards their thousand yard range to release R4M rockets. A new diagonal flight of P-51's from the 332nd opened up with a wall of 20mm cannon and .50 caliber machine gun fire. Once more, tracer bullets and small cannon shells ripped holes into the German jets, tearing away an engine on one fighter plane and part of the tail on the second. The two German jets wobbled erratically before the pilots regained control of their 262's and zoomed away. The jet pilots never got in a single shot at the droning B-17's.

Now the six P-51's arched up and away while the next diagonal chain moved up to meet a new duet of jet fighter planes. The next pair of ME-262's came soon after, led by Colonel Joseph Kammhuber. The colonel and his wing man roared toward the 463rd's port Charlie Squadron, but Kammhuber and his companion met a barrage of .50 caliber and 20mm fire. The wingman was killed when the plane's fusilage and cockpit received a deluge of .50 caliber hits. The jet slid left and downward before spinning dizzily to earth. Colonel Kammhuber's jet had also been hit, but he held his position, determined to strike the bombers or to die in the attempt. He had almost cleared the gauntlet of fire, but as he released four of his R4M rockets, a near miss from a 20mm shell bounced his jet fighter plane and disrupted his aim.

Any one of the four released rockets could have destroyed a B-17, but the R4M's whooshed high and sailed above the Charlie and Able squadrons. However, one rocket dropped far enough to slam into the fusilage of the starboard Baker Squadron Fort. The explosion nearly blinded Big Jenny's turret gunner, Marty Walsh. Suddenly, the two segments of the B-17 fell downward and disappeared. Walsh saw no chutes.

Several more pairs of ME 262 pilots tried to reach the bombers, but they too failed to hit a B-17. The six-plane diagonal defenders had badly disrupted their flights and their aims because of the withering gauntlet of firepower. While the P-51's knocked no more jet aircraft out of the air, they did damage several more of them. The diagonal defense pattern seemed to be working.

The frustrated Adolf Galland now turned on the P-51's themselves. The bombers would soon reach their target and the JV 44 kommodore could not allow them to reach their objective unmolested. He had to scatter the P-51's and open a path to the bombers. Colonel Ben Davis and the black pilots of the 332nd, the port vanguard of the protecting escort, would be the first target of Galland's altered strategy.

"Zeig Jagdverband!" Galland cried into his radio.

Colonel Ben Davis had been waiting to open another gauntlet of fire against the next duet of jets, but he gaped in astonishment when he saw the jets zoom downward and then veer right into his diagonal six-plane flight. "Bandits coming at us! Right at us!" the 332nd commander yelled into his radio. "We've got no choice. We'll have to take them on!"

Davis quickly opened fire on the oncoming jets and his fellow 332nd pilots followed suit. Soon the two air units clashed, twisting, turning, zooming, arching. And diving about the sky. Rattling machine gun fire, thumping 20mm cannon shells, and whooshing rockets shook the very sky. The crews of the B-17's, staring in awe from their stations in the tight bomber formations, suddenly understood a naked truth: if the Red Tails failed, the B-17 airmen would suffer the same fate as the 3rd Air Division on that abortive 18 March flight to Marienfelde.

Thirty ME-262's took on some fifty odd P-51's of the 332nd Fighter Group in a dogfight that ranged between 30,000 to 24,000 feet, almost directly above the smoke-screened Daimler-Benz complex. During the initial clash, the Red Tails quickly damaged two ME-262's, punching holes so badly in two jets that both German planes staggered away from the fight. At about 1237 hours, a pair of jets came towards Davis and his wingman, but chattering fire from several other P-51's smashed into the attackers. One of the jets exploded and fell to earth. The other, hit several times, veered left and away.

But the initial success of the 332nd was short lived. The experienced jet pilots, with faster and more maneuverable aircraft, soon took their toll. A pair of jets with Colonel Joseph Kammhuber in the lead, got on the tail of a Red Tail and Kammhuber loosened a barrage of rockets that literally tore the P-51 apart in a series of explosions. Then, as three Lonely Eagles got behind a pair of 262's, the jets merely soared away and moments later were on their pursuers.

"Eight o'clock high! Eight o'clock high!" somebody yelled over a radio.

Too late. Lieutenant Bob McDonald of the 99th Squadron looked around, but he had only time to scream, "My God!" before a pair of rockets smashed into his cockpit. The plane burst into flames before it fell to earth.

Now Colonel Davis himself tried to attack. He took his entire 99th Squadron, over a dozen planes, to meet a flight of seven ME-262's. Both sides loosened a flood of shells, rockets, and machine gun fire, but the jets had the advantage of speed and maneuverability. A rocket slammed into the plane of Lt. Jim Wheeler, knocking off the right wing of his P-51 and sending the plane plummeting to earth. Before the P-51's could react, another pair of jets tore into the 99th Squadron, releasing more rockets. Another P-51, this one piloted by Lieutenant Frank Wright, exploded violently, the pieces falling to earth like silver confetti.

But Captain Bill Mattison came into the melee with his entire 100th Squadron, machine guns and cannons blazing. Mattison missed, but Lieutenant Roscoe Brown caught a jet as it zoomed past. One of Brown's 20mm shells ripped off a wing of a Snowbird, stopping the ME in mid-air before the jet cartwheeled to earth.

Only seconds later, Colonel Bill Daniels joined the fray with a squadron from his 31st Redneck Group. Daniels tore into a flight of jets with sixteen P-51's and his pilots knocked two ME-262's out of the air.

In the vicious dogfight that lasted only a minute, the 332nd had suffered the loss of four planes and pilots, with damage to sixteen other planes. The 31st had suffered damage to a half dozen P-51's, but no losses. Galland had lost only three jets with damage to several more in the furious, one-minute dogfight with the 332nd and the 31st. Without doubt, if Galland had continued the dogfight, he might have knocked a dozen P-51's out of the air.

But Galland had lost six jets with damage to a dozen others in these initial engagements over Marienfelde and he was forced to break off the fight. Despite his higher score of kills and damage in the dogfights with the P-51's, Galland could not afford this loss in the face of more than 250 American fighter planes. The JG 44 kommodore took his jagdverband high in the sky to consider another strategy. The 332nd had been battered, but they had stopped a jet plane attack on the B-17's that might easily been a replay of the 18 March debacle.

The withdrawal of the jets brought relief to the B-17 crewmen. Bombardier Perry Ford sighed gratefully before he glanced at his compass. He had almost reached target. "IP in thirty seconds," he cried into his intercom.

"Open doors," Captain Ball said, "we're on correct PDI." When the hum of opening bomb bay doors ended, Ball called the waist gunners. "Check bombay doors."

"Open, sir," Sergeant Pete Cody answered.

Then, Captain Ball and Colonel McGregor craned their necks to look at the smoke-screened target. Suddenly, Ford cried again into the intercom. "Twenty seconds! Ten seconds!"

"Release flares," Ball cried.

A series of thumps slightly jarred Big Jenny as the direction flares, six of them, dropped from the lead B-17 and arched like fiery Roman candles towards the Daimler-Benz target. The signal put every bombardier in both the west and east columns on alert. Seconds later, lead bombardier Perry Ford looked carefully at his instruments. The H2X radar meter was on target. He was exactly at 26,500 feet and his location compass registered exactly 50.05 north by 13.1 west, air speed 215 mph, and axis at 20 degrees. If the readings were accurate, he could not miss.

"IP! IP!" Captain Ball cried suddenly.

Captain Perry Ford's own instruments checked out, and he pressed the bomb release button, sending the first two bombs whistling towards the smoke-screened Daimler-Benz complex. The screen did little good because Perry had pinpointed the target perfectly in his radar sights. The bomb landed squarely on the main assembly building 2A, blowing away a portion of the roof on this most northerly structure of the complex.

Other bombardiers of the 463rd Bomb Group, using the directive flares as an adenda to their own radar readings, released their own bombs. Another 38-thousand-pound bombs sailed downward like a spray of giant confetti. Seconds later, a series of explosions shook the thousand-square-acre target area. The rest of the 2A roof collapsed and the four walls crumbled in a thick cloud of dust. The exploding bombs also ripped neatly lined machines and lathes from the concrete floor. Tank parts, cams, threads, and crankshafts flew about the huge building, clanging against each other, twisting and breaking, and then clunking to the ruptured concrete floor. The accuracy of the 463rd bombardment had been devastating, thanks to the escorting fighter planes' ability to keep the dreaded jets away from the bombers. Of the more than forty tons of RDX bombs dropped by the 463rd, 56% of them hit the target.

The devastation wrought by this first group of American bombers shook the 262 pilots high in the sky over Marienfelde.

Galland cringed in his cockpit. "We must stop them. We must. We will attempt an attack on the bombers from the east."

"At once, Herr Galland," Major Hartmann answered.

Major Hartmann led the jets of his Staffel III in a huge arch, and from 30,000 feet, ne came sweeping down from two o'clock high at the next group of bombers, the 97th.

Colonel Gunther Lutzow followed Hartmann with his own Snowbirds of Staffel IV. The 97th Bomb Group was ready to drop its fifty-odd tons of bombs when Hartmann came sweeping towards the B-17's. But Colonel Daniels and his 31st Fighter Group pilots did not fail.

Daniels waited with the first diagonal six-plane line, and the flight opened fire as Major Hartmann came tearing towards the bombers in several two-plane sweeps. The P-51's met Hartmann and his Staffel III with withering .50 caliber and thumping 20mm cannon fire. Again, the American firepower punctured the wings, fusilages, and tails of the zooming jets. The Snowbirds remained aloft, but they had been effectively disrupted by the P-51's. The jet pilots released a dozen or more R4M rockets, but only knocked down one B-17 from the 97th Bomb Group.

Major Erich Hartmann squeezed his face in agonizing disappointment as he worked frantically to regain control of his punctured jet fighter plane. He finally straightened his aircraft, but he was too badly damaged for further combat. He was out of the fight.

With determination, Colonel Gunther Lutzow came next towards the 97th Bomb Group bombers, bracing himself for the gauntlet of fire that came from the 31st's other six-plane diagonal formation. Lutzow felt his lead ME-262 shudder from a stream of .50 caliber bullets, but he never waved. He continued on, his plane finally afire from an array of hits. Still, he roared into the 97th formation and released four rockets. Two of the missiles slammed into a B-17 and the Flying Fortress simply exploded. Flaming fragments tumbled to earth, with no crew member able to avoid death. Lutzow glanced for a single moment, smiled, but then saw his own precarious position. His plane was ablaze and he could not open his cockpit to bail out. Then his engine pods exploded and he plunged downward and crashed into a clump of trees in a ball of fire.

The man who had dared to call Field Marshal Kesselring a pompous ass, the man who had dared to insult Hitler and Goering, the man whom the Nazi hierarchy had exiled from Germany and Italy, had passed into eternity. In these closing weeks of the war, the outspoken colonel had given his life for those who had disparaged him. Lutzow no longer needed to worry about a home if the Allies took Holland.

Now, despite the loss of the B-17's and damage to other Forts from R4M rockets, the 97th made its bomb run. The thousand-pound bombs followed those of the 463rd to complete the destruction of main building 2A. Whatever was left of the machines, stock, walls, and equipment in this mainplant went up in twisting debris. Fire and smoke poured out of the factory, with no way to stop the flames or secondary explosions. Building 2A was a total wreck.

And there was no respite. Next came the B-17's of the 483rd whose bombardiers had accurately sighted the railroad yards of the Daimler-Benz complex with H2X radar. Another confetti of RDX bombs sailed downward. Now the shuddering explosions ripped up railroad sidings, switches, control buildings, signal towers, hoisting equipment, stock, oil, and water tanks. Flat cars with newly loaded tanks along with switch engines went up in smoke. The wreckage here had been as total as the wreckage of building 2A.

Next came Colonel Bob Bivro of the 2nd Group with the 301st and 99th Bomb Groups behind him. The bombardier of Bivro's lead B-17 also dropped his direction flares before the first two bombs from the lead east column Fortress dropped on the building 9A assembly plant in the center of the Daimler-Benz complex. Fifty more RDX bombs followed the first two, most of them landing squarely on target. The heavy, quick concussions even ripped away thick cement walls, leaving the reinforcement rods jutting out of the smashed concrete like huge, twisted worms crawling out of gray earth. More than forty tanks, fully or partially assembled, flew outward or skyward in contorted fragments. Wheels flew about like hundreds of erratic discs. Tank treads slammed against crumbling walls. Turrets slammed into the exploding metal ceilings and fires erupted in the bowels of the tanks. The roofs and walls of building 9A collapsed, creating tons of dust that settled over the smashed tanks.

High in the sky, Galland was stymied by the new P-51 tactic that had successfully thwarted his attempt to disrupt the B-17's. He winced with each new explosion on the Daimler-Benz complex below. Still, the JV 44 kommodore would not give up. He took his jets high in the sky again to remuster them for a strike at the last two groups of B-17's still coming over Marienfelde.

As Galland began this new move, the eleven ME-163's of JG 7 loomed out of the sky, zooming down from 30,000 feet. In pairs, the smaller 163's roared towards the tail squadron of the 483rd Bomb Group. But another barrage of .50 caliber and 20mm fire spewed out at the zooming Komets that tried to run the gauntlet. Lieutenant Ed Lester of the Red Tail's 102nd Squadron got a broadside 20mm hit on one of the swishing Komets. The 163 exploded like a firecracker and simply vanished in a puff of fire and smoke. And, oddly enough, B-17's gunners got two more of the speedy Komets.

However, other Komets swished on, loosening streams of 5cm fire. Two rockets from Major Schnaufer's Komet struck a wing and tail of one B-17. The wing fell off and the tail disappeared before the B-17 flipped over and tumbled to earth in a sheet of flame. Another pair of 5cm rockets hit a second 483rd B-17 in the belly before the Fort exploded and flip-flopped to earth.

Fortunately for the 483rd, the Red Tail and Redneck fire had ruined the aim of most of the 163 pilots, and the eleven Komets had only made these two fatal hits while suffering quite badly themselves. Besides the three losses, Colonel Johannes Steinhoff had suffered damage to three other Komets and JG 7 was at least temporarily out of the fight. Steinhoff took his remaining 163's high in the sky to reorganize them, but he found he had only six Komets still serviceable for combat.

Galland now cried into his radio. "All units will attack the second wave of bombers." Galland knew he was too late to do anything about the west column that had already dropped its bombs. His only hope was to disrupt the last two groups of oncoming bombers, the 301st and 99th, to salvage whatever he could of Daimler-Benz. He left the remnants of Staffel II to cope with the P-51's still covering the west column, while he took the rest of the JV 44 jets to attack the 301st and 99th.

But Galland was thwarted again. The P-51's of the 325th and 52nd Fighter Groups held their ground, forcing Galland and his airmen to run yet another gauntlet. As the determined Galland zoomed downward, five other 262's behind him, his plane caught several .50 caliber holes in the fusilage. Further, a near miss from a 20mm explosion tore away his right engine pod. Galland lost control of the aircraft and the jet teetered downward. The plane fell to 10,000 feet before Galland straightened and moved steadily on one engine at reduced speed. The JV 44 kommodore could only glance up at the air battle still raging far above him. Dejected and beaten, Galland picked up his radio. "Colonel Kammhuber, you will assume command of JV 44. My aircraft is too badly damaged to remain with you."

"What do you suggest, Herr Galland?"

For a moment, Galland remained silent. What could he tell Kammhuber? Galland knew the battle was over. He knew that neither his jets, their conventional aircraft, nor the ack-ack guns would make any difference. The enemy had already knocked out most of the tank assembly plant, and the tail groups of this American air armada would surely knock out the rest. After all the planning, all their enthusiasm, all their confidence—they had failed. He had personally failed; his pilots had failed; Germany had failed. In his lonely patch of sky, inside his battered Snowbird, Germany's most eminent Luftwaffe kommodore realized he could not stem the Allied tide. The hope had been a futile dream. The war was over.

"Colonel," Galland spoke softly into his radio, "do whatever you can."

But, neither Kammhuber nor any of the other jet pilots could do much. The tail groups of the east column, the 301st and 99th, were already over Daimler-Benz. At exactly 1247 hours, the bombardier of the 301st's lead B-17 pressed bomb release buttons. Other group bombardiers followed and fifty tons of high explosives fell on building 10A, the gun plant on the south acres of the Daimler-Benz complex. Once more, rattling, concussioning bursts tore through the huge building in deafening explosions. The neat lines of 88, 105, and 155mm tank guns erupted from their cradles and flew outward or upward, slamming into the cascading roof and walls. The exploding bombs had transformed the long barrels into hot, twisted metal debris.

And a moment later, a new confetti of bombs from the 99th Group, the last unit of the 80A armada, descended over the same building. If any of the guns or material of building 10A had escaped the 301st barrage, none escaped this second deluge of RDX bombs from the 99th. The explosions twisted more of the huge gun barrels, tossing them about in clanging, banging disarray. The explosions also ripped away electrical equipment, tore open temper tank furnaces, and ignited huge fires in the shattering building.

Soon, expanding fires and high columns of gray and black smoke, some as high as 10,000 feet, rose over the debris that had once been the Marienfelde Daimler-Benz complex. Not a single roof remained intact, on even the smallest building. No walls stood erect, and not a single piece of equipment, machinery or stock escaped destruction. In the leading yards, no platform stood upright, and the switch engines, rolling stock, and tracks were damaged beyond repair. No tanks would ever leave these plants again. Daimler-Benz was finished.

In the air, the P-51's moved close to their bomber charges as the B-17's turned southward to start the long flight home. As the air armada droned south, anti-aircraft fire resumed. But now, the B-17's soaring at nearly 30,000 feet, were quite safe from the ack-ack.

Colonel Joseph Kammhuber made one last effort to hit the 80A armada. He took the remnants of JV 44, now less than 30 serviceable aircraft, and pounced on the American armada as the 5th Wing droned along the east side of Berlin. This time, Colonel Daniels and his pilots of the 31st took the brunt of the ME-262 attack. But the contest was not much of a battle. The devastation over Daimler-Benz and the loss or damage to so many jets had taken the fight out of the German pilots. The ME-262's came down on the retiring B-17's with little determination, but they did knock another 483rd B-17 out of the air.

However, Daniels had tightened the diagonal patterns of his P-51's and he had let off a barrage of deadly .50 caliber and 20mm cannon fire at the swishing jets. The Americans caught a dozen Snowbirds in their sights and in one swift minute of action, Colonel Daniels and one of his pilots had knocked down two more jets.

Only Colonel Steinhoff, Major Schnaufer, Captain von Brauschitsch, and three more pilots of JG 7 still harassed the returning 5th Wing armada. The colonel's half dozen Komets jumped the east column of bombers. Remarkably, JG 7 knocked two more B-17's out of the air, one from the 301st and one from the 99th, with Schnaufer scoring his 134th kill of the war. Another rocket slammed into Colonel Bob Bivro's lead plane and tore away the underbelly, along with the ball turret and its belly gunner. However, the 2nd Group commander held the bomber steady as the waist gunners quickly spread canvas tarps over the gaping, elongated hole in the open floor of the fusilage.

But Steinhoff had suffered the loss of another Komet and damage to another pair of 163's. Captain von Brauchitsch had become the final fatal German statistic over Marienfelde on 24 March. The captain's Komet had caught a 20mm hit in the fuel tank and the plane exploded, leaving no trace of him on the aircraft. The famed Mercedes-Benz racing driver would never again settle behind the wheel of a Grand Prix racer.

At 1255 hours, Colonel Johannes Steinhoff took the battered survivors of JV 7 back to Lagar-Lechfield. Major Schnaufer squeezed his face in grief. He had lost a good friend in von Brauchitsch.

Soon a quiet settled in the skies over Berlin. After a mere half hour of furious action, the aircraft of both sides were gone and the ack-ack guns had ceased. Only the billowing smoke, crackling fires and belching, intermittent explosions from the ravaged Daimler-Benz plant marred the silence that now prevailed over Marienfelde.

Chapter Sixteen

The long line of B-17's and their escorting fighter planes had moved nearly fifty miles south of Marienfelde before Colonel George McGregor took stock. His own Group, the 463rd, had severe casualties: four B-17's lost to flak, one to jets. The 463rd had also sustained damage to twelve other planes, many of them sputtering homeward with feathered props, shot-up fusilages, wings, or tails. McGregor's own B-17, Big Jenny, now had a snub nose from the flak burst, although, miraculously, neither Bombardier Perry Ford nor his equipment had been damaged.

The 97th Group had also lost five B-17's and suffered damage to some eleven others. The 483rd, hit hardest by the jet attackers, had suffered the worst: six B-17's lost, damage to all but two of their other Forts, fifty airmen killed, and more than a hundred flyers wounded. The 483rd Pathfinders would need a field hospital itself to accommodate their injured when they finally returned to Sterperone.

The east column under Colonel Bob Bivro had not fared as badly as the west column, probably because the lead column had taken the brunt of the German ack-ack and Luftwaffe fighter attacks. However, the lead 2nd Group had suffered one B-17 lost to ack-ack and another presumed lost trying to reach Russia. Observers had seen German fighter planes pounce on the damaged Fort like wolves after a wounded deer. The 2nd had also sustained damage to several B-17's, including Bob Bivro's lead Fort. Bivro's plane had the underbelly shorn away and he and his crew were flying home on a prayer.

The last two groups of the east column, the 301st and 99th, had also sustained losses, three from flak and two from jet fighter planes. The 301st and 99th had also suffered damage to several other planes.

Among the fighter groups, Colonel Ben Davis's 332nd Lonely Eagles had sustained the worst loss. They had engaged Galland's jets in a furious dogfight when Galland decided to scatter the escorting American fighter planes to reach the bombers. Four of the Red Tail pilots had fallen victim to jet fighter planes: Lieutenants Jim Wheeler, Frank Wright, Norman Golden, and Bob McDonald. A dozen more Lonely Eagle P-51's had suffered aircraft damage. And, at 1315 hours, a fifth 332nd P-51 had fallen out of formation from aircraft damage and crashed in Germany. The pilot had bailed out to become a prisoner of war for the remaining weeks of the conflict.

The 31st Fighter Group had also engaged the German jet fighter planes, but Colonel Bill Daniels had enjoyed nothing less than a miracle. Of his fifty-seven P-51's that left Mondolfo Field, three had aborted, but all the remaining fifty-four Mustangs returned safely to base at 1530 hours, although several of the Redneck P-51's had been damaged.

"We were just goddam lucky," Colonel Daniels said later.

Among the other three escorting fighter groups, the 82nd had lost three P-38's and suffered damage to a dozen others from the running twenty-five mile dogfight with 109 and 190 fighter planes. A fourth P-38 had fallen victim to an ME-262. However, Colonel Joe Holtroder and his pilots had mauled the 109 and 190 geschwaders so badly that these units had not been able to effectively lure off the P-51 escorts or attack the B-17's.

The 325th and 52nd Fighter Groups had also engaged the German jet fighter planes, but they had suffered no losses. They had met with JV 44 and JG 7 planes after these Luftwaffe units had heavily engaged other American fighter units. One 52nd pilot had scored the kill of Captain von Brauchitsch, but other 163's had dropped two more B-17's out of the air. However, the pressure exerted by the 325th and 52nd Groups on the Komets had enabled the east column to drop their bombs accurately on the Daimler-Benz target.

Now, as the air armada droned back to Italy, the 5th Wing columns veered south by southeast, passing over battered Dresden, the city the British bombers had destroyed block by block in a retaliation for the Luftwaffe attacks on London and Coventry during the blitz. As the 5th Wing passed over the ruined city, Colonel McGregor spoke into his TDS.

"Keep the formations tight. Keep them tight." Then he looked at Captain Ball. "We okay?"

The Big Jenny pilot nodded. "We're in pretty good shape. Nobody hurt."

One by one the bomber and fighter group leaders reported to the 80A Mission commander. The armada had lost twenty-one bombers, 15 from ack-ack and six from the German jets. The air fleet had also suffered damage to over sixty planes, many of them quite badly. Some of the pilots of these impaired aircraft were not certain they could make it to Italy. Among the five fighter groups, the 82nd had lost four planes, the 332nd five, the 325th one, and the 52nd one. The five escort groups had also sustained damage to twenty or thirty fighter planes.

Colonel McGregor frowned on these losses, but they had been less than half of those suffered by the 3rd Air Division of 18 March. But most important, the 5th Wing had totally succeeded where they 3rd Air Division had totally failed. The railroad yards at the target complex had been nearly demolished. All traffic had ceased with countless yard locomotives and rolling stock a mass of wreckage. All three plants, 2A, 9A, and 10A, had been obliterated by direct bomb hits and near misses.

Lesser structures had also sustained heavy damage. The boiler house had probably been destroyed. The four or five workshops and administrative building had suffered damage from direct hits and near misses. Fires still belched from a building next to 9A as the bombers left the target.

Not until 1340 hours did the all-clear sirens wail through Marienfelde. Then streams of executives, supervisors, foremen, and workers filed out of their concrete and slag pile air raid shelters. Most of them felt numb from the nearly 250 tons of bombs that had rained on the tank assembly complex. Their ears still rang from loud concussions and their heads still spun from the shattering explosions. However, the air raid shelters had safely protected them from the heavy bomb attack. The aerial assault had not killed or seriously wounded any of the Daimler-Benz employees. But, as the 21,000 employees came into the open, the hanging dust and thick smoke that clouded Daimler-Benz made them cough, and they perspired from the hot fires that still crackled within some of the buildings.

The employees stared in disappointment at the destruction around them, but none were more disheartened than the firm's director, Dr. Wilhelm Haspel, and the firm's chief engineer, Dr. Fritz Nallinger. The two executives had found a new vitality during the past week, as new Tiger tanks rolled steadily off the assembly line. They had beamed optimistically after the abortive American attempt to destroy Daimler-Benz on 18 March, certain that Galland had spoken the truth when he said that no American bombers would bomb the plant. Now the utter destruction around them had brought to these Daimler-Benz executives the same sober reality as today's aerial failure had brought to Galland. They had wallowed in a futile dream.

"It is over, Herr Haspel," Dr. Nallinger said. "The war is over."

"Yes," Dr. Haspel answered softly. He kicked away some debris in his path, and he walked towards the ravaged structures with Dr. Nallinger. A civil defense worker stopped the two men.

"You must come no farther," the helmeted man said. "We have many fires in the ruined buildings and we can expect more explosions."

Daimler-Benz was out of business and the 21,000 employees under Haspel were out of work. He squinted to the left, at the rows of apartment houses and cottages that housed the Daimler-Benz workers. He saw many of these employee quarters ruined or damaged from errant American bombs. Not only were his employees out of work, but many of them were homeless.

At München-Riem, General Galland was among the first to return from the air battle over Marienfelde. He landed his damaged jet gingerly, but the plane wobbled erratically before it rolled to a safe stop. Ground crewmen hurried to the plane and expressed sympathy when they saw the agonizing look on the general's face. "Let me help, Herr General," one of the men said, leaning in the cockpit.

General Galland nodded.

When he left his riddled Snowbird, Galland walked across the field and climbed the steps to the control tower. Here, he waited and watched other jets of JV 44 and JG 7 return to the field. One by one or in paris, the Snowbirds and Komets touched down on the runway. Many planes had suffered damage: punctured wings, fusilages, and tails. Other planes had been riddled with shorn wings and shorn tails. A few landed precariously by one jet engine. The control tower clock read 1330 hours before the last plane returned, a battered 262 that belly landed on the airstrip and luckily did not explode.

By 1345 hours, Galland stood in his München-Riem headquarters and peered into the bright afternoon. Major Rudolpher, Colonel Kammhuber, Major Hartmann Colonel Steinhoff, and Major Schnaufer sat glumly at the table or stared at the silent Adolf Galland. For nearly five minutes the general stood immobile and stared out the window. Finally, Major Rudolpher spoke.

"We are ready for a report, Herr General."

Galland nodded, turned, and sat down.

"There are certain regrets," Colonel Steinhoff said. "We lost Colonel Lutzow. He crashed in the midst of battle. We also lost Captain von Brauchitsch. His Komet exploded in mid-air from an enemy cannon hit."

Galland pursed his lips. "Two good men."

The damage reports only heightened Galland's dejection. JV 44 had lost eleven of their ME-262's and suffered damage to twenty other Snowbirds. JG 7 had lost four Komets, with damage to five more. After today's battle, Galland had only twenty-eight serviceable ME-262's and two ME-163's. The defeat had verified Galland's worst fears—the imaginative Americans had indeed come up with an innovative way to deal with jet fighter planes. Only later would Galland learn from General Peltz that the conventional 109's and 190's had suffered brutal losses.

General Peltz had not come to München-Riem this time to congratulate Galland and his pilots: nor did any congratulatory calls come from Fliegerkorps Reich headquarters. In Berlin, everybody in the Luftwaffe, from the lowest clerk to Reichsmarshal Goering, knew that today's defeat over Marienfelde marked the end of Germany's efforts to stop the Allied tide, either in the air or on the ground.

And, in fact, at his headquarters in Osnabrück, both Field Marshal Von Rundstedt and the pesky kommodore of KG 51, Lt. Hans Kowaleski, saw no reason to smile. Kowaleski's Arado jet bombers would not be enough and Von Rundstedt could do nothing without tanks. Von Rundstedt's generals—Von Klüge, Von Maunteufel, and Dietrich—sat silently and watched the Commander of the Army of the West pace the floor until he finally turned and looked at his subordinates.

"I fear we have indulged ourselves in an unwarranted

surge of optimism, a delusion. We should have known that not even the determined efforts of Oberstleutnant Kowaleski and General Galland could really change the course of events. I can only ask that each of you do the best he can, not for those who babble about the invincibility of the Third Reich, but for ourselves and for the millions of good Germans who have entrusted the Fatherland to our care.

Nobody answered the field marshal.

Then Von Rundstedt rolled open a map on the table. "We must plan whatever strategy we can."

"Yes, Herr Field Marshal," General von Klüge answered.

A hundred miles away, in Cologne, General Omar Bradley pranced about his headquarters with a gusto bordering on intoxication. The reports of total destruction at Daimler-Benz had left him with an unrestrained optimism and he eagerly ordered go on Operation Overtone. Neither the Luftwaffe nor Von Rundstedt could any longer interfere with his jump off from the Rhine bridgeheads. The English and Canadians would drive north towards Bremen. The First Army would thrust out from Remagon towards Leipzig. In the center, Patton's Third Army would push towards Frankfurt. And finally, the U.S. Ninth Army would push out from Cologne towards Berlin itself. Allied ground troops would overrun Germany before summer.

Shortly after 1500 hours on 24 March 1945, the first aircraft of the 80A Mission reached their Italian bases. The P-51's of the 31st landed at 1510 hours at Mondolfo. Next came the pilots of the 52nd who landed at Piagilolino at 1530 hours; then came the 325th at Rimini at 1545 hours and the 82nd at Vincenzo at 1550 hours. The last fighter Group, the Red Tail 332nd did not reach Remitelli at Cattólica until nearly 1800 hours because Ben Davis had decided to lead his group in a strafing raid against rail traffic in Czechoslovakia on the way home.

The bomb groups had all reached home by 1800, with

most of the B-17's alighting safely on their assigned bases around Foggia. However, two B-17's which were badly damaged could not clear the Alps. The B-17's turned back and the crews bailed out of their aircraft in Austria, hopefully to spend the last weeks of the war as mere prisoners. Other B-17's, unable to reach Foggia, made emergency landings on some of the fighter strips in northern Italy. One aircraft, Colonel Bob Bivro's landed at the Remitelli field in Cattólica at 1810 hours, just before dusk. Red Tail ground personnel took the 2nd Group colonel and his crew to the messhall for a hot evening meal. Later, Bivro met with Colonel Ben Davis.

For a long, uneasy minute, Colonel Bivro fidgeted before the Red Tail commander. Then Bivro pursed his lips. "I don't know what to say, Colonel, except that I'm sorry, sorry as hell for all my criticism and complaints against you and your pilots. We lost a lot of Forts today, but we'd have lost a hell of a lot more if you and your pilots didn't mix with those jets."

"You mean there's hope for us niggers in the air corps?" Davis said acidly.

Bob Bivro rose from his chair, leaned forward and then looked at Ben Davis squarely in the eye. "I realize now that you poor bastards had to accomplish twice as much as the rest of us to prove your worth. It wasn't fair." Bivro raised his hand. "Davis, I'm making a vow before God. I'll spend the rest of my career working for equality for blacks in the Army Air Corps."

"I appreciate that, Colonel," Davis nodded. "How about a cup of coffee? I assure you, our black cooks make it as good as your white cooks."

"Thanks," Bob Bivro answered.

Elation on this early evening of 24 March spread up and down the boot of Italy, with jubilant celebrations throughout the campsites of the 5th Wing units. They had finally shown up the glory boys of the 8th Air Force and they wallowed in their success with smug satisfaction. Two days after the raid, the 5th Wing commander,

General Charles Lawrence, received a telegram from General Ira Baker, the CO of the Mediterranean Allied Air Forces.

"The 15th Air Force operation Saturday, 24 March 1945, penetrating the vital installations in the enemy's capital, was brilliantly executed. The 5th Wing has my warmest congratulations for this telling blow. The damage inflicted on the enemy from such a great distance in the face of heavy fighter and anti-aircraft oppostion is further proof that the air attacks were well done. I am proud of you."

The high brass showered 5th Wing units and personnel with an array of awards for the 24 March raid on Daimler-Benz. All eleven participating air groups in the attack on Marienfelde won DUC's for their efforts. Dozens of men earned medals, from the Distinguished Flying Cross to the Air Medal. Perhaps not so strangely, the 332nd won more individual awards than any other group. Colonel Ben Davis, Captian Bill Mattison, Major Al Turner, and Lieutenant Ed Lester won Distinguished Flying Crosses. A dozen other Red Tail pilots won considerable recognition, with Colonel Bill Daniels and two other pilots winning Distinguished Flying Crosses, while six others of the 51st Fighter Group won Silver Stars.

Colonel Bob Bivro remained true to his word. Shortly after the war ended, the air corps promoted Bivro to general and assigned him to the JCS of the Army Air Corps. In March of 1946, the air corps became a separate branch of the U.S. armed forces and immediately announced a policy of total integration. General Bivro brought Colonel Davis some pleasant news.

"Ben, the success of your 332nd pilots weighed heavily in the decision to totally integrate the new Army Air Force. You're getting a promotion to Brigadier and you'll be commanding the new 447th Air Wing at Lockburne Air Base in Ohio. Good luck."

The 332nd commander was grateful for the opportunity to head up an integrated unit of white and black airmen. He vowed to treat equally every man in his command. The capable Ben Davis did act without bias and with efficiency. During the Korean War, he received command of FEAF. He then became commander of the 13th Air Force in Formosa. And, on 10 April 1965, Davis reached the apex of his career when the Pentagon promoted him to head of the U.S. Air Force. Ben Davis held this post until retirement from military service in 1970. His replacement was another black, General Daniel James, who held the post until he retired from military service in 1978.

And what of the losers in the vicious air battle over Marienfelde on that aggravating 24 March 1945?

Colonel Lutzow and Captain von Brauchitsch had, of course, lost their lives in the 24 March air fight. Major Earl Rudolpher was killed in late March of 1945 during a dogfight with P-51 escorts over Ruhland. Major Hartmann and Colonel Kammhuber became Allied prisoners when U.S. infantry units overran the airfield at München-Riem in late April, but both men were released after the war. Major Schnaufer simply vanished after P-51's knocked his plane out of the air during an engagement over the Elbe River on 18 April 1945. Fellow pilots had seen him bail out of his jet, but the Luftwaffe's greatest fighter ace was never seen again.

On the same 18 April air battle over the Elbe River, Colonel Steinhoff never got into the fight. His jet plane crashed on take-off, but Steinhoff, severely burned, managed to escape from the burning plane. Medics took him to a hospital bed in Munich, where he was still in bandages when American GI's captured the hospital. American officials had treated Steinhoff with respect, because the Luftwaffe colonel had been responsible for training the best jet fighter pilots. Steinhoff never came under suspicion as a war criminal, and the Allies released him after the war. But his adept ability to train and lead men won him a place in the postwar West German government. In 1950 the Bonn government gave him command of the new, but much smaller, West German

Air Force. Steinhoff held this post until he retired in the 1960's.

General Peltz had apparently found himself trapped in Berlin when the Russians entered the city. Several Berliners said the Red Army had taken him prisoner, but no one saw nor heard of Dietrich Peltz again. Either he was killed in the Berlin fighting, or he was killed by Russian captors.

General Galland, after the 24 March 1945 debacle, reorganized his JV 44 unit as best he could and continued to challenge the hordes of Allied aircraft during the rest of the war. He and his JV 44 pilots still rose from München-Riem to intercept the waves of Allied bombers and fighters that droned constantly over Germany. By late April 1945, Galland and his handful of JV 44 pilots had knocked over a hundred Allied planes out of the air.

On 26 April, Galland himself flew his last combat mission. He led six ME-262's, all that remained of JV 44, against a formation of American Marauder bombers near Neuburg, Germany. Before the mission he had talked with his handful of pilots.

"The war is lost. Even our actions today cannot change anything. But we must continue the fight because we should be proud to be Luftwaffe pilots to the last. Only he who feels as I do should man his Snowbird."

Every pilot went.

On this 26 April day, Galland had personally shot down two of the Marauders, his 123rd and 124th kill. But then a P-51 caught him napping. The Mustang sent a 20mm shell into the forward section of the cockpit, shattering the instrument panel and slashing Galland's left knee. The aircraft wobbled out of control, but Galland managed to right his battered Snowbird and come bouncing into the runway on one engine. However, he landed smack in the middle of a P-47 fighter-bomber attack on the airfield. Still, Galland crawled out of his plane and hobbled across the open field amidst exploding bombs and strafing fire.

A ground crewman reached Galland and dragged him

to a sheltered ditch until the American attack ended. Medics then took Galland to the same Munich hospital as Colonel Steinhoff. Allied authorities took Galland to Nuremberg, but the Allies never indicted him as a war criminal. After the war, Galland became an executive for a new Lufthansa commercial airline until he retired in 1965.

Thus, the participants of both sides in the hard-fought air battle over Daimler-Benz faded into history.

MEET JIM RAINEY, MERCENARY SOLDIER. HE'S AS TOUGH AS THEY COME, AND HE KNOWS HIS BUSINESS. HIS BUSINESS IS WAR.

2089-0	SOLDIER OF FORTUNE #1: YELLOW RAIN	$2.50
2107-2	SOLDIER OF FORTUNE #2: GREEN HELL	$2.50
2124-2	SOLDIER OF FORTUNE #3: MORO	$2.50
2144-6	SOLDIER OF FORTUNE #4: KALAHARI	$2.50
2169-2	SOLDIER OF FORTUNE #5: GOLDEN TRIANGLE	$2.50
2190-0	SOLDIER OF FORTUNE #6: DEATH SQUAD	$2.50
2212-5	SOLDIER OF FORTUNE #7: BLOODBATH	$2.50
2240-0	SOLDIER OF FORTUNE #8: SOMALI SMASHOUT	$2.50
2261-3	SOLDIER OF FORTUNE #9: BLOOD ISLAND	$2.50

Make the Most of Your Leisure Time with
LEISURE BOOKS

Please send me the following titles:

Quantity	Book Number	Price
_____	_____	_____
_____	_____	_____
_____	_____	_____
_____	_____	_____
_____	_____	_____

If out of stock on any of the above titles, please send me the alternate title(s) listed below:

_____	_____	_____
_____	_____	_____
_____	_____	_____

                                Postage & Handling   _____

                                    Total Enclosed $_____

☐ Please send me a free catalog.

NAME_____

                          (please print)

ADDRESS_____

CITY _____ STATE_____ ZIP_____

Please include $1.00 shipping and handling for the first book ordered and 25¢ for each book thereafter in the same order. All orders are shipped within approximately 4 weeks via postal service book rate. PAYMENT MUST ACCOMPANY ALL ORDERS.*

*Canadian orders must be paid in US dollars payable through a New York banking facility.

Mail coupon to: **Dorchester Publishing Co., Inc.**
                       6 East 39 Street, Suite 900
                       New York, NY 10016
                       Att: ORDER DEPT.